Order of Vespers

Order of Vespers

Elyse Reyes

Irrisoria Publishing

Copyright © 2016 Irrisoria Publishing

All rights reserved. No part of this book may be reproduced or transmitted in any form or by any means, electronic or mechanical, including photocopying, recording, or by any information storage and retrieval system, without the written consent of the publisher, except where permitted by law.
Printed in the USA.

Cover art by Amygdala Design
© 2016

DEDICATION

To my amazing husband, Omar, and my tribe of extraordinary women for keeping balanced.

CONTENTS

CHAPTER 1 10
CHAPTER 2 35
CHAPTER 3 45
CHAPTER 4 50
CHAPTER 5 56
CHAPTER 6 74
CHAPTER 7 92
CHAPTER 8 101
CHAPTER 9 107
CHAPTER 10 110
CHAPTER 11 130
CHAPTER 12 149
CHAPTER 13 159
CHAPTER 14 165
CHAPTER 15 174
CHAPTER 16 181
CHAPTER 17 188
CHAPTER 18 196
CHAPTER 19 212
CHAPTER 20 223
CHAPTER 21 235
CHAPTER 22 243

Epilogue *254*

PART 1

Elyse Reyes

CHAPTER 1

From the moment I woke up there had been flashing neon signs warning me that danger was coming. An alarm that never went off, the stabbing pain in my temple, an unsettled stomach, a dead cell phone and a tear in my pants. Worse, the fingers that itched and a tingle in my arms.

A smart person, a sane person, would have heeded the caution. She would have listened to her father and gone back to bed and realized it was the perfect time for a mental health day. She would have told him the truth, begged him to stay home in case it happened again. She'd do everything to protect those around her. She'd avoid blowing up the west hallway of her high school.

Unfortunately, I wasn't that selfless or self-aware.

Order of Vespers

The explosion occurred, allegedly, shortly before the lunch period ended. Most of the lockers in the hallway were redecorated in scorch marks and snazzy divots and holes. The ones closes to the blast site featured partially-melted locks. Shards of the fluorescent lights littered the ground, warm and reflecting a strange, prism-like glow.

And in the center of the destruction, unconscious and untouched by the violence of the explosion, was me. Theories flew among the student body as the police combed over the "crime" scene. They searched me, my bags, my clothes and my locker, but found nothing that could have caused the blast. I pleaded innocence and ignorance, but no one believed me. A full detail of police accompanied me to the principal's office, on school arrest until they found a reason to charge me with arson. Attempted murder. Terrorism.

My incarceration in Mr. Conner's office wasn't the worst punishment. The ode to secondary education on a budget had been a second home for the last year. Its plywood furniture with cracks where someone drilled too much and its cheap, paisley carpet were as familiar as the plain, violet quilt on my bed at home. The room was a testimony to the pathetic efforts to modernize the school on a budget.

While I wasn't opposed to some renovations, I thought the money could have been better spent. Like on new floors that didn't catch fire when there were surprise explosions.

There was no use losing my temper again. No one believed me, not even after my twin brother, Jude, came to my defense. We were inseparable, two peas in a pod. Although we bickered constantly, seeing Jude come to my defense was the only thing that kept me sane.

A new police officer, a woman with a slight build and kind eyes, walked into my temporary prison and sat down in Mr. Conner's chair. She placed her hands on the

Elyse Reyes

desk, palms up and gave me the pleading puppy dog eyes.

I crossed my arms and sat back with all the teenage insolence I could muster. I've never backed down and I wasn't starting with this twit.

"Ms. Jasper Lee Andrews."

"That's my name. Don't wear it out," I drawled. "Look, Detective, I have nothing else to say."

The woman sat back and met my raised-eyebrow stare with one of her own.

She was dressed in plainclothes but everything about her screamed "cop." Black clumps of leather I recognized as orthopedic shoes, comfortable and serviceable black pants, a button down shirt and a jacket to cover her holster and gun. "Jasper ... May I call you Jasper?"

"No."

Her head jerked back. "No?"

I picked at the loose strands of the knee of my black jeans, the only victim of the explosion. It was the one day all school year that I'd worn all-black clothing. It probably didn't help my case.

"Jasper, you have to talk to me. I can't help you if you give me nothing to bring to my bosses. What did you use to cause the explosion?"

"I didn't cause the alleged explosion," I said calmly, even as my fingernails dug into my knees hard enough to draw blood.

"You were found at the scene."

A familiar shift came over me. My skin warmed and, if I were a dog, I'd say my hackles rose. I wasn't lying and I certainly wasn't an arsonist.

"I was unconscious."

"Knocked over by your own handiwork."

And just like that, *She* appeared in my mind. *She* was that inner primitive being hell bent on protecting me and mine. We existed in the same space, and she almost

Order of Vespers

always let me give input, although she ignored me most of the time.

We raised my head slowly and pinned the detective with a stare that dared her to mess with me. Us.

"No," I responded. "How many times do I have to tell you that I didn't do anything? You're interrogating me like I'm the only person in the entire school who might pull a prank like this. You should be asking if I'm in danger from some lunatic."

There was no lunatic, unless you counted my potentially split personality. *She* wasn't just a bad ass weekend warrior with an iron will and the self-preservation of a feral creature. *She* was insolent as all get-out and I had a sinking feeling she was about to make things worse.

The detective drew herself up to her full height in her chair, an impressive five foot three inches, if I had to guess. "Well, *Ms. Andrews*, there's no evidence that you didn't cause the explosion. This attitude isn't going to help you."

"Yeah, well, I have a major problem going to jail for an alleged crime that I didn't commit. Going to jail isn't on my bucket list."

"Here's what I don't get," she mused. "You're an honor student, a former cheerleader, pretty and athletic. Your brother is one of the most popular kids in this high school. What's your deal? Silly teenage prankster? Or are you part of something much bigger than you realize?"

The snort just came out. Couldn't help it. "Like what? Terrorism?"

"You used the word, not me."

My hand twitched and both my warrior chick and I stowed our urges to slap the woman. The young detective caught the big bad terrorist in the act and was going to get a commendation. I saw it in her face, the way her lips curled into a sneer and her body practically vibrated excitement.

Elyse Reyes

"Detective ..."

"Bryant."

"Bryant. Haven't you heard of the concept of innocent until proven guilty? Because as far as I'm concerned, you've got nothing. So do us all a favor, clear the crime scene and let me go home. I've got an exam tomorrow."

"You were the only one in the area and the scorch marks originated from you. Yet, there's not a smudge on your clothes...no burnt hair...?"

"I was unconscious!"

"I'm sorry, Jasper. We're not letting you go."

Although it would have been more satisfying to throw something at her, the rational part of my brain took over. "Let's review the facts." Each statement was punctuated by a tick off one of my fingers. "There was an explosion in the school. Two: No one was hurt, except the girl with a huge bruise on her forehead who was found in the middle of the wreckage. Three: You found her unconscious. Four: There was nothing on her person or in her belongings that could cause an explosion. Five: The police didn't wait for my lawyer to badger the only victim. Six: Miranda rights were never said or explained. Seven: the victim has not been allowed access to medical care."

Officer Bryant wasn't happy with me if the flared nostrils and hands gripping the edges of the armrests were any indication. "You haven't asked for medical care."

"Oh, but I have. Twice. Number eight is my favorite. Wanna hear it?"

She eyed me warily but nodded.

A slow smile crossed my face, all teeth and no kindness. "Nothing here adds up to probable cause, which means you're not going to arrest me. Unless you want my lawyer bringing those facts to your captain —"

Order of Vespers

My giggles interrupted my monologue and made me look like the psycho everyone seemed to assume I was anyway. "Hell, of course we're reporting it to your captain. How about you go fetch me a nurse, something to eat and my lawyer? I'm starving, you know, considering I was knocked unconscious and in the middle of an explosion. Chocolate and a can of pop would be fabulous. Bye, now."

With a dismissive glance, I shut her out of my world and grabbed my calculus textbook. Potential arrest or not, I had a test the next morning and I refused to fail.

§

The boredom was damn near tortuous. I finished studying for calculus. Twice. I memorized the new titles on Mr. Conner's bookshelves. I chipped off the nail polish I had so carefully applied the previous evening. Heck, I studied the weaving in my backpack until my eyes burned.

My cell phone was confiscated as if the plans for my elaborate "stunt" were written in code on some app called "Explosions are Cool." It was irrational, but the loss of my cell phone upset me more than anything else. It was worse than listening to the rumors that flew around the school.

Jasper's such a freak. She's probably a Satanist.

What's next? Is she going to sacrifice puppies in the cafeteria?

She was homecoming queen. No one dropped blood on her. Why's she doing this?

Dismissal had been an hour ago. Given the rumor mill at our small high school, I figured my latest stunt was likely the subject of dinner conversations in town.

Elyse Reyes

My parents were most likely furious. They had probably already decided to ground me for life. Again.

Yep. *I kept passing out and blowing things up around me for fun. It was a blast, pun totally intended.*

Not for the first time that day, I laughed at the absurdity of it all. The police and fire departments combed my school for hours. I was being held in custody, for lack of a better term, in the principal's office. My lawyer was on her way over to spring me and I was positive my parents planned to lock me in my room for the foreseeable future.

Buh-bye, senior prom. You'll be missed, high school graduation. Toodles, college next fall.

I liked to think I was a good person, if one overlooked the random, uncontrolled explosions. I was a responsible student who made honor roll every semester. Debate teams throughout the county feared my name. Hell, I would have been class president if I hadn't accidentally set the ballots on fire.

Mrs. Stannish, the school secretary, stomped into the office and glared at me. Her perpetual bad mood was amplified a hundredfold because Mr. Conner hadn't let her go home. "You keep quiet in here, Jasper Andrews. You've made enough of a spectacle today."

"Gotcha. No noise, no explosions. I can handle that." My bladder screamed at me. "Mrs. Stannish, I need to go to the bathroom. May I please go? It's right across the hall."

"No, you may not. You should have thought about that before your disgusting rampage. If it were up to me, I'd send you straight to Sing-Sing and throw away the key. Sit in it."

I closed my eyes and banged my head against the wall. The stabbing pain above my left eye reminded me of the lump that had formed when I fell to the floor.

The school nurse poked her head into the office with a small smile. The appearance of Ms. Davis, a sweet

Order of Vespers

woman with a pixie-cut, blue eyes, a model's figure, and a bad habit of wearing tie-dye outfits, was a huge comfort. She was the only person allowed in my cell who showed an iota of sympathy.

"How's that head doing, Jasper?" she asked as she stepped into the room.

"It's been better." I winced when she pressed on the orange-sized lump on my temple. "Passing out and slamming my skull against the floor kinda killed my day."

She laughed and shined a light into my eyes. "Somehow causing almost one hundred lockers to explode and scorching the west hallway didn't impact your mood? Go figure."

An unexpected giggle burst out of me like the purging of phlegm from the system. At least, judging by Ms. Davis' expression, that's the sound I made. But I couldn't stop. She was the funniest, most adorable thing, the best part of my day. Someone poking my head and making jokes about my arsonist ways.

What had I expected? Someone to give me a hug and send me to bed with milk and cookies? Kiss my boo boo and tell me it would be just fine?

Nope. They were going to send me to jail, and when one of these explosions happened, I'd end up right where Ms. Stannish wanted me — the upstate New York prison in Ossining, affectionately known as Sing-Sing. The other option was too horrifying to give more than a momentary consideration: sedated like a zombie and locked up in a psychiatric facility.

That's what society did to people like me. Locked us away and pretended we didn't exist. If horror movies were to be believed, they turned a blind eye to the awful experimentation that occurred. We were nothing, no one. We were anonymous souls with no voices.

I was going to be turned into a mutated lab rat.

Elyse Reyes

Thankfully, my mental breakdown was cut short when she clapped her hands in front of my face. Instead of an unkempt, smelly lab assistant staring down at me, Ms. Davis' blue eyes radiated concern.

"Sorry, sorry," I muttered, embarrassed at my short trip down the rabbit hole of what-ifs. "The stress is finally getting to me."

"Humph. Let me check this," she said as she pressed on the lump.

That throbbing, protruding thing became such a presence in the few hours that he'd become sentient. His name was "Boom," and lived up to the hype. I yelped and scooted away. Boom didn't like her, and for a second, neither did I.

Ms. Davis sat down next to me and patted my knee. "Honey, you're a good kid. What's going on? Why explosions? What are you trying to accomplish?"

Tears threatened to ruin my carefully cultivated mask of flippancy, which had survived the principal, Troll Stannish, a full squad of police and a house of firemen.

Actually, the firemen might have been the highlight of this awful day. Mom always said that my tastes in men leaned toward big, muscular and hot as hell. Sue me. I had a type.

Dreams of hot firefighters who belonged on calendars was only a momentary distraction, another break from reality.

Back on planet Earth, I was in high school and I'd committed the ultimate sin. From a young age, it had been drilled into my head that I had a single responsibility: protect the family by keeping our secrets. Our family's special abilities were too big and too dangerous to share. It was bad enough that I had put my family in danger. This incident threatened to expose us all.

"Nothing. I'm not trying to do anything. I didn't do this, Ms. Davis."

Order of Vespers

She cupped my chin with her palm. "You have so much potential, Jasper. Whatever you're trying to prove, it isn't worth this kind of trouble."

Bitterness roses like bile in my throat. Why was it so impossible to understand that I was the victim here? Injured and framed for a crime I technically didn't commit. There was no way they could blame me for an accident that happened while I was unconscious and completely unaware. That I was going to face furious parents who knew what was going on but had zero sympathy wasn't making my day any better.

She confessed she didn't know how to help. "But I do have some good news," she said. "Well, Gossip, really."

My ears perked up and, for the first time that day, I felt a flicker of hope. "Yeah?"

She smiled slightly. "You're driving the police crazy. There was an argument over who gets to interrogate you next because no one wants to do it. Jasper, I'm fairly certain that they won't arrest you. You need to take this opportunity to turn your life around."

That flicker of hope? Squashed. Obliterated. Gone.

§

Detective Bryant drew the short straw and dropped off a snack. The can of orange pop was hot to the touch, as if someone deliberately left it on a windowsill and saved it just for this moment. The chocolate was melted, but I was hungry and I needed the calories. Whatever caused the explosions required massive amounts of fuel.

Shouting from the antechamber to the office was music to my ears. My lawyer had arrived and was about to tear the local police new ones. When Jude had come by earlier, I had given him my list of issues to relay to

Elyse Reyes

Olivia, our older sister and attorney-at-law. She'd been practicing law for a year and I was her best client.

"You're holding her without cause! This isn't a jail, Officer. My sister was unconscious and the only person you've let in is the school nurse. You can bet your badge that your unconscionable behavior will be included in the lawsuit we plan to file. Wanna try to keep me from her, too?"

I love my sister.

"Ma'am," I heard Detective Bryant say, "Jasper has been defiant and uncooperative."

Olivia used her best ice queen voice on the officer, the kind that made even the bravest, most confident person shrivel into a ball and question their self-worth. "If you were walking down the street, were rendered unconscious and woke up in the midst of a crime scene, you'd be upset. Then imagine you're denied medical attention and are treated as a terrorist. I'd be pretty pissed off too."

The hallway filled with the clacking sound of Olivia's heels coming toward me, although her perfume arrived first. That overbearing floral scent that smells like the tissue paper that comes in every perfume box made me double over as my stomach tried to crawl out of my stomach.

It suited her. Olivia was a damn good lawyer whose reputation preceded her. She didn't threaten lightly, and when provoked, Olivia annihilated them. It was annoying to be a little sister with a penchant for getting into trouble. But as her client?

I harbored a strong dislike that only a little sister can maintain. But considering her skills as my pro bono legal counsel it was worth trying to maintain that sisterly love.

The heels clacked down the short hallway. Hope flared in my belly. My heart of hearts appeared in the

Order of Vespers

doorway, one hand on her non-existent hips and the other clutching her briefcase.

Olivia was terrifying in her perfection. Her black page boy haircut brought out the otherworldly paleness of her skin.

Lawyer-slash-part-time-assassin. Olivia, or Livie as I called her, reminded me of one of those hit men in the movies. Deadly calm, physically imposing and bad ass.

"Well?"

"They have my laptop and notebooks. My cell phone, too." I raised my hands in a helpless shrug. "I didn't read it on the list of things psychotic bombers should leave at home."

"Shut up," she hissed. "You're not exactly making it easy to defend you, idiot. Pack up your stuff and meet me by the secretary's desk. Don't dawdle."

I gave her a thumbs-up and picked up my scattered belongings. My messenger bag was lighter than it should have been, but then again that made sense since my gadgets were gone.

"Was there anything incriminating on the laptop, Detective?" Livie was in flighty sweetheart mode. He was so screwed.

Detective Lattimeir's first week with a golden shield was ruined, or made, by my untimely fuse shortage. Every time he came into the principal's office to interrogate me, the corners of his mouth fought to stay in place. He was the one who rifled through my bag and confiscated everything. The good detective took my phone apart because he was convinced that I had an incendiary device hidden somewhere. I was close to giving him a reason to arrest me when he knelt, grabbed my foot and tugged on my boots.

Detective Lattimeir's eyes darted around the room in an effort not to look at Livie. Small beads of sweat appeared on his upper lip and his hands trembled.

Elyse Reyes

Livie and I exchanged incredulous looks. Not many people lasted this long when she laid on the mind games. I nodded my approval and watched her work.

"Is there something wrong, Detective Lattimeir?" she asked in a practiced, sultry purr. "I really don't want to keep you any longer. You've been here all day."

"I, uh," he stuttered, "I decided it was better to keep her in the school instead of at the station. We have enough protection here, and, well, look at her. She's tiny. Any of us could take her out."

Olivia flashed the smile that wrapped most men around her pinky, took my arm and led me out. "Eww. If you tell *anyone* I flirted with him," she told me as soon as we were out of earshot, "I'll murder you."

§

The ride home was silent, and by the time Livie parked her silver Jetta in our driveway, fear had crawled its way into my stomach. Without the need to maintain my bravado, I was left with the sickening realization that I could have hurt someone. Killed them.

I didn't know how keep these explosions from getting worse. Hell, I didn't even know how to control them. Most of the time, I wasn't even conscious when they happened.

Jude had a theory that stress heightened my nerves and caused a buildup of kinetic energy. When it reached a critical level, my body expelled it with explosive force. It was an interesting concept. The *why* made perfect sense. It was the *how* that still eluded us, despite Jude witnessing the ordeal on more than one occasion.

Olivia shut off the engine with a world-weary sigh. "Mom and Dad are freaking out, Jas. Have you thought about what you're going to say? Do?"

I shrugged uncomfortably. "No idea. This is bad, Livie, with the police involved."

"Yeah, it is. I'll spend the next few days meeting with everyone associated with the case and, with luck, they'll blow it off and move —"

Those damn psychotic giggles burst out again. "Dude, you just said, blow it off. Get it? Explosions? Blow it off?"

"You're such a child," she snapped as she opened the door and stepped out of the car. She waited for me to follow suit and picked up her tirade. "I thought you were working on controlling yourself. And you know you're not allowed to show off your abilities."

"Of course I'm working on it. The problem, in case you didn't notice, is that I was unconscious. Unless you know something I don't, there's no good way to control anything when you're not awake." I crossed my arms and stomped toward the house.

Olivia grabbed my arm, her talon-like nails digging into my skin hard enough to draw blood. "I don't think you understand the severity of what happened or the implications for the rest of us. You know damn well what's going to happen."

We stared at each other balefully, neither of us willing to back down. *She* poked at the corner of my mind, silently pleading for permission to handle Olivia. I was amused by the courtesy; *She* only asked for permission when it came to my family. But since I didn't want my lawyer walking around with a black eye, I politely refused the offer.

"Let go of me," I warned. "Livie, *She* has been itching to do something since I woke up."

"Don't you think manifesting a split personality right now might not work in your favor?" Olivia released me and frowned at the droplets that formed. "Sorry," she murmured.

"You should be sorry. Look, I'm not oblivious to the impending shit-storm coming our way. But the other

Elyse Reyes

stuff? Livie, that's just boogieman crap that mom says to scare us."

"Is it?"

My eyes were drawn to the bay window of our Cape Cod style home with its blue paint and white trimmings, through which I could see my mother pacing and yelling into her cell phone, unaware that I was a few feet away. While most of the conversation was unintelligible through the glass, Olivia and I caught a few words.

Must get her out of here.
Too dangerous.
They can help. They have to help.
Hiding. Make her anonymous.

Olivia made a sweeping gesture with her right hand. "Are you sure this isn't a big deal?"

"Shut up," I snapped and stormed up the stairs and into our kitchen. There was no food on the stove, and no takeout bags, which meant I had to fend for myself. My cooking skills were sub-par at best. We had nothing of the heat-and-eat variety. I hated being sent to my room without dinner.

"Jasper Lee," my mother snarled from behind. "You are in so much trouble."

I turned around slowly, finally afraid. My mother was a nice woman, if prickly. But when she was angry, her shout echoed in my head for days. "Hi, Mom."

"Hi Mom? *Hi Mom?* You blow up your school, have an attitude with the police and all you can say is *hi mom.*" Her voice kept going up, finishing about two octaves higher than it started.

"I'm sorry," I said, ducking my head. "Mouthing off to the police was poor form. But Mom, *She* wasn't thrilled with the way the police treated me."

Mom inhaled sharply. "*She* made an appearance? At school? Did *She* do this?"

Order of Vespers

"Doubtful. *She* didn't emerge until the police interrogated me." I leaned back against the refrigerator. "There's the possibility that *She* was around earlier, but I wasn't aware."

"Okay," she said, her shoulders sagging. She crossed the kitchen in three strides and hugged me harder than she had in years. "My baby girl. I'm so sorry."

"Mom, stop squeezing me."

She let go with a laugh, then opened the refrigerator. "What would you like for dinner, sweetheart?"

I narrowed my eyes. We didn't do mushy affection in my family. Mom almost never asked me to decide on dinner. My tastes were experimental at best and I was a vegetarian at the moment. The other shoe dangled and waited to drop.

"Why?"

"Because I need to cook and you're here." Mom pulled out an armful of vegetables, washed and set them on the counter, and diced with enviable precision. "The spring pasta you like. Is that okay?"

"Yeah, sure. So...are you going to keep me hanging? What's my punishment?"

Mom's eyes, the same chocolate brown color as mine and Jude's blinked rapidly, as if to rid themselves of grit. "Honey, we'll deal with punishments and such over dinner. Why don't you go to your room and relax?"

When she hugged me this time, I sensed something disconcerting. Sadness. Regret. It felt like she was saying goodbye.

§

"Jasper!" My dad's voice boomed across the house and up a flight of stairs. "Dinner's ready."

Elyse Reyes

I bookmarked the website on kinetic energy manifestations, shut my laptop and made my way downstairs with the naive hope that things would be okay. Dad tried to smile as I walked into the dining room and held out a chair for me.

Holy crap. I'm still unconscious. Maybe this has all been a dream. Dad never holds out my chair anymore.

"Hey, Dad," I said uneasily. "How was work?"

"Fine, sweetie. How's your head? Livie told me that you were injured in the ... accident today."

"Daddy? What's happening? Something's off. You're acting weird."

Mom put a pause in our conversation as she served generous portions of pasta, salad, and my favorite biscuits. "Hope you're hungry, sweetheart. Jude and Livie are out for the evening, so it's just the three of us."

"What the hell is wrong with you? No one has yelled at me or punished me for the next century. You're making my favorite foods and calling me pet names. Can someone please tell me what's happening?"

"Eat," Dad said, his tone an unspoken threat.

Ah, yes. Back in familiar territory.

Without thinking, I put a napkin on my lap and began to inhale my food. The explosion had left me famished and it occurred to me that the only thing I'd eaten was the melted candy bar and can of pop.

"Jasper," my mother said quietly. "What happened today ... it's a problem. Olivia won't be able to manipulate the entirety of people involved."

My father cleared his throat. "Your mother—"

"Mark," my mother snapped. "*We* are afraid of the attention that this will bring to the family. Jasper, this has put us all in danger. Do you remember the stories I used to tell you about our people? My mother's distant family? My aunt and her friends?"

My mind raced as I thought of the countless tales of our boogieman, cautionary stories about a group of people who hate people like us. A group whose sole purpose is to find and kill those with our abilities. People like me, Jude and Olivia."

"Some of them. But those people aren't real, Mom. They can't be real."

"Jasper, honey." My father wiped his face with his napkin, yet managed to miss the bit of tomato in his beard. Despite everything, I smiled. My dad was the epitome of absentmindedness, barely keeping track of our schedules and letting my brother and I come and go as we pleased. He was also my biggest cheerleader, as if he forgot the severity of my problems until the next incident came along. I knew my father would fix this.

"Dad, your beard," I said as I reached over and picked out the food stuck on his face. The normalcy was the thing that turned this all around. I was sure of it. If I pretended everything was okay, then fate had no other choice but to make things right again. "Okay, okay. These people. Even if they're real, which I don't believe, they can't just come and kill us. They'd be exposed."

"My point is that we're no longer safe here. More importantly, you're no longer safe."

"What does that mean? Dad, do you agree?" I turned to my father, but he refused to meet my eyes, staring down at his plate.

"Yes, Jas. And I agree with your mother. Our safety ... you can't stay here anymore. We've been trying to reach some of your mom's family who have closer connections to a group that can protect you. Hide you."

"No," I exclaimed. "Mom, no. You can't just send me away. It's the beginning of senior year. My college applications are ready to send out. I have a calculus test tomorrow."

My lungs couldn't get enough air, nor could my eyes or ears take a second more of this ludicrous conversation. Bile rose in my throat and the world grew darker, quieter, until I was gone.

Elyse Reyes

§

Minutes or hours later, I surfaced from the glorious realm of unconsciousness, where reality simply didn't exist. But reality had come for me and I had no choice but to deal with it.

Someone had tucked me in properly, the lilac quilt brought up to my ears and my favorite pink teddy bear in my arms. My shoes had been removed, and in their place were fuzzy socks.

They'd gone through my belongings. Everything was out of place, stacked into neat piles against the wall across from me. I jumped out of bed and took stock of the changes.

Someone had stacked my underclothes, organized by type and color.

Mom.

My father was still too weirded out after two daughters to touch my unmentionables, as he called them. Only Mom was capable of this type of organized chaos.

Socks according to thickness and length.

Long sleeved shirts, short sleeves, tanks, sweaters. Jeans. Skirts. I suspected she organized my shoes by season, starting with my winter Uggs and ending in a pair of flip flops I loved. Next to all of that sat my camping bag, my big messenger bag and a suitcase.

And on my desk was a note held in place by a new cell phone still in the evil clam shell plastic that would take me hours to open. I picked up the note with shaking hands.

Jasper, we love you so much. You're a wonderful young woman whose generosity, humor, and sharp brain make us proud. Please know that if there was any other way of keeping us safe, we'd do it.

Order of Vespers

We've managed to get in touch with your great-aunt Jody. She made some calls and someone will be here tomorrow evening to take you somewhere you'll be safe.

I'd love to say that this was just until this mess blows over, but I can't. You can't come back to this town. Between the police and these awful people, you'd be hunted.

We started to pack for you, but figured you'd want to have the final say. Fill up the camping bag with the most important essentials. The suitcase is for items that aren't pressing - like your fifth favorite pair of jeans. The cell phone is pre-paid. It's not safe to have a way to trace your location.

Come downstairs when you're ready to talk.

Nope. Not happening. I refused to believe that twelve hours ago, my biggest concern was my calculus exam and now my parents were sending me away with strangers. I thought of every spy show I could imagine to find the right phrasing.

Jack Bauer, James Bond, Nikita.

They were going to disappear me. Tuck me into the shadows somewhere, make me an anonymous face in the crowd.

My eyes swept the room wildly, as if each pass would reveal my belongings back in place. But nothing changed. Nothing would change.

No more school. No more falling asleep in the room next to my best friend and biggest pain in my ass. No more arguing with Olivia when I borrowed her clothes. No more ogling at Adam, Jude's closest friend, and hoping he finally asked out. Images of what would never be flashed across the back of my eyelids.

I exhaled and began to organize my belongings according to Mom's instructions. My barely-used camping bag stored my basic toiletries, clothes I could layer and carry over seasons, two boxes of tampons because my mother is a planner like that, a small makeup bag, my Converse All-Stars sneakers, and accessories like gloves, a winter hat, scarves and a pair of fluffy pink earmuffs.

The suitcase filled up just as quickly with a few versatile dresses and skirts, sweaters of varying weights, my favorite pajamas, and swimsuits.

My mother and I clearly had different ideas of what sending your youngest child to live with strangers meant. I had a feeling that, wherever I was going, it wasn't going to be a five-star resort.

Exhaustion began to overwhelm me. I climbed back into bed, reread the note, closed my eyes, and succumbed to the darkness.

§

"What?" I yelled at the door. "Sleeping!"

The fist knocked again. "Open the goddamn door, Jas."

I sat up and brightened. Jude was home and he'd distract me from the disaster that was my life. My brother was a pain in my ass, but he was the best. He was the guy who beat up my ex-boyfriend for talking smack about me. He'd also dragged me out with him and his friends on the weekends if I didn't have plans. Jude had some idea that it was unhealthy for me to go more than a day or two without spending time with friends.

"It's unlocked."

Jude walked in and plopped down on my bed. "Ya did it now, Sparky."

I should throw sparks at you, goddamn it. I hate that name.

"Livie said it was fixed. She did her mind control voodoo and no one is pressing charges. I'm not even suspended."

"I don't know if you noticed, but today wasn't your usual narcoleptic boomer."

Order of Vespers

My fingers itched with the desire to curl up into a fist and plow into my brother's eye. His refusal to meet my eyes and gentle tone made him seem shifty. Worse, it made me wonder if he was on my side.

"Thank you, Captain Obvious," I snarled. "I'm aware. The throbbing lump on my temple is a constant reminder. What would I ever do without your insight?"

Siblings fight. Twins fight harder. Us? We were close to an all-out, hair pulling, kicking, calling-mom-to-referee death match.

Jude weighed his choices. "You're so lucky this shit is serious," he said. "This was a big one, Jas. How long do you think it will take before this story is in the local newspaper? Regional?"

Jude mentally, possibly telepathically — we weren't exactly sure — poked at me and conveyed his fear that today's incident had sent up a flare signal and announced to the world that we were here. If they were real, and they showed up, they would ... Neither of us wanted to finish that thought.

My sleep-drugged mind finally caught up to the conversation. I rubbed the sleep out of my eyes and stared at Jude. "You don't know."

"Know what?"

"Jude, they're sending me off with these strangers who are supposedly like us. Mom thinks it best that I go into hiding."

My brother pulled his knees to his chest and pulled some of my quilt over his body, as if the thin blanket could shield him from the truth.

"No."

I shook my head, my hair tumbling into my face like shadows attempting to hide me from the world. "Read this."

Jude snatched the note from me with shaking hands. His eyes ran back and forth across the page; his lips moved as he read the note to himself.

Elyse Reyes

Once.

Twice.

"No, Jas." He shook his head until I thought he might hurt himself. "*No.*"

"As soon as they find these people, whoever they are, they're disappearing me. Permanently. Jude? What am I going to do?"

"What are *we* going to do? Did you really think I'd twiddle my thumbs and watch a mysterious unknown take away my best friend? Did that lump scramble your brain?" Jude shook his head again. "Did you go back downstairs to talk to Mom and Dad?"

"I couldn't," I admitted in a small voice. "What if they repeated themselves? What if they insisted that everything was real, that they were shipping me out?"

"Jasper, I don't think you get it." Jude met my eyes and did something unexpected. He reached across and held my hand in his. "You're not going anywhere without me. Twinsies, remember? Your big brother isn't going to let anyone hurt you."

I smiled slightly. Jude was exactly ninety seconds older than me. He was also five inches taller and twenty pounds heavier, so he called me his little sister.

"It's not going to happen. Jude, you to do everything we've always discussed. Go to college. Join a fraternity. Don't let me ruin your future."

"It's not happening," he said flatly. "And you're an idiot for thinking otherwise." The worry lines on his face deepened. It seemed to age him, the weariness of protecting our secret carried the weight of the world.

I closed my eyes and thought about the ways we'd exposed ourselves in the past. Once puberty hit and Jude and I came into our abilities fully, we were walking billboards outside of school. We'd drive out to the woods near us and practice using our powers safely. Being the giggling idiots that we were, practice meant creating sparks of electricity that Jude blew around. It

Order of Vespers

was all good until one of those sparks hit a tree and set it on fire.

Jude commanded the wind to torment the people who messed with us. Gossips, ex-boyfriends and bullies were inexplicably pushed around, lifted into the air and bothered by "ghosts" that brushed against their skin.

Thanks to Livie, we had always been able to keep things quiet. She used her mind control to convince people that certain events never happened or that we weren't where they said.

That was just how the Andrews clan rolled.

"We're screwed, aren't we? But do you really think they'd kill an eighteen year old who wasn't doing it on purpose? Who didn't even know how it happened?"

"The fact that your powers are growing more unstable is probably enough reason to take you out." Jude curled three fingers into his fist and pointed at me like a gun. "Pew, pew, pew."

Our eyes were perfect matches, down to the flecks of hazel inside the chocolate brown. We stared at one another for a moment before bursting into laughter. Only my brother had the ability to make me laugh when I was facing such traumatizing circumstances.

"Jas," Jude said quietly. "I'm not letting anything happen to you. When are they supposed to be here?"

"I got the impression that it would be before the end of the week. Don't look at me like that," I snapped. "I know we only have twenty-four hours. Why do you think I did most of my packing earlier?"

Jude blew out a breath, his hair that was overdue for a cut floating horizontally for a moment before falling in his eyes. "Okay. We can handle this. Tomorrow I'll..."

We stared at one another helplessly.

"Move over."

I turned off the light and held my brother's hand tightly. For longer than I remembered, whenever one of

Elyse Reyes

us was scared, we'd lie side by side in the dark, squeezing hands and praying for a different outcome.

"It's going to be okay," he whispered.

"No, it's not. I'm going to miss you so much."

The sobs finally wrenched themselves from my chest and Jude put an arm around me. It wasn't until I hovered on the edge of sleep that I realized the tears weren't all mine.

§

"Mom!" I shouted from my bedroom. "Did you at least get a name?"

"No," she shouted back from her room down the hall, where she'd sequestered herself to hide her devastation. "All I was told was to expect a black Lincoln Towncar."

Fan-frickin-tastic. Taken away by strangers in the single most generic car in the state of New York. Not sketchy at all.

I wondered why my parents didn't seem concerned about the shadiness of this venture. Jude and I had spent the last twenty-three hours researching what little information we could on this mysterious group. Neither of us were surprised when nothing came up, not even on the dark web.

Jude snorted from his spot on the paisley rug on my bedroom floor. He was painstakingly writing in a notebook he refused to show to me. "Nope, not at all suspicious. Do you remember your self-defense class?"

The pounding at my temple continued even though the lump named Boom had shrunken significantly. I rubbed it absently. "Yeah."

"Do you have my number programmed into your new cell phone?"

"Yeah, of course."

Jude's eyes glittered with protectiveness and his hands curled into fists. "You call me the second anything

Order of Vespers

seems shady. When you get wherever you're going. I don't care if you can't tell me the location."

"I know."

The last twenty-four hours had gone similarly. My parents avoided me, the shame of shipping their daughter away too much to handle. Olivia hugged me once and was cooking up a storm. She said she wanted me to have a little bit of home wherever I went. And Jude peppered me with questions every few minutes.

"Jas, as soon as you get there, find the exits."

"Goddammit, Jude! We've gone over this a million times. If you don't stop I'm going to junk-punch you, rip out your pomade spikes and tell everyone that you wet the bed last year."

"I was sick, jerk," he hissed. "And asleep for twenty hours."

"So was I, but I didn't pee on myself."

I exhaled and shook my head at the absurdity of it. I had less than an hour left to spend with my twin and we were arguing about teenage bed wetting.

Keep classy, Andrews Twins.

Jude jumped up and ran to his room, slamming the door behind him. A single wall of plaster and particle board separated us, but he felt miles away. I hated that we were arguing.

Before I decided on a course of action, Jude stomped back in with a parcel in his hands. He plopped down next to me on my bed.

"Here. I'd feel better if you had this."

I stared at the bulging manila envelope full of ten- and twenty-dollar bills and watched him rifle the cash with his thumb. "Jude," I breathed. "That's our life savings."

He smiled slightly. "Just about five thousand dollars. I have a feeling you'll need it more than I will."

"Can't. Won't. You'll need it for college."

Elyse Reyes

"Don't be an idiot," he retorted. "I'm not going to college. Once we figure out where the lair of anonymity is located, I'm coming for you. We'll figure things out from there."

The lump in my throat refused to go away. My brother was giving me the money we'd been saving for a post-graduation vacation. Frugal to a fault, he handed me the result of years of painstaking budgeting.

"Yeah," I whispered. Something told me that Jude wasn't coming for me or, if he tried, his chances of finding me were nil. "Okay, I'll take it. Jude, do you have that pit in your stomach?"

"The one that comes from my little sister getting ready to leave home for good? Yeah. Why?"

I shook my head. Forty-five minutes.

CHAPTER 2

My bags were piled next to me on our front patio. After an awkward and painful goodbye, I refused to go back inside our house. Their house.

The restlessness, the fear, and the anger were too fresh and I was afraid I'd trash the house.

Ironically, *She* was silent, possibly absent. My anger was sufficient for the both of us.

My mom came outside and sat next to me. "I love you, Jasper."

"Love you, too," I replied woodenly.

"Your grandmother swore that these people were friends of friends. Or something like that. In any case, you should be fine. And you call me as soon as you get wherever to let me know you're okay."

"Right." I shivered and wrapped my arms around my chest to protect myself from the chill of the September air. "Call mom as soon as I get to the place where I'm going to be held prisoner."

"Jasper, stop. It's not imprisonment. Hopefully, we'll be able to see each other soon. There's always email. Skype. Text messages."

"I'm not going off to college, *Mother*. Would you please leave me alone? I need to take a walk. I can't handle talking about this, not right now."

T-minus twenty minutes.

"Practice walking with your camping bag," my dad offered from the door. He looked worse than any of us. His normally smooth face was covered with uneven stubble and his eyes were bloodshot. "Just in case there are secret tunnels to traverse."

I scoffed, "Glad to see you find the humor in this. Gonna stay on a bender for a while?"

My mother looked at my father for a long moment. "Mark? How long have you been drinking? What on Earth made you think that being blind drunk was a good idea? Really."

"Why do you care," he slurred. "One kid gone, Delia, I heard you talking to your sister. Thanking god for these people. Can't wait until she's gone, you said."

"Asshole," she hissed. "That was a private conversation. You're taking things out of context."

Mission get-them-to-leave-me-alone accomplished.

Ignoring the ongoing conversation, I swung the heavy camping bag up onto my back and took off for the meadow behind my house.

By the time I reached the far edge of the clearing, the midday sun had warmed my skin. Yet, it wasn't enough to get rid of the chill in my bones. Something was wrong.

The gut feeling that had been nagging at me all morning told me to go back home immediately. *She* even made an appearance to warn me that something bad was about to go down. *She* was there to protect me.

I turned and headed back to the house, quickly breaking into a jog. The bag was too heavy for a full-out run, but it didn't occur to me to remove it.

My heart was pounding, but it wasn't driving my blood hard enough to get my legs up to speed...at least not to the speed I wanted. I felt like I was about to stall. *She* stepped up, finally, and we were jogging again.

Searing heat washed over me and knocked me to my knees. I threw my hands over my eyes and threw myself to the ground, hoping it would pass over me. But the heat seemed to flow into and through my body, hotter than anything I could imagine. And with the heat came a blinding white light. Even after I slammed my eyes closed, the light pulsed around me, shining through my lids in a pure, bright red.

There was no roar, no snapping or hissing. Just a shrill sound that pierced my eardrums in a horrific pop. I cried out and slapped my hands over my ears, but it made the pain worse and did nothing to block the sounds. Worse, slick, sticky liquid dripped down my cheek. The viscous substance had to be blood.

Blood spurted from my nose.

Fire engulfed me. Enveloped me. Poured into my every cell.

I wanted to die. The pain was more than I thought I could ever feel. If I ever opened my eyes, I knew that my skin would be blackened, hair gone, the little blood left oozing out of my orifices.

My life flashed in front of my eyes, something I had always thought was a trite falsehood. But I saw myself sitting in our playpen with Jude, fighting over toys and napping on opposite sides of the mat, connected by our clasped hands. My mother beamed at me and Jude on the first day of school. That embarrassing first kiss seemed to play in slow motion; Raul's lips mashing into mine was as real as his teeth almost breaking the skin. I was present on the night of junior prom when Michael and I giggled like idiots as we entered the hotel room he rented for the night.

Tears, or possibly blood, spilled down my cheeks as a good, relatively normal life was taken away.

The fire began to withdraw just as suddenly as it had spread. It flew out of my body, millions of fiery pinpricks shooting out of my skin. The bright light retreated, as did the scorching pain searing every inch of my body.

I gasped for air as the last of the heat retreated, leaving me cold and aching.

My hearing was muffled, the siren sound still present, but I swore I heard a scream. I propped myself up and looked on horror.

Images from history class flew through my mind as my brain tried to give me something to compare to the destruction in front of me.

That searing heat, the undulating light?

It had passed over me and driven into my house.

My home exploded with such force that a cloud bloomed above it, reminding me of the pictures I'd seen of nuclear bomb blasts.

The fire raged for a scant few seconds before it revealed its destruction.

There was nothing left. The foundation of the house and precious few support beams remained, charred and on the verge of snapping. The second floor was gone. Most of the first floor was gone.

My home, my family, my life had just been incinerated.

§

I climbed to my feet and tried to run, stumbling as my unsteady legs threatened to betray me and my mind refused to believe the macabre sight in front of me. My legs did eventually give out, so I crawled into the blackened grass of our backyard, made it past the spot that held our secret playhouse, the non-existent vegetable garden and the laughably melted patio furniture.

The smoky smell that flooded my nostrils mixed with something else, something that I'd recently experience.

Charred flesh.

I turned my head and vomited. One of my relatives, unrecognizable and seared through to the bone, lay twenty feet in front of me.

My throat worked and I felt a scream burst from my chest.

"No, no, no, no, no," I wailed.

One out of four, Jasper. Someone must have survived. Get up and move!

She infused my limbs and gently let me know it was okay to take a backseat. *She* had this.

We pushed to our feet and clumsily weaved through the wreckage. Nothing made sense. My life was reduced to indistinguishable shards of wood and metal and melted plastic. There were no walls or doors to tell us where to go, and if there had been, most of the first floor was submerged under the detritus of our bedrooms.

She cataloged each detail with dispassionate precision, sorting and filing each bit of recognizable flotsam. We didn't have the time for a full analysis of the data. Our family was missing, possibly injured. They were our first priority.

§

I sat in what used to be my front yard with my knees pulled to my chest and stared at the smoldering remains of my house. The only traces I'd found of my missing family members amounted to one of Jude's baseball cleats, half of my mother's antique sewing machine, and a black trunk that must have come from the attic.

Despite its crumbling exterior the trunk, its lid and the latch connecting them were unyielding, and I didn't have the mental wherewithal to pry it open. Coordination was a fool's wish: even sitting, my body weaved and jerked like a drunkard after last call.

My head throbbed and ached. Poor Boom, my bump from the other day, suddenly had to contend for my attention. Cuts, bruises, and other lumps fought their way to prominence on my skull.

"Crap, crap, crap. Stupid jeans," I grumbled, poking a finger through the hole in my left knee. It separated fabric from skin with the grace of a three-day-old Band-Aid and left a coating of blue fibers like an alien mole. "Gotta beg for a ride to the mall this weekend."

Right. That's not gonna happen. Focus.

I scoffed at my choices: contemplating the destruction of my life up until this moment or worrying about the imminent future. My one good ear gave me hints of sirens coming toward me.

"Jasper. Jasper." Like my crumbling, destroyed house, the robotic voice couldn't have been real.

A blond woman squatted in front of me and said my name. I wanted to respond, but both *She* and I were cowed by the violence and losses.

"Jasper Andrews?"

Light flooded my pupils, blinding me. Latex-covered fingers pressed on the inside of my wrists and carotid artery. Someone noticed the blood dripping from my right ear and cleaned it with gentle fingers. Those same hands checked me for bruises, poking and prodding.

But I kept staring at my house, waiting for my parents, Livie and Jude to come running out from some hiding place. But after the fire marshal and the police detectives combed through the ashes, my family still hadn't appeared.

Grief welled in my chest at the sudden acceptance that they were gone. My eyes blinked rapidly and I burst into gut-wrenching wails.

§

"Jasper, honey, let's wrap this blanket around you, get you nice and warm," said a young EMT. The scratchy wool blanket took away the worst of the chill and I nodded my thanks.

"Not leaving," I reminded her in a scratchy voice. "Can't make me."

"Jasper!" A desperate male voice cut across the crowd of law enforcement and spectators.

Hope flooded me. "Jude!" I jumped up from my perch on the back of the ambulance and spun around. "Jude, where are you?"

"Jasper?"

"Jude! I'm over here by the ambulance." I bounced on my toes and waved my hands wildly above my head. "Jude!"

The crowd parted. I fell to my knees and clutched my stomach, the grief attacking me all over again. "Adam," I whispered. "I-I-I thought ... you sound like Jude. Is he with you?"

My brother's closest friend from school, Adam Norwood, knelt down next to me. "No, Jas. He's not. You're the only one."

"I didn't know. One minute I was there and then noises and heat and I couldn't see. Then I could and the house blew up and it looked like a mushroom cloud. Where are they?"

Adam's lip quivered. He looked like his five year old self after Jude ate one of the roses on his birthday cake. "Jasper," he said slowly. "Jasper, what did you do?"

I stared at him blankly. "What do you mean? Adam, my family. They're *gone* and I need to find them. They might be hurt. You have to help me."

He grasped my shoulders and shook me roughly, the transformation sudden and frightening. His face was splotchy red and his body shook.

"What did you do?" he shouted. "What did you do to them? I know it was you. Why did you kill them?"

A nearby firefighter pulled Adam off me. "Son, what the hell is your problem? She's injured, for Christ's sake."

From my vantage point, sprawled out on the sooty, wet ground, I saw Adam struggling, spitting and snarling. "It's her fault! Didn't you see the high school earlier? She did this! She killed her family!"

"Whoa, son. That's a huge accusation. Come with me."

The same EMT who wrapped me in the blanket helped me to my feet and brought me back to my perch.

I frowned and pointed to my bandaged ear when her lips began to move but no sound reached me. She tried again.

"You had us scared for a while. Nod if you understand me. Good girl. What's your name?"

"Jasper Andrews."

"Do you know today's date?"

I stuttered over the month and day. "I didn't do anything. My family."

"I'm here to treat your wounds, but I can send for someone who can take your story."

No. Shit. Shit. Shit. This is just like earlier. They don't believe me. Only this time, I really didn't do it. It. Blow up my house. Kill my family.

"Oh, my god," I said as it all sank in again. What little was left in my stomach came up with force before I could turn away and hit the poor EMT. The saint of a woman sighed and sanitized me to the best of her ability before leaving for what I could only assume was a decontamination unit.

"My family. They're dead."

"Ms. Andrews."

Shit. Shit. Shit.

"Detective Lattimeir. Detective Bryant," I said wearily. "My family's dead. My home is gone. I don't know what more I can add to your reports."

The burly detective knelt before me and tapped my shoulder. "Where were you going?"

My camping bag was a sack of rocks I'd forgotten.

"Oh." I pressed my lips together as my mind raced. "My parents, after the incident earlier this week, they thought it was best that I finish up the school year with one of my relatives. I was waiting for them to arrive."

"Who was coming to get you?"

"*Them*. My mom called them. I don't know their names. I think Mom knows. Knew."

In the back of my mind, *She* sent me a warning. *Watch those words Jasper. They already thing you're unstable. And that shit head, Adam. I swear he's next on our list.*

44

Next?

Next as in asses we need to kick after these detectives.

"Ms. Andrews?"

Fingers snapped in front of my face, startling me.

"Sorry. They're my mom's people from where she grew up or something. All I know is they were supposed to arrive in a Lincoln Towncar. My dad said I should practice walking with my bag, since we didn't exactly know where I'm headed. So I took a walk in the meadow. Then something felt off and I was hit by this ... concussive blast that knocked me to the ground. But it wasn't until I got up and started running toward the house that it exploded."

"Were you angry about being sent away?"

She wasn't the only one who was angry. The implication of *her* warning and the detective's tone sunk into my thick skull. "What? Are you saying that I did this? Destroyed my life? My family?"

That smug jerk, Detective Bryant, crossed her arms and jutted out her hip as if she had just found Carmen San Diego. "You said it, not me."

Big mistake.

She gave up all pretenses of civility and tossed me to the backseat, leaving me to watch with horror as *She*/I hauled ourselves to our feet and punched the good detective in the jaw. With the exception of Jude, I'd never gotten into physical altercations and the thrill of punching him had gone away a long time ago.

But this? The bones and muscles in my hand tightening into a compact fist, pulling my arm back and launching it forward with extreme velocity.

She purred on contact, relishing the way Detective Bryant's skin rippled under the force of the assault. The raw, physical gratification nearly overwhelmed me.

Detective Bryant wasn't expecting the punch. She screamed shrilly and cradled her chin. I swung again, this time connecting with her temple.

The sickening crunch of bone, the parting of flesh and slow oozing of blood from the wound *She/I* inflicted ...

Glorious.

"Let go of me," I shrieked.

"Jasper Andrews, you're under arrest for assault of a police officer and suspected murder of Jude, Olivia, Mark and Delia Andrews. You have the right to remain silent..."

CHAPTER 3

Detective Bryant hauled me into the station, her arm a vise around my bicep. The big bad detective brought in the evil arsonist, all five and a half feet and less than a hundred and forty pounds of me. My hands cuffed behind my back made me a real danger.

Her chest puffed out and her face almost split from that shit-eating grin. That, and the barely-healed cuts on her lip and just above her ear. She shoved me into a chair and handcuffed me to it.

I bared my teeth and snarled at her. "Let me go," I spat.

"Right. Officer Rodriguez, please book Ms. Jasper Andrews. Watch out, though. She's vicious and she can make an incendiary out of anything."

"My family's either hurt or dead, moron. Do your job and find them."

Detective Bryant smirked and walked away, leaving me with a terrified Officer Rodriguez who couldn't have been much older than my tender eighteen years.

"Did you go to Clarkson Senior High?" I asked.
"Yeah, class of 2013. You?"
"Would have been the class of 2016."

47

"Yeah, huh. Sorry about all that." Officer Rodriguez pulled up the booking software and straightened in his seat. "Full name, age, sex, occupation?"

"Jasper Lee Andrews, eighteen, female. Depends on who you ask. Arsonist. Terrorist. Murderer."

My tantrum garnered more attention than I anticipated.

"You tell 'em, sweetie. We're all innocent in here," jeered a middle-aged man with a bad comb over and cheap polyester pants. "Bet you could set me on fire."

Your name shall be Landlord in a low-rent adult movie.

I hissed at him. "Fuck off."

"Jasper. Ms. Andrews. Did the arresting officer tell you why you've been arrested?"

"Huh? Sure." Landlord and I were engaged in a staring contest, only his anger was laced with lust. Mine was laced with murder.

Come at me, bro.

Officer Rodriguez's questions buzzed around me. "Were you read your rights?"

"Yup. Do I get a phone call?"

"No, not yet."

Landlord's thin lips flapped again. "Who ya calling, Sparky?"

Kill him. Murder him. Tear his skin from his flesh and separate his bones. No one calls us Sparky. No one except Jude.

Jude.

My chest heaved and sweat poured down my face as three officers tilted my chair, with me in it, upright and shouted at Landlord to shut his mouth.

"Listen, Andrews," a furious police officer snapped. "You're already facing charges of arson, manslaughter and assault of a law enforcement official. Keep this shit up and I'll tell everyone that you're trying to kill yourself. You'll be on a 5150 before you can say boo. And that's before you go to jail."

I stared at my wrists in horror. The struggle to get to Landlord had been violent enough that I had cut

48

myself on the handcuffs and was bleeding. The rest of my body bloomed in pain and bruises. "I didn't, I don't know," I babbled.

My unit of watchmen marched me over into the nearest holding cell. Some officer told me to cool off, that they'd send someone to finish my booking away from the pervs and junkies.

Nothing but the finest for Clarkson's top criminal.

They took off the cuffs and left me alone in the tiny room with nothing but memories that flashed across my eyes as often as the florescent lights above my head. Nothing made sense, no matter how I tried to arrange the facts and mix in circumstantial evidence. I had blown up. Less than two days later, as I waited for strangers to hide me the boogieman, my house had blown up and my family died.

Open and shut, as the television shows always said.

I curled up in the corner of the cold metal bench and closed my eyes. There was no fight left in me. I knew that they had all the evidence that they needed for a conviction. I was going to jail.

She woke up abruptly and told me, in no uncertain terms, that we were not going to jail. We had a family to avenge. Murderers to find. Neither of which could be done from a jail cell. We had to get out.

I began to feel hot from inside my body, a heat that wanted to expand outward, past the barriers of my flesh. It took the form of millions of tiny needles, ready to lance me at *Her* signal.

"Officer Rodriguez!"

Don't work against me, Jasper. You'll regret it.

Shut up and stop being such a psycho.

Doesn't work like that, little Jas. Stop pretending like there was any other way.

"Officer Rodriguez," I screamed again, as he came into view I collapsed with relief against the wall. "Officer, you have to either get me out of here or clear the station. It's important to clear the area right away."

His Adam's apple bobbled as he tried to speak. "Is that a threat? Do you have a device on you?"

"No, no, no. Just ... trust me. Please. You have to get out of here. I don't want anyone to get hurt," I begged.

Millions of white-hot pinpricks were at the surface, ready to go. *She* had her finger on the detonator and had picked her moment.

My camping bag hadn't yet been searched or logged into evidence; instead, it sat next to the chair at Officer Rodriguez's desk. That meant they hadn't found the thick envelope of cash with our life savings. Money, he had told me that would get me by until we could reunite. I needed my bag. I needed to get out.

Officer Rodriguez took a cautious step backward.

Heat and anger burst out of my skin in a frightening concussive blast that knocked over anything that wasn't bolted down, blasted glass windows and electronic screens and rendered unconscious everyone around me.

"Run, Jasper."

I looked around wildly for the source of the genius advice, but I was alone. Since it was good advice, I pushed the holding cell door open and picked my way across the floor littered with bodies. I picked up my camping bag and quickly divested an officer of his weapon. I turned the safety on and stuck it in my jacket.

One last look and I was gone.

§

I rubbed my hands together and breathed on them to keep the circulation flowing. Escaping a police station that I was already being accused of bombing made getting out of town more difficult than I thought.

I spent the remainder of the day running through the woods along the Harlem River and making my way toward Manhattan. Although we didn't visit often, Jude and I marveled at the anonymity to be found in the City

That Never Sleeps. I didn't have a plan, but Manhattan seemed like a safe bet. With my brother's foresight, I had the cash to find a cheap, sketchy motel to hide until a bright idea came to me.

But I was running and hiking over twenty miles; I had to make camp or I'd be wandering in the dark. I found an overgrowth within a mile stretch of forest between the river and the Bronx River Parkway and set up camp as best possible. I ate jerky and protein bars and washed it down with a few sips of water.

Although it wouldn't have been easy to spot, I didn't put up my tent. I'd have to leave it behind if I had to leave suddenly and I refused to risk my only reliable shelter. Instead, I unzipped my green sleeping bag and wrapped it around my shoulders.

September winds whipped through the trees, scattering leaves and pine needles danced around me. It reminded me of something my dad and I talked about the first time he took us camping. Jude snored next to us, but I was scared of the noise.

"Daddy, there's too many things out there trying to eat us," my eight-year-old self had whispered.

Dad had laughed and put an arm around my shoulders. "Nah, only a handful of things want to eat us, Jas. Most of the creatures are like us, moving around to keep warm."

"Why does Jude get to be a hibernating bear?"

"Because your brother isn't scared of much, is he?"

Shame had warmed my cheeks that night. "No. I'm the scaredy cat."

Dad jutted his head toward my twin. "But you're cleverer in some ways. He'll do anything, but you have to get him out of those messes."

"Don't tell him. He doesn't like to think I help him. But I do because he beats up kids who try to mess with me and my friends," I said, proud of our complementary natures.

"You keep sharp, Jas, because I have a feeling you two are going to end up in some crazy situations as teenagers."

CHAPTER 4

Manhattan welcomed me with open arms. From the moment I stepped out of the bus terminal at 181st Street and Broadway, I breathed easier. No one looked for an upstate New York teenager in the middle of the city. No one was that dumb.

Safety was accomplished, so my inner Maslow began the search for sustenance and rest. Sustenance was easy. Washington Heights had more smells and scents than I had ever experienced. I walked into the first store and ordered a plate of rice, beans and chicken. The waitress smiled kindly at my bad Spanish and came back a few minutes later with water, bread with butter and garlic, and a bowl of grapes.

I nodded my thanks and demolished the grapes while keeping an eye on the television, where the Spanish newscaster talked about everything but me. Tension melted from my body at the realization that I was safe in this neighborhood.

The chicken melted in my mouth, salty and juicy with a hint of lime. The rice was just as good and even more filling. I shoveled the food in my mouth, rice falling on the table and my lap. I ate voraciously because I didn't know when I'd eat something this good again.

Crap. Living from one day to the next was awful.

I paid as soon as I was done and made my way to a park down the street from the restaurant. I'd reached the point where recklessness and adrenaline would suffice. Any plan would have been better than none at all.

Two teenagers ambled by the bench where I was sitting. They were gossiping about a friend.

"She had to leave, son. Her moms wasn't gonna let her stay there pregnant," one of the young men told a younger, lankier teen. "It's crazy."

The other guy responded in Spanish. The only words I understood were *dormir, bañar,* and *comer.* Sleep, bathe and eat.

Gold.

Upon hearing those words *She* nudged my consciousness after several hours of petulant silence. Apparently, disagreeing with her about blowing up a police station was out of line in our relationship.

Too easy. Why is everything so easy?

Her advice had been terrible thus far, so I made the executive decision to ask the guys about a place to stay. I pretended to be a tourist, which they must have encountered all the time, because within minutes I had the name of two hostels and a few homeless shelters.

§

The shelter where I showered, took a nap and ate a quick lunch was no longer an option, not after my face showed up on the afternoon, mid-afternoon and evening news reports.

I grabbed my belongings and jumped on the first bus that looked like it was headed toward a crappy neighborhood, the kind where they only ask for identification if you're buying beer. Not that I had any firsthand experience with crappy neighborhoods, but my knowledge of television had paid off thus far.

My first stop was a questionable-looking salon, where I cut five inches off my hair. The second was the bargain clothing store across the street where I undressed and packed my clothes and slipped into a pair of skinny jeans, boots, a too-tight sweater and a faux-leather jacket. Makeup was the last step. The mugshot showed a fresh-faced, scared girl with long hair.

I was saucy, showing off my curves in tight clothes and was rocking a short, darker hairdo. I was also hoping that the police were dumb enough to fall for this ruse. Based on the gossip of women in the salon, I learned that the area was rife with homelessness and crime. I'd have to switch bags again, but I was confident that I could lose myself somewhere even the police avoided.

Welcome to Hunts Point, Home of the World's Largest Flower Market, the Bronx River and a Vibrant Community.

I scanned the statistics on the temporary sign nailed to the side of the train station entrance. It housed plenty of youth shelters and community organizations. Good enough place as any to get lost for a while. Dark was falling again and I couldn't stand the idea of sleeping outdoors, not in that cold, so I trudged my way up a hill with lights bright enough for a football field beaming up top.

Ahead of me, a guy wearing a baseball cap and a hooded sweatshirt exited a building on my right. Although his hands were in his pockets and headphones blared in his ears, he gave me the shivers. I couldn't avoid him and his eyes were all over me.

"Sup, sweetie," he murmured as we passed each other. "Looking good."

"Thanks," I said uneasily. *She* watched him and poked at something I couldn't see. *She* wanted to know if he was like her.

"I don't know you," he said flatly. He stopped walking and stared at me. "I know everyone in this neighborhood. Where are you going?"

"Don't know what to tell you. I must have one of those forgettable faces." Flippant and scared tones warred with each other. Fear won and my voice shook. "Have a good night."

The man sighed and closed the distance between us. "For what it's worth, Jasper," he said quietly as he whirled me around and wrapped his large arm around my throat. "I'm sorry about this."

The last time Jude and I wrestled and he tried to put me in a headlock, I junk punched him and ran away.

This man wasn't my brother. His muscles had muscles and they were all currently restricting my airway.

"G..get off m..m..me," I wheezed. "Asshole." Adrenaline and my flight impulse kicked in as *She* roared to life; we kicked, punched, and scratched until my vision started to fade and all I could hear was the music coming from his headphones.

The sonofabitch was listening to Beyoncé.

PART 2

CHAPTER 5

We laughed at the darkness/so scared that we lost it/ we stood on the ceilings/you showed me love was all you needed.

I woke up by degrees. With sharpening consciousness, however, came growing awareness of an unexpected numbness in my limbs. Voices around me grew louder until I could make out distinct words.

"She ... called to ... too late ... poor girl."

"So? She's still ... threat ... neutralize."

"Don't be idiots. If she poses that much of a threat, then put in the work. Train her. She's raw, without any sense of how to control herself."

A woman's voice, low and kind, said, "I think she's waking up. We should probably take the hood off her head."

Hood? On my head? Holy shit. I'd been abducted by the boogieman. They found me. My family died and they found me anyway.

I fought a valiant battle with the crust gluing my eyes shut. It clung to my lashes and cemented closed my tear ducts. Somehow, it created a level of itchiness I didn't know existed, the kind one had no way of knowing until they were unable to use their hands.

Hands. Feet. Shit. Can't move.

Nope. Not happening. Not a real thing. If I said it enough it would be true. So I did the same thing any reasonable person would do.

"Help! Someone help me!" I struggled against the restraints. "Get me out of here!"

"Jasper," a calm, almost detached voice said. The same voice that abducted me. "Listen to me carefully because your safety depends on what you say next."

"Is that a threat?"

"No," he replied. "For the record, I don't threaten. Now, how did you find us, Jasper Andrews?"

"You drugged me and kidnapped me. I haven't the faintest clue who you are or where you've taken me. Dude, untie me. This situation will get a lot worse."

The room sucked in a collective breath and held it.

The man in front of me laughed. "Impressive set of *cojones*. If I remove this bag, do you promise to behave yourself?"

"As much as you'd behave in my situation." I closed my crust-filled eyes again and tried to extend my senses.

Big guy is the muscle. The woman ... potential ally or designated good cop.

I growled despite myself. I wasn't on the best terms with law enforcement at the moment. The feeling was mutual.

Two other men and one woman inside the room. More just outside the door. People who are okay with abducting and restraining me.

The boogieman found me.

"The correct response is, 'yes, of course, I'll behave because I recognize the severity and direness of this mess.' Got it?" The man leaned forward and lowered his voice. "I didn't drug you. You went down quickly with minimal effort on my part. Remember that when I remove the hood."

The man who kidnapped me was in charge of this interrogation. The guy who listened to Beyoncé while attacking a young woman.

He was gentle as he divested me of the black hood and shielded my eyes for a moment. "Take your time and don't fight. You'll only injure yourself and hurt your pride."

Lovely, classic perfume wafted toward me, a fitting introduction to the voice that followed.

"You've terrorized our guest enough, Jordan. Go sit in a corner."

"Still don't trust me, *Cecilia*? I'll keep that in mind when I get a call in the middle of the night because someone needs a ride home."

"Hate to interrupt the marital discord here, because it's amusing. But can I open my eyes, answer your ridiculous questions and get the hell out of here? I have someplace where I'm expected."

"And? Your dinner plans are the least of your worries, Jasper Andrews. How did you find us?"

"Jordan," the woman hissed. "One thing at a time. Go on, now, and let me work."

I heard Jordan huff and guessed those were his heavy footfalls moving away from us. His retreating footsteps provided a moment of relief. Whoever he was, the guy had an overwhelming, eclipsing presence. He was also the guy who drugged — sorry, choked — me and threatened my life. He was also a jerk to his girlfriend.

Cecilia applied a warm washcloth to my face, wiping away the sweat and eye crust.

"Done?" Jordan snapped.

"If you value your life, you'll leave or stop asking asinine questions. I don't disagree with your actions, but there's no need to treat her like a criminal."

"Hey, guys," I said, "I haven't seen your faces and I have no idea where —"

"We treat her however I decide. Until you're in charge of keeping every person in this compound safe, don't offer your advice. It's not wanted."

Cecilia dropped the washcloth, whirled around and jabbed her finger in the chest of a tall blond man with blue-green eyes. Jordan.

Yep, still terrifying.

"Maybe you should excuse yourself. Clearly, this case is messing with the minuscule amounts of decency you have left. The poor kid has suffered enough."

"Kid? Lady, I'm eighteen. I saw my family being murdered and might have killed an entire police station's worth of people. Please don't treat me like a child."

Jordan, who stared down at Cecilia with something akin to amusement, raised his eyes to meet mine. "Haven't seen my face? Couldn't help yourself?"

"Shit."

"Enough!" The voice boomed from a black man I hadn't noticed before. "Shelve your personal issues for a later time. You're supposed to be debriefing her and preparing her to meet with the High Council."

Jordan's lips twisted into a scowl and he spoke stiffly. "Exactly."

"Good," the black man said. "Shall we return to the matter at hand?"

"Can Cecilia stay?" I asked Jordan quietly. "No offense to you, big guy, but you're terrifying. If possible, I'd love to use the restroom and I'd appreciate it if you weren't the one watching."

The black man nodded his assent. The room cleared out save for a handful of people — Jordan, Cecilia, the black man, a young, Latino guy who reminded me of middle management at my part-time job, and two older women.

"My name is Dakarai," he said as he removed my restraints. He gently massaged my ankles and wrists. "My apologies for the way you've been treated."

"Am I a prisoner?"

Jordan snorted to himself, but leaned back against the wall with his arms crossed instead of answering.

"Depends on what you mean by prisoner," the Latino man said. "Jasper, I know it's hard to believe, but you're safe here. We need to assess whether or not you're a threat to our people."

Too many questions flashed in my head: good questions, but the least intelligent was the one that escaped. "Can I go to the bathroom?"

Dakarai smiled, offered a hand and helped me to my feet. "Of course, my dear. You'll probably want to clean up, shower and nap. Are you hungry?"

"Yes, thank you."

"Alright. I'll try to expedite the process. You've already met Jordan and Cecilia. This," he said, waving at the Latino man, "is Daniel. He'll be your point of contact for the duration."

"Why can't you be my contact?" I refused to let go of Dakarai's hand. He was the nicest person I'd encountered since the incident in school and there was nothing that could make me give that kindness away.

"Because I'm in charge," Daniel snapped.

My lips curled into a disdainful snarl. In the last week, I'd blown up a hallway in my school, watched my family murdered, was arrested, blew up a police station and escaped from custody and managed to get lost in Manhattan.

I was having a terrible week, but I was coping.

Daniel's response broke me.

Two men, short and indistinct, walked into the room. They were followed by two women.

§

Jordan clucked. "He's all bark, Jasper. You can stop crying now. Please stop crying."

Sobs mixed with incoherent words I didn't even understand as I curled into myself against a wall.

Only walls weren't warm, nor did they move with steady breaths. They didn't wear t-shirts or cradle me like a child. They certainly didn't smooth hair back from my forehead or hand me a handkerchief.

"J-j-Jordan?"

Captain Obvious, reporting for duty.

He leaned against the wall, pulled me onto his lap and held me against his chest. "I won't lie to you, Jasper. You're not going to wake up and realize this was all a terrible nightmare. You're not going to see your home or bed again."

"Smooth, Jordy," Cecilia said. "Let's completely traumatize her today."

"And since when did you develop a soft spot for prisoners?"

Daniel, jerk face, asshole, mean piece of —

"Danny, listen closely because we're not discussing this again. There were better, more humane ways to bring Jasper here. I provided a list of those ways in my assessment, all of which were rejected. There's no point in being cruel to her, especially now."

"Why?"

"Why what? Why now?" Jordan shrugged. "Because, aside from being untrained, she's not a threat. Right now, she needs a bed, a shower and food."

"Are you sure this has nothing to do with your savior complex?" Cecilia's voice was bitter. "She needs a friend, not a pit bull."

"Never claimed to be either," Jordan responded evenly. "But you're more interested in arguing with me and Danny will likely torture her to death."

"Not helping," Dakarai added. "Jordan and Cecilia, why don't you show Jasper to a room and get her something to eat? Danny, you can utilize the time to prepare your report for the High Council."

The unexpected shift in dynamics was confusing enough to halt my sobs. I thought and had been told that Daniel was in charge. Yet, everyone seemed to defer to Dakarai. And no one had bothered to introduce the wizened older women sitting in the shadows. A small part of me wished that I wasn't too devastated to make smartass comments. The other part was excited to be alive.

Jordan complained, but picked me up and cradled me in his arms. "Ceci, will you slip her bag over my shoulder?"

"I've got it," she replied. "And Danny, you and I will discuss this later."

Daniel ran a hand through his hair and swore. He nodded, kissed her cheek and stomped out of the room.

"Is there a particular room you'd like us to give her?"

Dakarai pursed his lips. "I thought she might be comfortable in the new residential wing. There are several unoccupied rooms at the moment."

Jordan finally grinned. "Danny's going to have a heart attack when he realizes she's a few doors down from him. Cecilia and I can manage from here. Just shoot me a text message with the time of the meeting with the High Council."

§

Despite my protests, Jordan carried me through the huge industrial-looking complex.

"You're barely standing," he pointed out unnecessarily. "The residential wing is on the other side of the compound. I'd appreciate not having to stop at the infirmary because you cracked your head open or fell down a flight of stairs."

Cecilia scoffed behind us. "Yup. That's the only reason."

Except for the slight deepening of a single breath, Jordan didn't react. "Besides, you don't weigh enough to be an inconvenience."

"Okay," I replied meekly and hid my face in his shirt. "Sorry."

"Don't apologize. We'll get you settled in shortly. You'll have a room and a private bathroom. There's a laptop with limited access to the internet. Someone will bring you food."

"Why?"

"Why are we feeding you and letting you sleep? Because we're not monsters, Jasper." Cecilia's tone was just on this side of frosty, as if I were encroaching on unwelcoming lands. "Protecting our people is our primary focus. Dakarai decided you're not a threat, so now we'll tend to your needs. Are you injured?"

"No idea. And thank you."

"Is there anyone who might be searching for you?"

I laughed. "The police? My brother's best friend who wants to literally kill me? Small town folk with pitchforks? Other than that, no."

"Other than that," Jordan mocked. "They can't find you or hurt you."

"Right. You're nice."

"No, I'm not. Don't mistake decency for innate goodness. If you want nice, talk to Cecilia or Dakarai. Even Mikael. Just don't come to me." Jordan stopped in front of an elevator bank and pressed the call button.

"Who's Mikael?"

"You'll meet him soon enough."

"Did someone say my name?"

Jordan smiled widely. "Ask and ye shall receive. What's up, bro?"

The tall, lanky man raised an eyebrow and spoke with a noticeable Russian accent. "A present? You shouldn't have, *brat.*"

Cecilia glared at them. "She's right here, idiots. As in don't ignore her or speak about her as if she's not here."

Pot meet kettle much?

Mikael bowed his head. "Forgive me? That was unspeakably rude."

"Hi, Mikael," I squeaked, feeling ridiculous talking to him while being toted around like a puppy. "I'm Jasper."

He smiled kindly. "Welcome, *sestra*. Once you're settled, I'll give you a proper tour."

Somewhere in the back of my mind, the word *sestra* bounced around, looking for the meaning. Although I

65

barely knew the language, *sestra* sounded like a familiar, almost intimate, term of endearment.

"Thank you."

"They gave you trouble, eh? Has anyone bothered to tell you anything?" Mikael stepped closer and peered at me, the infant in Jordan's arms.

"No. Jordan?"

"Hmm?"

The rat bastard was humming Beyoncé songs to himself.

"Put me down."

"No."

Cecilia put a restraining hand on my shoulder. "Jasper, speaking from experience, you'll have an easier time if you allow him the caveman routine. You're Jordy's responsibility, something he —"

Jordan stopped humming to himself. "Shut up," he said quietly. "My reasons are my own. Make yourself useful or go away."

Cecilia squared her shoulders. "I've let your attitude slide in the past. Don't push me."

He burst out into laughter. "Screwing Danny doesn't give you authority here. Last time I checked, the safety of this facility and everyone here is my responsibility. I can be nice or you can sleep without worrying about getting kidnapped or murdered. Your choice."

The elevator chimed and the doors opened, a perfect desuetude to the conversation.

§

The door locked from the outside.

True to his word, Jordan delivered me to a nondescript room in the residential wing, whatever that was. He held on to me as I regained my equilibrium and showed me around while Mikael and Cecilia watched from the open door.

"This," he said, waving a hand, "is your room. Door on the left is your bathroom. The hot water takes a minute. Everything else is self-explanatory."

"Yeah. Desk, chair, laptop and lamp. Got it."

"Good." Jordan stuck his hands in his pockets and stared above my head. "Uh, if you need anything, just ask someone."

"Who?"

The man might have choked me unconscious, but he also carried me because I'd been crying. I didn't understand him. Yet, somehow it seemed he was my only ally.

He shrugged. "No idea. Well, have fun."

Cecilia stared daggers at his retreating figure. "Asshole," she hissed.

"Ah, *solnyshka*," Mikael said, rolling his eyes at her. "You never fail to impress me with your good manners. Jasper, please excuse Jordan and Cecilia. They devolve into poorly behaved children when they disagree."

"Okay," I said slowly. "I won't claim to understand, but my brother and I are …" I turned away. These strangers didn't deserve to know anything about Jude. They didn't deserve anything.

"Grief comes in the most unexpected ways, *da*? You have no reason to believe anyone here. If you trust nothing else, please know that you will be given the time and opportunity to honor your family's memory."

"Get out." The lump in my throat grew. I couldn't handle the pain much longer.

Mikael bowed his head and walked away, whistling a sad tune to himself.

§

"Well, this has been delightful," Cecilia drawled. "Unfortunately, I have other obligations, so I'll make this quick and tell you what Jordan refused to share. You can't escape. This door can only be opened from the outside and the windows are shatterproof. I suggest you shower and nap. Someone will deliver your meal shortly."

I pressed my lips together and nodded. Cecilia had to have been the third or fourth person to suggest a shower, so either these people were hideously rude or I reeked. A warm shower and nap sounded heavenly.

"Great. Fantastic. Anything else I should know?"

Cecilia smiled, the corner of her thin lips notched to the right. "Yes. Don't trust anyone or anything. It's naive to think the man who rendered you unconscious will hold your hand."

"Got it."

We took one another's measure, a staring contest, the first round of what I imagined would be several pissing matches.

She broke first.

"Wonderful. Someone will retrieve you later. Tomorrow. Whenever."

The door shut and I was blessedly alone, away from the strong personalities and overbearing physical presences of these insane people who knew what I was. For a moment, I'd been naive enough to think I'd been found by my mother's people, those mysterious protectors.

But protectors didn't imprison people they swore to protect.

Or did they?

I was laughably out of my league, unprepared, ignorant and physically inferior. I quickly realized I should have been spending my time devising some ingenious escape plan or crafting some MacGyver-like weapon. The room had to contain clues pertaining to my location. Something.

I prowled the room like the super-sleuth I was undeniably not, turning over the mattress. Underneath was a simple frame with a note attached.

Stop wasting your time. If we wanted to harm you, you'd already be dead.

Fear and anger hit my system, rousing *Her* from her slumber.

"About time," I grumbled aloud. "Where the hell have you been? Why didn't you save me from tall, blond and scary? And do *not* tell me you're curious about him."

Don't be an idiot, Jasper. One of us had to handle this with some detachment. I'm curious about him and everyone else here. Didn't you feel it? The hum of electricity? Power?

I did not.

Everyone in this building is like us. They have abilities that I don't dare mess with, not yet. Tall, blond and scary? He's packing major power. Mikael, too.

"What about the two women who didn't speak?"

Speaking out loud to myself did nothing to make me appear sane, but *She* was the only connection I had to my reality. She saw what I was too emotional to process and was our best bet of survival.

Powerful, but not a threat. I'm inexplicably drawn to the rest of them. Cecilia, Daniel, Jordan and Dakarai. Stay alert.

"Lie to me. Tell me everything's going to be okay."

I'm sorry, Jasper. Truly. Stay strong. And for cripes' sake, take a shower, woman. You look like a three day stale hooker.

"Ouch." I replaced the mattress and dumped my camping bag on the bed. Somehow, it was still meticulously organized, so I fished out my toiletries and a new outfit and entered the bathroom.

Holy shit. My own bathroom bigger than the one I shared with Jude. The sole ray of sunshine in the midst of this nightmare. Deciding it would be poor form to whoop at the small pleasure, I stripped and jumped in the shower.

The icy cold water hit me with the force of a fireman's hose. I shrieked and jumped right back out. "Son of a ... damn piece of ... all lies. I hate them," I growled at my reflection in the mirror above the sink. "I hate the lies, the secrets, and the freezing effing water. I should punish them with my stench and insolence. I'm good at insolence."

My tirade lasted as long as it took for the hot water to arrive. I stepped back into the shower under the protest of my inner crybaby, then moaned from the perfect temperature and pressure. The crybaby disappeared.

She was gone. The inner crybaby was gone. Hell, my anger and indignation had fled in their wake. For the first time in recent history, I was alone in my head. My father used to call moments like that "where the rubber meets the road," the true test of a person's character.

I wasn't afraid of much, or at least I hadn't been until a few days ago. I was smart, clever and in good shape. I also knew something they didn't — this prison wasn't my last stop. Grief crippled, I'd learned. But revenge motivated.

§

When the knock at the door came, I was ready. I'd scrubbed my skin pink, washed my hair until it was squeaky and brushed my teeth until my gums hated me.

The shower comments bothered me. I was vain and didn't care if they thought poorly of me.

"Jasper," Mikael called softly. "I brought food."

He did me the courtesy of not entering unbidden and waited for me to open the door. In his hands was a tray with burgers, fries, onion rings and milkshakes.

"I can't eat that much."

Mikael tilted his head to one side. "*Da, da.* I hoped you would tolerate some company."

"Sorry." *So not sorry.* "You seem kind enough, but it seems like a terrible idea to share a meal with one of my captors."

"I argued against that plan. Jordan and Dakarai, as well. But we're only three voices amongst many. Have patience, Jasper."

He placed the tray down on the small bedside table and stepped back into the hallway.

"Thank you for the meal," I said, then gently closed the door in his face.

I pressed my ear against the door and waited until his footsteps faded before turning my attention to the tray.

The big, juicy bacon cheeseburger drew me in with its siren song. Intellectually, I knew there was a chance that the meal was poisoned and would kill me. Emotionally, I needed comfort food. Being a vegetarian wasn't a luxury I could afford.

The burger was everything. I cut the monstrosity in half and bit down. Flavors burst into life on my tongue — the sharpness of the cheddar cheese complemented the saltiness of the bacon and the sweet ketchup. The meat, cooked to a perfect medium rare, dripped its juices down my chin. It might have been the best burger I'd ever tasted.

The entire meal was gone in less than ten minutes. Once I was comfortably full, my eyelids began to droop. The bed called my name and, since I'm no fool, I listened for once. The sheets smelled like sunshine, that fresh smell that can only be achieved by drying them on a line. It reminded me of home.

§

"Jasper," Cecilia called through the door. "Wake up. We have preparations to deal with, the least of which is your appearance."

I sat up with a scowl. My appearance? Cecilia thought that was a priority. History couldn't provide weirder captors.

"Go away."

Cecilia knocked again. "I'm being polite. Open the damn door."

Sighing, I climbed out of bed and opened the damn door. "What do you want?"

"To prepare you." She stared at me. "Did you not hear me? Anyway, we should get started. Time's ticking."

"Holy shit, can you be any vaguer? Someone needs to start speaking in some sort of coherent language or I'm going to lose my shit."

"The High Council is ready to see you. One does not meet with the High Council in wrinkled jeans and a t-shirt. Neither does one use foul language. Therefore, I'm here to make sure you're dressed appropriately and briefed."

The tightness around her eyes hadn't faded, nor had the lack of warmth in her smile. The only other woman I'd encountered was my stylist.

"This is such bullshit."

She raised one of those perfect eyebrows and crossed her arms. "Exactly what part is bullshit? The fact that you're here? Or that I've been relegated to being your babysitter? Trust me, I'm not happy about it either."

"Oh, good. At least we're on the same page."

Cecilia's shoulders relaxed. "For now. I had to guess your sizes, but I have an appropriate outfit in your closet."

How had I missed the closet?

Inside, I found a pair of classic black pants, a crew-neck black shirt and sensible flats. "You can turn around now."

She smirked and closed her eyes. "Modesty is highly overrated. Besides, the human body becomes less interesting the more you study it."

"And you do?" I asked as I slipped on the shoes. The mirror in front of me revealed someone different — a confident, proud, dangerous young woman. I wished I had claws like Wolverine or mind control like Jean Grey or my sister.

"My field of study is bio electromagnetics. Before you ask, it is the examination of the interactions between electromagnetic fields and biological entities."

"Thank you, Captain Obvious. You can open your eyes."

Cecilia took in my appearance with a single, sweeping glance. "Sit down so I can do your hair and makeup."

"How'd you go from a biophysicist to my personal stylist? Don't get me wrong, your personal style is fantastic. But I don't think it's a stretch to say that something is off."

I wasn't lying. Cecilia was gorgeous in her unique way. She was model thin with mousy brown hair cut into a sleek bob and pale skin. She reminded me of Anne Hathaway without the benefit of her own beauty squad. She wore a black sheath dress and three-inch heels with enviable grace.

"Men are idiots. There are layers of leadership here. I belong to one of the upper echelons, as do Jordan, Mikael, Dakarai and Danny. There are a few others, but we comprise the core group. Despite their collective intelligence, which I question some days, they have the misguided belief that we'll be best friends right away because we're women."

"Morons."

She grinned at me through the mirror and attempted to tame my hair. "Exactly. Yesterday wasn't a fair representation of our relationships. We disagree on how to handle you."

"Yet again, we're on the same page. I have so many questions."

"Ask anything you'd like. Should you ask something you're not ready to hear, I won't answer."

I closed my eyes and allowed myself to enjoy the sensation of the brush running through my hair, untangling the knots and giving it a healthy sheen. *She poked at my consciousness.*

Enjoy the simple things, buddy. We both know this is the last moment of normality you'll have.

"How many layers of leadership exist? Do you have to donate obscene amounts of money to progress?"

73

"This isn't Hollywood, Jasper," she snapped. The tightness in her voice returned. "I'll let the High Council explain, but suffice to say that we are a large ... organization with a strict mission. The top layer of leadership is the High Council. Underneath is the Circle, which I described."

"The High Council is like a board of directors and you're division heads?"

"Something like that." She patted my shoulders. "Hair's done. Makeup time."

"Fabulous, dahling. Transform me into a star."

"Your sarcasm isn't appreciated."

Cecilia took a deep breath and unzipped a large makeup kit. Primer, foundation, concealer, blush, eyeshadow, mascara and lipstick covered the desk like an explosion of the beauty counter in a department store. She tapped her chin.

"Light olive. It will bring out the natural rosiness in your cheeks. Pretty eyes, by the way."

"Thanks. So you're a division head. Does that mean people report to you? What do they do? What is this place?"

"All good questions, none of which I'll answer."

I clenched my fist and, for the first time since the explosion, my hands warmed and glowed. Although it was accompanied by the usual pinprick sensation, it felt good. I felt alive and in control.

Cecilia looked down and stifled a laugh. "Ooh, the glow worm thinks she's a bad ass. You may have been a big deal in the outside world, but here you're just another person."

She snapped her fingers and emitted a faint glow. It was nowhere near as effulgent as mine, but it was there.

"What the hell is this place?" I asked breathlessly.

"This place may very well be your new home. Welcome to the headquarters of the Order of Vespers."

§

Vespers. I'd heard that word before, possibly from my mother. I vaguely remembered hearing it a few times within the context of a boogieman story.

"My mom ... she said there were people like me. They were supposed to help me. I was waiting for someone to pick me up when my family was ... when the explosion happened."

I wrapped my arms around myself and rocked.

"I'm sorry, Jasper."

"You never showed up. It's your fault that my family's gone. If you'd been there, you could have stopped all of this."

"It's time," Cecilia said gently and held out a hand.

"Time for you to get the answers you deserve."

CHAPTER 6

Danny met us at the elevator and gave me a curt nod of acknowledgment.

"Is she ready?"

"As prepared as one can be for this kind of shock. She didn't know about us, Danny."

"That's not possible."

"Hi. I'm standing right here. It would be groovy if you'd talk to me directly. Please." I tucked my hair behind my ears self-consciously, but maintained my bad ass posture.

Ooh, you're so tough, Jasper. It's the perfect image considering the last time he saw you, you were bawling like a baby. Time to put up or shut up.

Danny reduced me to a child in trouble with a single, withering glare. "When I need your opinion, I'll tell you. Otherwise, shut the hell up."

"Oh, fuck you," I exploded. "Enough with the secrecy, the talking about me like I'm not here, and the judgment. Tell me what's going on or I'm walking."

He let out a derisive laugh. "Really. Exactly where are you walking? You have no idea where you are and you have no idea how to exit the building. No one intends to hurt you unless you give us a reason."

"Danny!" Cecilia slapped his arm, her lips pressed in a thin line and nostrils flaring. "Stop it."

"Don't give me a reason to hurt you, Jasper."

The elevator's timely appearance may have saved us from an imminent brawl, but its confines made for some thick tension. I flexed my glowing fingers.

It did nothing to impress them.

Danny rolled his eyes and ignored me.

She showed up and was murderous.

Don't show weakness, Jasper. He's a predator and will exploit your fears. Take him out before he hurts you.

"Thanks, but I've got this one," I muttered to myself. Or *Her*. Lately, it was hard to keep track of who was in charge.

When the elevator doors opened, I pushed past them and exhaled. Danny reminded me of Jordan with his intensity and presence. I needed air that wasn't drenched in testosterone and animosity.

"Let's go," he said. "We're not there yet."

I wished I had a single ally in this place, someone who would show an ounce of compassion. Hell, I'd take a pat on the back or a Xanax. I wasn't picky.

Cecilia patted my shoulder sympathetically and smiled. "This place is huge, almost overwhelming. I've been here for years and I still get lost on occasion."

I frowned, my eyebrows nearly meeting at the bridge of my nose. What kind of madness was this? I wished for a friend and Cecilia's attitude changed.

Livie used to influence kids in school. Even though she was snotty and cliquish, she was the most popular student in her year. When we were young, she explained it by saying she wished really hard and things just worked out for her.

Try it again. I have a theory, but we need more evidence.

"We're going to a sub-level. It houses the High Council's chambers, the Circle's meeting rooms and the —"

"Interrogation rooms."

Danny's tough guy act didn't intimidate me. I had no doubt that he could hold his own in a fight. His physique indicated that he worked out regularly; his flat eyes hinted at a lack of restraint. But I had one thing he didn't. I was a loose cannon, untrained and even I didn't know what kind of damage I could cause.

Great. Find a way to mimic the school explosion and we should be groovy. Try some mind voodoo.

I wished Danny would shut up and hold doors like a gentleman. I wished that they'd tell me exactly where I was and point out the exits. The universe, or whatever higher being, laughed at me.

Danny held the door for Cecilia and chatted with her about their dinner plans, ignoring me completely.

There was no way I'd sink into his level of pettiness, so I took in my surroundings. From what I could tell we were in a complex of several connected buildings. The residential building, where I'd been relegated, was located at one end. We seemed to be walking through a school of sorts. Teenagers sat at cafeteria tables and gossiped. Around us were doors that led to classrooms.

The first floor of the next building was more bizarre than the last. On one side was a bank of elevators and a sign that informed the casual visitor of the location of medical facilities. Another bank of elevators went to somewhere called the Command Center.

Although the windows were opaque, this was the brightest area I'd seen so far. The floors were white marble. The security desks, the conversation pits scattered across the open space and walls were an equally bright white. The only break in the monochromatic scenery came from the clothes of the people walking through and the brushed aluminum elevator doors.

Two young men crossed in front of us, talking loudly.

"Did you hear anything about the mission?" The first man nearly bounced with excitement, his fingers waggling with the need to do something.

The other man nodded. "Yeah. I heard McAllister had to wrestle her to the ground and knock her out. Someone else told me that —"

"Gentlemen," Danny said.

They froze, fear plastered on their faces. The first man's shoulders scrunched up to his ears and his arms wrapped around himself.

Danny's voice, usually a rough snarl, became toneless. "Spreading gossip is a sure way to get demoted. Do you want to spend the rest of your days in the filing room? With actual paper files?"

"N...n...no, Mr. Santiago," they said in unison. The guy with the scrunched shoulders clasped his hands together in supplication. Babbled apologies and pleas for their jobs spilled out.

"This is your last warning. Go."

When he turned back to me and Cecilia, there was a grim satisfaction in his eyes. He'd liked scaring those men. He liked scaring people in general and throwing his weight around. A bully. That's what Danny was.

Jude would have kicked his ass on principle. I imagined his invisible wind knocking Danny around, tripping him up and pushing him to the floor. The thought made me smile, one of those big, genuine, face splitting grins.

Then it happened. Danny's body flew to the left, then was yanked to the right. Another gust nearly dropped him on the floor, but he was pushed upright at the last minute. And, in typical Jude fashion, the episode ended with the autocratic jerk sprawled out on the floor.

I clapped a hand over my mouth to suppress a wave of giggling.

Danny looked for the culprit wildly. Cecilia was too stunned to move, but I had a tickling in my brain that told me she was just as amused. The guards stepped forward and stopped several times, not wanting to bruise Danny's pride but unwilling to lose their jobs to his temper.

The silence was broken by a small giggle. A child, no older than eight years old, pointed and laughed.

Danny's face, already red with embarrassment, turned a dangerous shade of purple. His hair, which had been meticulously gelled into place, stood at odd angles and his button-down shirt sported some impressive wrinkles where the wind had struck him.

The lobby was silent as Danny brushed himself off and took several calming breaths. He closed his eyes and turned to the young girl with a smile.

"I think someone's jealous because they didn't get to play," he teased.

The little girl nodded. "Can you do it again?"

"Nah, sorry, kiddo. I have a meeting now. Another time?"

"Yeah! Thanks, Danny!"

I didn't understand these people.

§

Danny took Cecilia's hand, kissed it and murmured something with a smile. She relaxed, straightened his shirt and said something that made him laugh. The activity that had halted like a screeching record picked up the tempo and it was as if nothing happened. All seemed right in their world.

I was torn between outrage at the lack of response and shock that Jude's abilities somehow manifested at my wish. Was he a spirit watching over me? Did he enjoy that scene as much as I did? No matter where he was, I was sure Jude was laughing.

But Jude wasn't there to protect me. He always told me that I spent too much time in my head and needed to pay attention to the world around me. I was smarter, he claimed, but would end up in a world of trouble because I tended to follow along blindly.

Damn. Big brother was right again.

I blinked twice and realized I stood alone in the middle of the lobby. Cecilia and Danny had almost reached the other side while I remained alone, in the middle of the lobby, like an idiot. I jogged over to them quickly and scowled.

"How often do you drag prisoners around that no one minds? You tease kids."

Danny shrugged and held open the door leading to the final building. "Children, for the most part, are innocents. I'm not in the business of hurting anyone who doesn't deserve it."

"Who decides which person gets to die?" I countered. "If you believe in a higher power, you'd believe there was a master plan. You'd be interfering with it, which, if I remember correctly from, oh, every major world religion, would be screwing with said plans. Isn't that a ticket straight to hell? As is murder?"

Cecilia and Danny exchanged apprehensive looks. "Jasper, expand that argument. Everyone has the power to decide who lives and who dies. It's the social contract that keeps people from being murderous, thieving jerks."

"Fine. Let's run with the social contract. You don't kill me and I won't kill you. When you hurt someone, you're violating that contract. What puts you above the one act that maintains what's left of civility?"

"Hold that thought. I promise we'll continue this conversation later today."

Whereas the previous building was blinding white, the transitional corridor slowly darkened to grey, a shade so dark it was almost black. The poorly-lit corridor set my already stressed brain into overdrive. Images of figures in the dark, creatures out to eat me, and excruciating death danced like sugar plums in my head.

Feather-light touches brushed against my skin, lifted my hair, and kissed my neck. My worst nightmares never included freaky ghost-monsters in a pitch black brothel with a penchant for foreplay. I bit back a scream of horror.

A large hand landed on my shoulder and that scream escaped. A high, shrilly, pathetic scream.

The deep voice accompanying that hand laughed. "You're scared of the dark, too? Ah, Jasper, you're going to be a lot of work."

Jordan.

"Dayte yey otdokhnut', brat. Nasha sestra zdes'... moya sestra. My uvidim, chto ona k vam. Da?"

Mikael.

"You're awful," I hissed.

The darkness seemed to thicken and become more oppressive as we progressed. My body locked in place, causing a pileup of bodies behind me. Not even Jordan's large frame could drive me forward. The idea of running through the wraiths' bordello alone was as appealing as blindly following this path.

Neither option was ideal. The weak girl in me opened her mouth as *She* curled her imaginary lip in disgust.

"Hold my hand?"

Jordan snickered but put an arm around my shoulder. I pulled away. "What? Holding your hand is fine, but this isn't? How old are you?"

"Last time you put your arm around me, you choked me unconscious. Bad idea. I'm fine." I snatched my hand away and berated myself for continually forgetting the choking incident. Fear was a powerful and odd motivation.

"Did I apologize for that? I meant to apologize. I wish it had gone down differently."

"But it didn't. This is insane. I'm following the guy who hates me and continually threatens me, his girlfriend who y'all think will be my new bestie, the guy who choked me and the guy who may or may not be a creep."

Mikael spoke. "No one hates you. Sure, it's been a rough start, but I promise it will get better."

"Right. I'm still a prisoner here."

"Tomato, tomahto." I imagined Jordan's shrug in the dark. "If you were in college and pledged a sorority, they'd haze you and you'd ask for another helping of shit."

"Where's Dakarai? He seems like the only sane one of this bunch."

"You'll see him shortly. He's meeting with the High Council," Danny called over his shoulder. "And stop bitching. Don't you ever shut up?"

Even in the dark, I knew everyone's relative position. Danny was about ten yards in front of me, close enough for me to close the distance and do something hurtful.

"Don't do it," Mikael said softly. "It's tempting. Trust me, I know, but it's not worth it."

"But I'd enjoy it so much."

He chuckled and squeezed my hand. "In this group, I am the least terrifying. Am I not?"

"Sure," I said doubtfully. "Least terrifying kidnapper and potential murderer isn't a title I'd advertise."

Mikael let go and stepped away without another word. I had the impression that I hurt his feelings, maybe even his pride, and felt surprisingly guilty. He was definitely weird and anyone who was friends with Jordan had to be suspect. But he'd only displayed kindness and understanding.

"Sorry," I whispered. "That wasn't ... you don't deserve my anger."

We walked the rest of the way in silence, though Mikael and Jordan were close enough that their body heat chased away the chill around me. If I hadn't been afraid, I'd have found the gesture comforting. Sweet, in the way that Jude insisted on sleeping next to me in our sleeping bags when the heater in our house kicked the bucket.

The corridor sloped and curved so frequently that I lost all sense of direction. I imagined the roots of ancient trees breaking through the ceilings and walls, loosening the earth and trapping me. The further we progressed, the worse the condition of the floor became. I tripped on loose stones, roots and something I never wanted to see in the light of day. It was squishy and wet.

Jordan alternated between low chuckles at Mikael's jokes in Russian and amused sighs at my constant attempts to become one with the ground. "Are you sure you don't want to hold my hand?"

"Shut up."

As we continued to spiral down into the Earth, I grew convinced that they were taking me like a lamb to the slaughter. I had been fed, cleaned and was coming along somewhat willingly.

I feel something kindred below. We need to find and study it. We can kill them later.

Apparently, my inner bad ass was becoming a soon-to-be psychotic killer. For the first time since I arrived, I considered the possibility that I belonged there. Maybe I *had* killed my family and I was sentenced to a terrifying prison in hell for my crimes.

No. My brain refused to accept that possibility. No matter how angry I'd been, I'd never hurt them. And hypothetically speaking, even if I hurt my parents and Livie, there was nothing in Hell or on Earth that would make me hurt my brother. Twinsies.

The ground gradually leveled out and the darkness gave way to light. Ahead of us was a set of massive wooden doors flanked by massive torches. Symbols, images and words were carved into the wood that was so old that it looked shiny and petrified.

She waited silently, attentively, almost as if in a trance, as we moved up to stand in front of the door. One image, out of possibly thousands, called to us. It was carved into a granite circle that appeared to seal the doors shut. On it, a hooded figure sat upon a simple, unadorned throne and watched us from beneath its cowl. No face or hands were visible, but I got the distinct impression that it didn't matter. It was everything and it was nothing.

I reached out my hand to touch it, but Mikael yanked me backward.

"Careful, *sestra*. Do not touch what you don't understand. Unchecked power, use of misunderstood power. It always ends in tragedy."

"Right. As if we can squeeze any more tragedy into my life this week," I sneered. "Touching a stone can't possibly make things worse."

"Oh, trust me. It can get much, much worse."

§

She bristled. The tickling in my mind, the one that reminded me of Jude, let out a threatening growl.

Me? I reached out and touched the stone, marveling at the silky feel and detailed craftsmanship. The artist must have spent months chiseling the tiny lines that made the robe undulate in the pale light. I could see that the throne wasn't truly plain: millions of words and symbols were compressed there to create the illusion of blackness.

"Jasper," a sibilant voice whispered.

I spun around and saw nothing. Pitch black in every direction. It reminded me of plays where the protagonist delivers his or her soliloquy, standing alone under the spotlight. Everyone else was gone. The door was gone.

Pay attention.

"Hello?" I called, ever the idiot in a horror movie who gives up her location. "Is anyone out there?"

The voice wrapped around me more intimately than the phantoms' touches. "As day falls into night and the Vespers Hours begin, the Black Knights become my vessels. You, child, will be the finest of my Knights, but you must embrace the balance."

"Huh?"

Smooth, Jasper.

The disembodied voice continued in an amused tone. "Fire creates and destroys. Its dominion is beyond the petty realms of Heaven and Hell."

Yes. We are home.

"What do you want me to do?"

"You are apart from the universal balance. Your deeds will no longer be classified as good or bad, right or wrong. Yours will neutralize and maintain the balance."

Because I'd never been the most subtle person in the world, I repeated myself. "What do you want me to do?"

An exasperated ghost was a dangerous entity and I had a feeling I'd depleted my reserve of good will.

"Liminality. Neutrality equilibrium. Sacred Geometry. Gnosticism. Read a book," it said irritably.

"Sure," I lied. "Crystal clear. Um, who are you?"

"The Black Knights are beyond judgment as their actions maintain the universal balance."

"How do I determine who threatens the balance?"

The voice sighed, a chilling wind. "A gift to see you through the darkest of nights."

Darkness overwhelmed me and I was alone.

§

"Jas," my brother whined. "Get up."

My eyes blinked several times before the world came into focus. I whirled around and gasped.

"Jude?" My heart stuttered as I looked at my brother. He wore his usual summer uniform of basketball shorts and a t-shirt with our high school's logo along with a pair of trainers.

"Duh. We need to talk and I haven't played ball in a while." He dribbled the basketball a few times before throwing it to me.

I caught the ball, dropped it immediately, and crossed my arms. "Where have you been? Do you know how badly I've needed your advice? Jude, I feel like I'm in a horrible nightmare and I can't wake up."

"It hasn't exactly been easy to get a hold of you. Even I can't get around certain rules here, sis. I had to wait for the right circumstances."

"I've missed you."

Jude's lips trembled as we wrapped our arms around each other. "I'm so sorry, Jas. I didn't want to leave you. I didn't figure it out until it was too late, and then..."

"You're here now. You can stay, right? We can see each other?"

He averted his gaze to somewhere above my head. "I'm not sure, but I don't think I can do this often. If you're in the in-between space I think I can reach you here, but nowhere else."

I frowned. "What do you mean, 'the in-between' space? Where am I?"

"Neither here nor there, not in the void, not anywhere." Jude kissed my forehead. "I don't know what that means, to be honest. But you're not dead. That's all I care about. Do you know how you got here?"

"No. If we're not anywhere and you're dead...does this mean I'm dying? Would you tell me if I was?"

"Jasperilla, if you were dying, I'd be there with you the entire time." Jude prowled the perimeter of the spotlight. "It doesn't hurt, not after the actual death. It's boring, though. Bright light, long tunnels, pearly gates, blah, blah, blah."

"Really?"

Jude snorted. "No, not really. It hurt for a while, but then I felt like I was floating. There's no bright light, no brighter than usual. We walked together, all of us. I thought we were going to heaven, but a giant dude in a cloak stopped us. Creepy as fuck, Jas. No face, no hands. His name is –"

Jude's eyes flew open as his back arched and he screamed in pain. He dropped to his knees.

"Jude! Jude, tell me what's wrong." I wrapped my arms around him as he writhed, his face contorted in pain. "Stop it! Stop hurting him!" I shrieked towards the sky, at whatever invisible force was doing that to him. "Jude, it's going to be okay. Forget them. Forget everyone else. You have to get better, Jude."

87

After several agonizing moments, his body slumped into me. "Jas?"

"Oh, thank God."

"Jas, where are we? What are we doing here?"

"No. No, no, no, no. Jude, we were just talking a few minutes ago about everything. How we're in this in-between space."

"I have no idea what you're talking about. Aren't you supposed to be outside? Waiting for your ride to the rabbit hole?"

The realization that my brother's memory of our time together had just been wiped away gutted me. From the way it seemed, Jude's brain reset to shortly before he died.

He didn't know he was dead and I was still alive.

I tried to hide my panic with a smile. "Don't sweat it. Twinsie dreams. We probably just connected."

Jude relaxed visibly and moved off of his knees and into a cross-legged position. "Oh. That makes sense. So, what time are they supposed to show up? Did Mom give you any more information?"

A gust of wind brought a chill as the light around us faded. "I think the dream is ending."

"Yeah. Jasperilla, I'm exhausted, drained, like there's nothing left in me. Don't know how long I'm going to be here. Sing to me?"

I laughed a little because neither of our parents sang to us. We used to set up a fort, hid inside and sang each other to sleep when we were scared. I motioned for him to stretch out and rest his head on my lap. Once he closed his eyes, I began to sing his favorite.

Hey Jude
Don't make it bad
Take a sad song and make it better.

"Nuh-uh. Next verse." Jude yawned, sounding much younger than the eighteen years he lived. He was the boy under the fort who begged me to banish his monsters. "For nightmares and stuff."

"Brat. You always make me skip verses."

"Yup. Works better. Please?"

I ran my hands through his hair, grateful he couldn't see my tears.

And anytime you feel the pain, hey Jude, refrain
Don't carry the world upon your shoulders

By the time I reached the last line, my brother had turned cold. He felt insubstantial, absent. I wept over his body until the darkness found me again.

§

Fire burned through my nose and throat, yanking me back to my unfortunate reality. I gagged at the smell and jolted into a sitting position. Jordan knelt in front of me with an ammonia inhalant and concern etched on his face.

A scream tried to claw its way out of my throat as I scuttled backward until I reached a wall. Slick, cold sweat coated my body. It was impossible to reconcile what I'd just experienced, spending time with my dead brother, seeing him tortured and losing his memory.

These people possessed knowledge of the entity or whatever-the-fuck it wanted to call itself. They were aware of whatever assaulted my brother. I felt the wraiths return. They kept their distance, observing my reaction with something that *She* recognized as concern.

He wouldn't let me go with you. You saw Jude? Did you feel Him? Jude's guy?

I hurled every swear word, insult and threat at her for leaving me alone. When I needed her most, *She* had abandoned me. *She* accepted the diatribe without argument. *Her* sole purpose was to protect me and she failed.

I'm sorry, Jasper. I tried, but I couldn't find you. I knew you saw Jude and I tried to find his location, from wherever he was sent. Something blocked me.

While I lambasted my inner bad ass, the Circle members tried to reach me. I fought like a trapped animal, arms flailing and teeth bared. I knew the answers I needed were behind those massive double doors. All I had to do was stand and follow them, but they were strangers, threats.

The wraiths pressed closer and became one with the wall. They joined my fight, tossing away Jordan and Danny as if they were nothing but pesky flies. Whispers touched my thoughts. Unlike *Her*, these were angry commands.

Throw them back with the wind. Tell them to retreat. Burn them. Kill them.

Whoa, buddy.

The last command jolted me out of my feral state. I whimpered and curled into a ball. My body felt like I'd been battered by hurricane-level winds. My poor brain was frazzled and refused to cooperate further. I stared at the retreating wraiths and the Circle members, but I didn't see them as they slowly recovered.

Danny rose, his lips pressed together in a furious scowl. This was the second time he'd been attacked by me and he wanted revenge. Cecilia cringed in his arms, her eyes wide and body angling away from me.

Jordan and Mikael regarded me with morbid curiosity. Their hands twitched as if they wanted to restrain me and scrutinize me in a laboratory.

It was a testament to my pathetic shape that their contemplation soothed me. Neither man was afraid. Mikael leaned forward with boyish fascination with his big eyes and mouth slightly ajar. He had a front row seat to a never before seen spectacle and loved it.

Jordan, however, narrowed his eyes as he approached slowly. He held his hands up and spoke. "Jasper, can you hear me?"

My head bobbed up and down.

"Okay, good. I'm going to sit next to you." He crept forward until he was a few feet away. "Promise not to gnaw on my arm? Use me as a punching bag?"

Although I hadn't worked up to speaking, my scowl was enough.

He chuckled to himself and sat shoulder to shoulder. "Shitty day, huh? I'll talk and you can join the conversation when you're ready."

The man had the calm of a lion tamer and a sense of humor that would have tickled me in any other context. My head bobbed again.

"Cool. Most of the kids here call me Jordy. It pissed me off at first, but I like it now," he said in a conversational tone. "In some ways, they're different people. Jordan is the guy who gets things done. The soldier, assassin, whatever you want to call it. He's cold and clinical, a strategist who executes without emotion. Jordy is different. He's human, if that makes any sense."

Kindred. Listen. Watch. Learn.

"Jordy is the guy who holds a kid over his head so they can dunk a basketball, hates horror movies, and — if you tell anyone, I'll have to kill you — teared up at the end of the last Fast and Furious movie. When I was younger, Jordan was my imaginary friend." He ducked his head. "I know, I know. He's a fucked up friend. He taught me how to fight, how to hide, how to protect. There were some days when he was in charge and all Jordy could do was watch in fascination or horror. Depended on the day."

I licked my dry lips and tried to speak. The words couldn't, wouldn't, manifest. I dug my nails into his arm and pleaded with him to understand silently.

Jordan, or Jordy, nodded. "I thought as much. It's okay, Jasper. You're both safe here. So ... by the time I was, oh, fourteen or fifteen, Jordan was loud and strong enough that it was a constant battle to stay in control. He needed an outlet, so I found a place that let him vent his rage. I wasn't a good person, Jasper. I hurt people for money and pleasure. As sick as I felt, I couldn't bring myself to silence Jordan. When it came down to it, no one understood me better and no one else protected me. Does she have a name?"

"*She*," I whispered. "Just *She* or *Her*."

"Oh, come on," he teased. "Eighteen years and that's your best effort? Jordan would have made my life miserable."

"Split personalities?"

"No, not exactly. Do you remember what happened?"

Fear returned, a stone in my stomach that would never dissolve. Confinement, interrogation, and torture were just a few of the promises in Danny's eyes.

Jordy touched my chin and brought my gaze back to his face. "Ignore him. You touched the stone and had a seizure that lasted roughly five minutes. When it was over, you were unconscious for another minute before you went feral."

Six minutes. I was *gone* for six minutes, but it had felt like an eternity. My brother's appearance eclipsed the big, bad shadowy dude, which was probably a terrible mistake, because that had also seemed like a lifetime. I tried to wrap my mind around everything. The seizure accounted for why I felt so battered and bruised.

"Oh," I said in a small voice. "What about the wraiths?"

"Those guys? They haven't been active in some time. I'm just as curious as you. Jasper, I know you're scared and tired. I wish I could tell you that your day was over, that you could crawl into bed and hide. But I won't lie to you. We're going to get up and go into the chamber. You'll tell the High Council and the Circle where you traveled during those six minutes."

"What if *She* objects?"

Jordy chuckled. "Tell *Her* that *She* can object when she has a name. Then she can deal with Jordan. And for the record? If you're willing, I'll teach you how to find that balance so you're not at odds with her all the time. You might hate me after a few days, but you'll learn."

"Promise not to choke me again?"

"I can't promise that," he replied as he rose and stretched. "But if I do, you'll know ahead of time and I'll have already taught you how to break free. Deal?"

Words failed. I took his proffered hand and prayed that I wasn't making a mistake.

CHAPTER 7

The overwhelming scents of stale coffee, incense, and wax candles filled my nostrils as the massive doors to the High Council's chamber swept open. The room was carved from the rocks deep underground, complete with glittering stalagmites hanging perilously from the high ceiling. My claustrophobia reared its ugly head and seized my chest. Oxygen was a luxury that my brain wasn't permitted.

Don't pass out. Don't pass out. Don't pass out.

Strong arms on either side of me supported my body and helped me along. Jordan. Mikael.

"We've got you," Mikael said in his lilting accent. "It's overwhelming, yes?"

"Yeah."

He leaned close and whispered, "It has always reminded me of the chamber from the Potter books. Where the trials were held? Sometimes, I imagine a mythical creature will traipse through the room looking for its owner. If I had to choose, I would like a white owl. Who wants a rat?"

Laughter bubbled out and echoed in the room. I froze. That had to have been sacrilege of the highest magnitude. Guards or wraiths were around the corner, my imagination told me, and they had devious methods of torture already planned. Out of the frying pan and into the volcano; it described my life in a nutshell.

Instead, Dakarai looked up from the conference table in the middle of the chamber floor and flashed me those gleaming white teeth, the laugh lines around his eyes winking. "Oh, I would pass on the animal, Mikael. There are other ways to deliver messages. I'd prefer a broomstick."

Cecilia scoffed. "Idiots, all of you. Hermione's time-turner is the best. I'd go back and get another degree, travel abroad and do absolutely nothing. In the wrong hands, it would be disastrous. Can you imagine someone like Jasper trying to rectify past mistakes?"

The heat in the room disappeared. In its place was bone-chilling cold. Tightly controlled anger and disdain hovered in the air, crystalline and ready to explode. I patted myself down, peered at my hands and wracked my brain for any memory of doing this.

It wasn't me.

Dakarai uncurled his body and stretched to his full height. Anger rolled off of him in undulating pulses, growing as it devoured any source of heat. Ice crackled around the room, but Dakarai was bathed in light and steam. He was raw power, unchained and converging at a single target.

Yes! This is power, Jasper. We could have this. We could be this.

I didn't envy the target of his inexplicable rage. I didn't particularly like Cecilia, but I didn't want to witness her death.

My intuition told me that Dakarai was one of the most powerful members of the Order, if not the strongest. Whatever he decided, no one had the ability to stop him or block whatever he threw at the shaking, crying Cecilia.

Dakarai's eyes lost their lovely normal brown pigment. Red and orange blended together to create the illusion of flames being stoked. He was the terrifying god of fire. Perun. Malakbel. Huitzilopochtli. Sulis. Yuyi and Ra. Helios and Agni. Akycha. Neto, Dazbog, and Hors. Ares incarnate. The names came to me unbidden, plucked from a repository of knowledge within me that I didn't know existed.

Gods and goddesses of ancient times with fire in their eyes.

Dakarai.

We were rooted to the ground, either paralyzed by fear or fixed by the thin layer of frost coating our bodies. When he spoke, his voice was flat and devoid of humanity.

"You mock power, yet you crave it. One such as Jasper has the ability to manifest and alter realities in ways you cannot comprehend. When the time comes, we will wield our abilities to save humanity. You will be of no consequence, except to cause the death of those you hold dearest."

Dakarai's hands glowed brightly. Unlike my own attempts, he was in full control. The fire in his eyes blazed crimson as he gathered the energy and heat he'd sucked out of the room and raised his arms.

Danny's eyes bulged. He was a mere six feet away from Cecilia but was locked into place by the crystalline prison.

To my right, ice shattered and shimmered in the air before pelting the ground and everyone rooted to it. Jordan moved with inhuman speed and threw himself in front of Cecilia.

"Dakarai," he thundered. "Stop. This is madness and unnecessary violence only you can prevent. We don't punish ignorance and you're not that flaming superhero from that awful movie you love. I'm not the sidekick friend. Don't make me hurt you, Sparky."

They were two gods on the eternal battlefield, taking one another's measure. Pure energy pitted itself against … whatever Jordan represented. The dimness of the chamber had distorted my vision because Jordan appeared larger, more menacing, something I hadn't thought possible. Even his voice was transformed. The guttural sound resonated through my body like a

96

powerful earthquake. Jordan was a warrior god and the only one willing to challenge Dakarai.

Doubt flickered in Dakarai's eyes. It was the first sign of humanity he had shown since he went all the Human Torch on us. He shook his head and growled, "Move out of my way, beast. This does not concern you."

Jordan broke the spell we'd all been under with a single derisive snort. "My ass. You're endangering everyone in this room. Including your protégé, Jasper. Do you really want to crispy critter her before you have a chance to train her? We both know you're the only one who can show her the path."

The doubt returned and Dakarai stared at me as if he'd never seen me before, like I'd been brought to this moment where the sole purpose of helping Jordan make his point. The fire in his eyes dimmed as did the brightness of his hands.

"That's it," Jordan said carefully. The lion tamer stalked forward. "That's right. You've got this. We can deal with the intentional misinformation and ignorance another time. She doesn't know, Dakarai."

A single tear rolled down Dakarai's smooth sienna clay skin as he fell to his knees. The fire and heat emanating from him stuttered and extinguished.

Just as suddenly as the episode had begun, our icy prisons dissolved and turned to steam, leaving nothing behind but a chill deep inside my bones. The chamber was warm again, as if someone had lit a fireplace for the sole purpose of warming us up after walking in a blizzard. I wrapped my arms around myself and wished I had a sweater.

Jordan knelt next to Dakarai and whispered softly. Although I couldn't make out the words, they resonated out to me. I was overcome by intense grief and guilt for something irreparable. Dakarai wept and leaned on his friend, the only person willing to challenge him, for support.

Danny pulled Cecilia into his arms and held her as she cried. He barked, "Get him the fuck out of here. This is why we don't let him out. He's too dangerous, and Jasper will be just as volatile. For once in your godforsaken lives, listen to me. We need to lock them both away."

The High Council, which had been silent up until this point, sprang into action. Four of them surrounded Dakarai and Jordan and spoke in hushed voices. Two men, nearly identical in appearance in their black pants and button-down shirts, graying hair and glasses, helped Dakarai to his feet and settled him in a chair near the head of the table. Another retrieved a glass of water and, bizarrely, a fruit tray. Two other High Council members, tall and regal in their bearing, usher Danny and Cecilia into an alcove I hadn't noticed before.

Michael and I stood side by side, holding hands and staring at the spectacle before us. It reminded me of my brother. I wasn't sure how I felt about that, someone reminding me of Jude and the comfort he always provided me, but in this madhouse I took whatever I could get.

"Exciting day, yes?" Michael grinned weakly. "I assure you most days aren't like this. Your arrival has turned everything into a bit of a circus. It will be fine, I promise you."

She smirked. We both doubted my arrival had been the catalyst for this insanity. From what I saw, there were dynamics and layers of politics that required years of study and acumen to understand.

"Can we leave and go grab a burger? Or do we have to stay here and wait for the dust to settle?"

Michael laughed softly. "I wish. There is a hole in the wall diner nearby that makes the most exquisite greasy burgers with egg on top. They call it a Texas burger. Fantastic for hangovers."

Jordan waved us over with an impatient hand. We made our way to the large conference table and sat down to Dakarai's left, while Jordan situated himself to Dakarai's right. Danny and Cecilia had yet to reappear but from the looks of it, I didn't think anyone cared.

The four of us were joined by the thus far useless High Council members. I hoped that they said something to set them apart, because I was very close to giving them random nicknames. The uniformity of the black outfits was distracting, probably not what was intended when instituted.

Dakarai, whose head was bowed, slowly reached his hand over towards me. I took it, since I was terrified that he would fry me for any transgressions. His trembling hand enfolded mine.

"I am so sorry, Jasper. My lack of control is inexcusable and I fear that I have done irreparable damage to your trust in me. I would never harm you."

"Hey, don't stress yourself over this. Everyone has a bad day, right? It just so happens that you and I blow up things on our bad days." I gathered my courage and peered at him until he met my eyes. "Can you help me?"

Dakarai shook his head sadly. "I had hoped to work with you, but it may be too dangerous."

Although we were whispering, the entire room was riveted by our conversation. Not a single person moved or even twitched.

Dakarai glared at them. "Don't you have anything better to talk about?"

The man at the head of the table smiled grimly. He seemed to be the leader of the group. There was something about his carriage that reminded me of Danny, imperious and unyielding. An asshole.

"Do not be a fool, Dakarai. You know why we're here, and what we need to accomplish." The man turned his attention to me. "Jasper, I'm sorry for this poor reception and their appalling manners. I trust your accommodations were comfortable."

It wasn't a question.

"Yes, thank you. Everything has been quite lovely." Michael vibrated with un-vocalized laughter and pinched my arm. I could almost hear his voice in my head saying, "You're so full of shit, Jasper. You've hated every single moment you have been here." Instinct told me that if he had a notebook in front of him Michael would scroll notes to me with the hopes of making me laugh.

"Wonderful. Now, onto our present agenda. We have assembled the High Council and the Circle here today because the existence of the Order, our mission and our members have been threatened. You, Jasper, are being included because we believe you are the weapon we need to end the threat from at least one of these unknown entities."

Too many questions danced on the tip of my tongue but before I could ask any of them, Michael cut his head to one side, a silent warning to listen and observe before I spoke. My fingers twitched in his hand, recognition and acceptance, and his hand relaxed.

The woman to the left of Mr. Talking Head smiled. There was no warmth or humor in her expression. "I'm sure you have questions, Jasper. However, we may not have time for those answers. We trust you to act on our behalf with the little information we provide."

"Wait. What?" I blurted. "You brought me here because you think I'm a weapon against some evil conglomerate that you can't identify? And you want me to blindly follow your orders?" I laughed bitterly. "You clearly don't know me. I'm not your lemming ready to go off a cliff."

Talking Head scowled. "You are a child of the Vespers," he scolded. "You are subject to the rule of the High Council, and therefore required to do as directed."

"Well, fuck you, buddy. I didn't know you existed until a few days ago. Therefore, unless you start talking, I will make it my sole purpose in life to disrupt your days and otherwise make your life miserable."

The woman who had just spoken put a restraining hand on Talking Head's arm. She returned her attention to me. "What do you mean? No one from the direct line grows up unaware of the Order of Vespers."

I crossed my arms and tilted my chair back. "Well, apparently it's happened. I don't know who or what the

Order of Vespers is, nor do I know or care about this direct line. Bottom line it for me, big guy."

§

"Impossible," Talking Head spluttered. "You are of the direct line. Your family should have primed you to become a member of the Circle, you and your siblings."

The mention of my dead siblings stoked the fire inside me, the one that Dakarai must have felt only moments ago. I leveled Talking Head with a stare and held his gaze until he blinked. "My siblings? We were supposed to be groomed for Circle? How? Why? Start from the beginning."

No one spoke.

"Please," I begged. "If I'm as important as you've implied, isn't it only fair that you give me some background?"

There were seven members of the High Council, and only one of me. I should have felt fear, but I was curious about these anonymous people. Were they sheep who were elected to the Council for easy votes? And where did this woman stand in the hierarchy of things? Was her purpose to support their leader? Did she use gentle persuasion to achieve her goals? More disturbing, were these the people who gave the orders for my kidnapping? Were they so committed to their mission that I would be confined to the complex?

Dakarai spoke in a low voice. "She doesn't know. Her family decided several generations back to deny their heritage. They wouldn't be the first."

"It's more likely that they wanted to shield their line and protect their progeny," Jordan remarked. "As she said, Jasper is ignorant of our traditions and our purpose. We're asking much of her with little in return. We owe Jasper a piece of her history."

Annoyance flashed over Talking Head's face but he did not dismiss the request. "Jordan is correct. We will ask much of you, nay, everything of you. It is only right to bestow upon you the knowledge of for what you fight."

My eyebrows shot beyond my hairline. "I have a choice? Huh, I didn't expect that."

This guy hated me. His face was mottled red and his fists clenched and unclenched. He spoke through gritted teeth. "We will tell you the history of our people. There is one condition." Talking Head held up a hand before I could respond. "Take notes if you will but be quiet. Listen. And most importantly, don't interrupt."

"Yeah, sure. Whatever." I extended my free hand in a sweeping gesture. "Shall we?"

Talking Head nodded, appeased. "Yes, well, my name is Charles. I'm the leader of the High Council of the Order of Vespers. In this capacity, I ensure that the Order stays true to its purpose and oversee our activities." He nodded to the woman on his left.

"My name is Miriam, child. I know the last few days have been difficult, and I wish I could promise you respite, but the storm isn't coming. It is here."

I bit the inside of my cheek. Just a few sentences into this explanation and I already had a million questions. I nodded and tried to smile, as if their condolences were worth anything.

The next person spoke. "My name is Liliana."

"Marcus."

"Yurina."

"Ivan."

"Carlo."

"Thank you," I murmured. I knew I would forget their names momentarily, as there wasn't much difference between them physically, and they didn't say anything to distinguish themselves from each other. My eyes went back to Charles.

He cleared his throat. "In the beginning," he intoned. "God said, 'Let there be light', and there was light. God saw that the light was good, and he separated the light from the darkness."

CHAPTER 8

"You're joking." My head swiveled from one end of the table to the other and back. "Right?"

Jordan shook his head, but I could see him fighting a smile. Mikael's eyes were wide and he cringed as if I just summoned the wrath of the gods. If hell and damnation were going to be rained down upon me, he was going to move the hell out of the way.

Talking Head pressed his lips into a thin line, flexing that hand several times until he managed to control himself.

In the beginning of this tale, Talking Head considered smiting poor little Jasper.

At least someone found this amusing. I planned to have a serious talk with *Her* as soon as I got out of the Bat Cave and had time to think. *She* hadn't exactly been helpful the last few hours. Look and listen. That wasn't my idea of good advice, nor had it worked in my favor. Protector, my ass.

"Yes, this is where the story begins. It's also where the story will end. Keep in mind, although you'll hear much that is familiar, this theological and philosophical territory is largely unrecognized by major religions."

Charles paused and I realized he was waiting for me to interrupt. When I said nothing, he continued. "According to the legend, boundary was created. This boundary represents an entity whose real name cannot be uttered: Il Separatio, or Annonnimus."

Miriam picked up the narrative. "This entity was regarded as perfect and absolute neutrality. What makes this dangerous, and relevant, is that the concept provides a third entity midway between God and the Devil. The medieval church, no church, wants to introduce competition, not when its people are so invested in a system that benefits them. Nor did they want to permit a discussion of which entity is the strongest—God or Il Separatio."

Her hypnotic voice transported me to the place of imagination, where her words came to life before my eyes. "Our history pre-dates the written word, but the first mention of us occurs in the Middle Ages."

I snapped my fingers. "When I was outside and touched ... there was a figure in black who said something about Black Knights. That I was the fi... an important Knight, and my actions were now outside of the flow of morality because I would help maintain the universal balance."

The silence that followed was pregnant with validation of this vision and a desperate urge to press me for more details.

"There was a lot I didn't understand," I admitted. "Something about liminality and Gnosticism. He told me to read a book."

"Well, that's a first," Dakarai said, breaking the silence. "What else were you told?"

"Nothing." Jude was my secret. Until I fully understood what had happened, I refused to give the thought of him over to someone else to dissect.

"Nothing?" Talking Head asked. "You were told to read a book. Nothing happened afterward?"

"It went dark and the vision was gone."

Nice evasion.

One of the Council Clones — Ivan, maybe — leaned forward and rested his elbows on the table. "Jasper, every detail is important, no matter how insignificant it seems. Is there anything else?"

"If there was something else, I'd tell you. He, it, whatever, told me to read a book and told me to maintain the universal balance. That's it," I insisted. "Why is this so important? Does he tell everyone something different?"

"He doesn't speak to anyone, Jasper," Dakarai said carefully. "Rather, the appearances are rare. Your vision is significant because it has the bearings of previous messages. I think —"

"No one cares what you think, freak," Danny spat as he strode back into the chamber, sans Cecilia. "There are only two possible scenarios. Either Jasper is lying about her ignorance or her abilities are strong enough to merit the attention of one who doesn't bother to speak to his children."

I raked him with a scathing look. "Hey. Don't take your pity party out on me. Boohoo, the new girl is more powerful than you. So sad, you're not important enough for a vision. Get over yourself."

"Atta girl," Jordan murmured. "There's the steel I expected."

Danny was apoplectic with rage. But unlike the men on either side of me, he didn't grow bigger or mythologically more impressive. He was weak and desperate to hold onto control. "Y-you...the balls...how dare," he spluttered. "Confinement. Jordan, take her away. Lock her up near Dakarai's quarters and make sure she can't escape."

Dakarai winked as if to say *I've got this,* and straightened. "You have no authority here and you were invited merely as a courtesy. Sit down and shut up, unless you want the entire compound to know you're terrified of ... what was it you called her? The scrawny little girl?"

"I am not scrawny!"

Talking Head slammed his fist on the table, but it didn't matter. We hurled insults and threats at each other, increasing in volume until I had no sense of who said what and to whom.

"Shut up!" Miriam roared. "Enough. I don't know what the hell is happening with your Circle, Dakarai, but I suggest you rectify the matter immediately. Jasper, do you understand the broad strokes?"

Stunned, I plopped back into my seat. "Broad strokes? There's God, who's thought of as good, the Devil, obviously bad. And there's He-Who-Shouldn't-Be-Named. And somehow we're the descendants of this entity?"

"Yes," she said, mollified by my grasp of the obvious. "The Order was created to ensure we, the children of Il Separatio, continue to exist and continue to maintain the universal balance. We are his Black Knights, if you will, separate from the moral and ethical judgments of the world."

"Right." I frowned. "Something terrible is about to happen and I'm supposed to stop it by whatever means necessary."

"Yes. With the help of the Circle, you will defeat this threat."

"Great. Super. Fantastic. Now, what exactly is this threat?"

§

"Finally," Jordan muttered. "Cripes, talk about circling the issue. May I?"

Talking Head, Charles, nodded wearily. Whether it was the bickering, the multiple shows of immense ability and power, or the exhausting conversation, he wanted to be done with the lot of us.

"I'll keep it simple. Someone is hunting our kind, our people. We haven't been able to establish a pattern for these deaths, only that families who have abandoned the Order are being targeted."

"Sounds like a pattern to me. Why can't you send an email or an owl to warn them?"

"Because," Danny said, "Like your family, they've shirked their duties and hidden themselves within humanity well. We wouldn't have known about you if Mikael hadn't begun to have visions of you shortly before we received a call from one of your distant relations."

My head swiveled to the right. To his credit, Mikael appeared chagrined. "Visions?"

He nodded slowly. "Under ordinary circumstances, you wouldn't be privy to this information, not yet. The Circle keeps our abilities a closely guarded secret. I have seen visions of the future, past and present my entire life. I saw you, but it was too late."

I pushed myself to stand on shaky legs. "I can't. I'm sorry, but I'm officially at my breaking point. Here's sanity," I said, drawing an imaginary line in the air. "And here's me, standing on the edge. Bottom line it for me before I start blowing up shit."

Danny began to speak, but Jordan silenced him with a look. "Among other things, Danny collects information through more traditional means. Between his intel, Mikael's visions and Dakarai's ... innate sense of the cosmic equilibrium, I've hypothesized that whomever is taking our people is trying to tilt the balance to their side."

"The Devil is trying to take over Earth?" I asked stupidly. "Isn't this the kind of problem *God* should handle? Why us? Why me?"

"In theory, yes. But neither the Devil nor God have been present or involved in some time. Il Separatio, the Entity of Neutrality, by his nature, doesn't get directly involved unless the existence of humanity is at peril. Without God or the Devil to counteract the other, society is in a free-fall. Humanity needs us and someone is trying to ensure that we can't do our job."

"When you shake your fist at a god or blame a devil, it doesn't matter. They're not there, wherever *there* might be, and they're not listening. Got it. May I be excused?"

"Not quite yet," Ivan or Carlo or Marcus said. "I will honor your request and bottom-line it for you. Yes, you are likely our best hope of eliminating this threat, but you can't be sent into the world untrained. Others will do what they can until you are ready."

"Entrance into the Order," Mikael interrupted. "You must undergo the initiation process, which will teach you control over your physical abilities, your cognitive processing, and the soul fire that burns in you."

Wind. Mind Control. Fire and Energy.

The truth smacked me in the face like a baseball bat and knocked me back into my seat. "Oh, shit. You're joking right? I'm the last option, aren't I? It was supposed to be the three of us: me, Livie and Jude."

Dakarai inclined his head. "You were always the most powerful of the three, even before your family's tragic deaths. Now, you're the repository for all three abilities."

"Jasper," Miriam said, "If you don't help us save the others of our kind, we won't be able to maintain the balance. The world will experience violence of unimaginable proportions. Humanity *will* die."

Nope. No pressure.

CHAPTER 9

I refused to discuss anything after Miriam's pronouncement. The fate of the world was literally my responsibility.

Find the people killing the Vespers and kill *them*. When I was done with that pesky task, they wanted me to become a super-sleuth, find the people who were trying to tilt the balance, determine how, and kill *them*.

No biggie.

But...

If I left, I had nowhere to go. I'd be a threat to whomever was kind enough to shelter me. I'd always be hunted. In a long list of terrible options, staying here, living with these potentially unstable and definitely murderous people, and honing my abilities was my best bet.

They could make me disappear from the world, out of the headlines and off of the police's most wanted list. Jasper Andrews would be no more. But Jasper Lee had a chance at a new lease on life, one where she was valued, protected and given the opportunity to do the impossible.

The answer had been there all along.

Choice? What choice?

I was going to save the world.

§

Blood, fire, and wind sealed my fate.

Dressed in a grey cloak, surrounded by the Circle and standing in front of the High Council, I pledged my life to the Order of Vespers and repeated the vows of an initiate.

Dakarai held my hand over a ritual fire, made a deep cut with a blade of obsidian, and let the blood flow. More words were uttered, none of which I remembered, and a wind of unknown origin extinguished the flames in the chamber.

I was home.

PART 3

CHAPTER 10

Dakarai knocked on the door of my new room. It was open wide, but he always extended the courtesy. A true gentleman, that one. It was part of his DNA, the impeccable manners and enviable grace.

"Hello, Jasper."

I sat cross-legged on my new plush couch and grinned. "Howdy, neighbor. How's it going?"

He cocked his head to the side, considering the question for a long moment. The movement revealed a thick scar on the side of his neck. It was easily six inches long, beginning somewhere behind his ear and snaking its way beneath his the collar of his sweater. The scar was thick and raised, a testament to a wound so vicious that it dared its owner to revisit the cause every time he looked in the mirror.

He must have noticed my probing stare and attempts to keep my jaw hinged. Rubbing his neck absently, he smiled. "I should ask you the same. Your accommodations. Are they to your satisfaction?"

"Are you kidding? Dude."

Said accommodations had changed the moment the initiation ceremony had ended. Actually, my entire existence at the Order changed. Before the guys could say boo, Cecilia had whisked me away and dragged me to a small room somewhere above ground. Inside was a treasure chest. Clothes, all in my size, were piled by function and color. Warm jeans and sweaters, dresses for every occasion, workout gear, and fuzzy socks were mine for the taking. And the shoes! Two pairs of trainers, chucks in three different colors, flats, boots, cozy slippers, and something that could only be called shit-kickers awaited my approval.

Who was I to turn down a new wardrobe of stylish, comfortable garments?

I was convinced that they lived by the motto, "go big or go home," because the gifts kept on coming.

Instead of the dormitory-style room where I'd been confined, I now lived across the hall from Dakarai in what we affectionately called Quasimodo's Tower. We each had a suite with a small living area, a kitchenette and a work station. The cool blue walls held generic hotel prints, but I didn't mind since decorating was the last thing on my mind. The bedroom, however, rocked my world. It was twice the size of the one I had at home. And the bathroom…

My eyes rolled back in ecstasy every time I thought about the sweet space I called my own.

Jude and I had always shared a bathroom, first because it had been easier for my parents to bathe and keep track of mischievous twins, and later because it connected our bedrooms. Jack and Jill, I remembered my father calling the style. We'd hated it during middle school. Jude was full of barely-teenage funk and I had been self-conscious about handling my period.

This bathroom? It had a tub big enough for a legitimate soaking experience, a separate shower, and a vanity. It was so big that I could have lined the back wall with tampons and no one would have been the wiser.

Shallowness became me. Even *She* was excited about the tub.

Saving the world has it perks.

Dakarai's suite of rooms was slightly bigger, but he'd lived there for years and seniority had its privileges. He'd kept his decor minimal with a few black and white photographs of cityscapes on the walls and stacks of books everywhere.

He extended his hand and offered me a three inch tome. "You should enjoy this," he said with the grin of someone obsessed with books. "History of ancient religions."

"Ooh, exciting."

"Good to see that enthusiasm."

I felt terrible that Dakarai didn't catch the sarcasm in my voice. He rarely did. The poor guy thought I was excited about reading something that dense. Heck, he was excited for each of my new experiences. He deserved better than the droll commentary on life. I tried again with real enthusiasm. "Yeah. Please pass along anything helpful. You're the best."

Dakarai's face lit up as he bounced on his heels. "Excellent. When you're ready, you'll accompany me to the Circle's library. It contains all of the books collected and written by Circle members since the dawn of the written word. I've slept there on more than one occasion."

He will remain loyal, even at the end.

The end? What the hell? I made a note to have a long conversation with *Her* about dropping cryptic messages while I was in the middle of a conversation with a corporeal person. The end. Pssh. As if *She* hadn't given me enough to ponder. *She* was making her way to the top of my shit list.

"Why on Earth would you sleep in a library? There are a million other places."

"The accommodations here are beyond expectations. However, I spend most of my time in the Tower, so the occasional change of scenery is a luxury." He grinned again. "Being Quasimodo isn't so bad, yes?"

"If I'd known this was part of the deal, I might not have put up such a fight. How does this all work?"

"The Order takes care of its own." He shrugged. "You should receive a new laptop and cell phone later today. Did anyone deliver your credit card and personal bank account information?"

"No," I said slowly. "I didn't know I was supposed to receive one. I don't have a lot of money, Dakarai."

"I know it's overwhelming. The Order understands the burden it has put upon its members, especially those of us in the Circle. To compensate —"

"Do you mean bribe?"

Dakarai snorted. "What's the expression? Six of one, half a dozen of another. The card is paid off and the account is refreshed at the end of each month."

"I can't bring myself to protest."

"May I?" Dakarai gestured to the seat across from me. When I nodded, he plunked down on the forest green marshmallow monstrosity and stretched his long legs with a groan. "Jordan was not kind in our workout this morning."

"Is he ever?"

"No, I don't suppose he understands the concept of kindness when it involves training. Don't mistake that for the entirety of his personality."

An uncomfortable silence stretched between us as we took one another's measure. At his most serene, Dakarai still exuded a nearly tangible aura of energy. *She* had been right about Dakarai packing serious power. The problem was that I still didn't know what his power entailed. He could have been a shapeshifter for all I knew.

The supernatural on a grand scale was too new for me to make any assumptions. I wondered if he had the ability to peer inside my brain and pick through my thoughts. I'd have died of mortification if Dakarai had access to the dream I had about Jordan sometime in the early hours.

"I'm not sure I want to know him. Period." A small voice in my head called me on my bullshit. The guy was an enigma in an attractive package. I reasoned it wasn't a bad thing as long as I didn't blurt out that he quickly made it to the top of my hot-guy list.

Sighing, I wrenched my attention away from the scary dude of my dreams and focused on the kind creature in front of me.

Dakarai was dressed in his usual attire of jeans and a lightweight sweater of the finest cashmere. His shoes, however, amused me. He wore a different pair each day, and they rarely matched his outfit. Today brought a pair of high-top Converse sneakers with a graffiti design.

"Your identification. You've dropped your last name."

"Yes." I frowned because it seemed like a logical choice. "Why?"

Dakarai shrugged and twisted the fingers of his right hand, a nervous habit I'd noticed. "It's a big decision to shed one's identity and become anonymous."

"Last names gives one a sense of belonging. My family is dead. Besides, the police want Jasper Andrews. She no longer exists."

"Nor does your long brown hair."

I touched my chin-length black hair. It was the only bit of my old life I mourned. Not my friends, not my hometown. My hair. Vanity became me.

"Well, we all make sacrifices," I said lightly. "What's up, Obi-Wan?"

He rolled his eyes, already exhausted by my Star Wars references. I'd already asked him if he'd call me his padawan, but he'd shot that down immediately. Nor did he consent to being the Yogi to my Boo-Boo, Batman to my Robin, or the Bill to my Ted in this most excellent adventure. The superhero capes had been rejected before I'd had a chance to show him my crude design.

"The Circle is worried about you. Your recent history and losses — anyone else might have crumpled. Yet, you're able to joke around and smile."

My head hurt. I'd spent years cultivating a mask of indifference. It had been my only defense against the rumors and outlandish allegations about my and Jude's unusual abilities.

"You don't understand. If I didn't laugh, I'd drown myself in my sorrows and that's not acceptable." I exhaled and plastered a grin on my face. "On another note, I don't have a high school diploma."

"Yes, you do," he replied. "Your records are being expunged as we speak. The police will assume you had been shipped off to a boarding school, the Vesparia Academy. Your diploma should arrive within the next few weeks."

"My friend Adam?"

Dakarai's eyes darkened. "Gone. He disappeared shortly after he confronted you. I hope I am the one to find him."

This one would use unimaginable power to destroy your enemies. Keep him close.

"Close or closer?"

"I'm sorry?"

Embarrassment warmed my cheeks. I had to get this under control. The Circle's worries would multiply a thousand fold if I kept talking to myself. They probably had a dungeon here exclusively for folks who lost their shit and babbled incoherently. "Just thinking."

"Ah. There's much to digest."

"Yeah." I looked at him. "I'm guessing this wasn't a purely social call."

"It's time," he said quietly.

My stomach sank. I looked around the room and my dreams of taking a few weeks to read, nap, and sneak around the compound dissipated like steam after a wonderfully steamy shower. The short romance with normalcy was over before it began. "I'm ready."

The grin returned as he clapped his hands together. "Fan-friggin-tastic," he said in his odd, lilting accent. "Under normal circumstances, you would be one of ten or so initiates and would progress as a class."

The word "class" put me in exam prep mode. I was good under pressure. I was better at test taking. (Screw you, Jude. My SAT scores were better.)

I pushed up the sleeves of the hooded sweatshirt I'd stolen from my brother and pulled my chin-length hair into a tight bun. My fingers itched for a pen or a laptop to take notes. Neurons fired on all cylinders and my mental engine purred.

Ooh, excited, are we? Try not to have the same kind of breakdown you normally have around finals. Your reputation as a hysterical little girl precedes you.

Maybe I didn't have to have that stern talk. She kept an eye on the details, like the fact that my circumstances were far from normal, even there. "Since I'm so powerful and unstable, I need individual tutoring."

"Yes. It may be hard to believe, but this precaution is for your safety." Dakarai's face tightened. "My tutoring was more restrictive that yours. Be grateful."

What had they done to this poor man? Why?

"Right. Okay. Can you tell me what's going to happen? Or is it one of those things I'll learn as I go along?"

"You'll receive training from the individual Circle members and shadow us as we go about our jobs." His eyes took in my body with frank interest. "Jordan is going to destroy you during training."

"Hey," I said, "I'm already in decent shape."

"Not by his standards. Cecilia will certainly find you lacking, and Mikael..." The corners of his lips twitched. "I have no doubt he'll surprise us. Please be kind in your dealings with him. Admittedly, he is odd and prickly, but in many ways, he's as alone as we are. More, because he cannot control his abilities."

"Why?"

"Because Mikael's visions are related to human decisions, which change constantly. He has little agency over his life and has difficulty functioning outside of the Order."

"That's awful. Is he okay?"

"If you're inquiring as to his emotional well-being, you'll have to talk to him. Mikael is quiet. Shy. He tutors the children here when he's not plagued by the headaches the visions cause. He may not say much, but being in the company of accepting people is good for him. When he does talk, he's quite interesting."

Mikael had clasped my hand like it was a lifeline. Mikael tried to reassure me that he was the least terrifying of the group. I'd rebuffed him. No wonder he hadn't visited.

"Oof, and I thought I had it bad. I'll be sure to chat with him the next time our paths cross. What about you?"

Dakarai slumped in his chair. The incident in the chamber of the High Council weighed heavily on his conscience, as did Danny's accusations. He'd told me as much the previous night over the simple dinner of chicken breasts, mashed potatoes and salad. His voice was tired, resigned even. "You might grow to hate me even more than Jordan."

"I don't hate him. He's nice enough when he's not terrifying. Should I be scared of you as well?"

"Yes."

These one word answers were going to make me torch a building. Yes. What the hell kind of answer was that? Bullshit. That's what it was. Jordan and Mikael had topped my list of scary dudes. Dakarai wanted me to add him as well. Fan-friggin-tastic, as he said. I threw my hands in the air. Be scared of me, Jasper. I won't tell you why, so don't worry your pretty little head about it, Jasper. You're the least scary person here, Jasper. Hell.

Too soon to torch. It may be an option later.

"Yes? Care to elaborate?"

"No. Your concern is what I can teach you. We will spend several weeks delving into the source of your abilities, the soul fire, and learning to channel it safely and at your command."

"Groovy. On to more important things. When do we begin?" It was foolish to hope for an answer of never. Hell, I'd have taken a week.

"Tomorrow. Be ready at five."

"In the morning?"

I wasn't a morning person. Never had been, much to the disappointment of my early rising parents. Getting out of bed before dawn was a cardinal sin in my book.

"Yes. Your day begins with Jordan. Good luck."

§

The door of my suite quaked under the force of a series of rapid blows, shaking the generic frames on my pale cream walls and jerking me out of the deepest sleep I've had in ages. I looked around for a weapon and, finding nothing obvious, I grabbed the lamp on my bedside table. It would do in a pinch and had the potential to gain me a few precious seconds in an attack. Or so I'd seen on television. I wedged myself behind the couch in the living room and waited.

The door shuddered again.

"This is your wake up call," Jordan called. "Ten minutes and I'm breaking the door down. Dress for the gym."

Jordan? Ten minutes? Gym?

My brain struggled to free itself from the dregs of sleep and comprehend what was happening. It was like studying calculus after midnight. Nearly impossible to process and unlikely to be remembered.

"Jasper, you're down to eight minutes. I will throw you over my shoulder and take you as you are. If you want to work out in pajamas and bare feet, that's up to you."

I scrambled to my feet, ran into my bedroom and shoved my limbs into the workout gear that had mysteriously appeared in my chest of drawers. Somehow, I managed to do everything and open my door with thirty seconds to spare.

He scowled down the nearly ten inches of height between us and bit back a sigh of exasperation. "When I say five, you're to be ready to go at five. That means dressed, fed, watered and prepared. Understood?"

My brain barely processed the words. It couldn't, not with the more pressing matter at the forefront of my thoughts. "Coffee?"

"You had your chance. It's now five-fifteen."

"Handle my own business before we meet. Got it. Should I meet you in the gym from now on? At five?"

"She can be taught," he drawled. "Yes. If I can wake up to train you, you can be there on time."

He turned on his heel and glided down the hallway toward the elevators with the grace of a predator on a hunt. In the silence of this corridor, his footfalls made no sound, unlike my own unintentional elephant stomps.

Jordan muttered under his breath about his cooling coffee and the time I'd wasted. I might have been imagining it, but his fists opened and closed a few times, as if restraining himself from punching me.

This guy was a poster-dude for aggressive tension. He pulsed with it, and if I could see auras, I was positive that his would have been an angry red.

If this was Jordan cranky, I didn't want to see him angry.

"Sorry, boss," I said meekly as we waited at the sleek white elevator doors.

"It's fine. Don't let it happen again," he said, seemingly mollified by the apology. Even though he had the distinctive bloodshot eyes of someone nursing a hangover, he suddenly appeared younger and less dangerous. He could have been any one of the guys who played against my brother in pickup basketball games. "We'll take it easy today. I'll have you run through a series of exercises to assess your overall conditioning. Tomorrow, we'll go to the armory. I need to see your level of comfort and ability to pick up skills with different weapons."

"Here's a dumb question," I said through a yawn. "I have the ability to cause explosions. Why do I need a weapon?"

"You have an enemy who wants to kill you. Do you wait for your erratic abilities to kick in? Or do you shoot the asshole in the head and move on with your day?"

Fair enough.

"I'd rather not shoot anyone in the head."

Jordan's unblinking azure eyes hinted at the ghosts of his victims who accompanied him night and day. "If someone threatens mine, I will do whatever is necessary to keep them safe. The people we're trying to find? They killed your family and they'll continue to kill other innocent people. When I find them, my abilities will be the least of their concerns."

Damn.

Being inducted into a mystical order I didn't fully understand and thinking of myself as a superhero-in-training had obscured my vision. The concept of saving the world had become an abstract overnight, divorced from the names and faces of the people who died. Separate from my dead parents and siblings. My cheeks heated as I ducked my head in shame. "I'm sorry."

"Don't be sorry. Pay attention, don't be afraid to ask questions, and execute." The corner of his lips twitched. "No pun intended."

"Dude!"

My protest broke his facade. He barked out a laugh. "Jasper, do you know why I haven't lost my mind? Killed myself?"

Time to back away. The beast is close to the surface.

"Beast?" I immediately regretted saying the word aloud. Jordan's eyes shuttered and the azure became cobalt. The optical illusion, where he appeared to increase in mass and size, was back. He was a bigger, fiercer, violent version of himself, otherworldly and awesome.

The elevator which had seemed spacious mere moments ago was suffocating. Jordan's anger pushed against the walls, squeezing out excess oxygen. Gone was his perpetual scowl. It had been replaced by a warrior's furor in the midst of a battle for his soul. He couldn't have been more terrifying if he turned blue, sprouted funky hair and exhibited claws.

"Beast," he spat in a guttural voice. "Watch yourself, *child*. We hate that name."

I blinked, and Jordan sipped his coffee once again, the slightest bit of humor in his half-smile.

"What ... Jordan, what the hell was that?" I tried to swallow but found that I had neither saliva nor tears to convey my growing terror. "You were ... I said ... blue."

"Explain."

The elevator arrived with a thud. Its doors opened silently and politely waited for us to leave its confines. I stepped out into yet another nondescript corridor and backed up against the adjacent wall.

Stepped was too kind. Jumped, stumbled backwards, and flailed as I landed on my ass was more accurate. Smooth as always.

I shrank into myself and willed myself invisible. When that failed to produce any results, I crouched into a ball and pressed harder, waiting for a magical secret door to whisk me away. I wasn't so lucky. I was stuck there with a monster. A literal monster. "You *changed*. Y-y...you told me to watch myself. Please don't hurt me."

He scowled and crossed his arms. Bad move, considering it brought back the visceral memory of being choked by the mother of all biceps. "Why on Earth would you think I'd hurt you?"

"What's wrong with you? You can't do something like that and expect me to stay calm."

Jordan rolled his eyes. "What did you see? Any heralds of the almighty? Dire warnings of impending doom? No? Good. Let's get moving. You're cutting into your workout time."

I shook my head and whimpered. "Nuh-uh. How do I know you won't Hulk out and attack me?" The cool white walls of the corridor cast eerie light around him in the pre-dawn hours. It illuminated the harsh lines of exhaustion. And if I wasn't mistaken, there were lines of grief and rage around his eyes. "If you can't remember what you said two minutes ago, why should I believe you?"

He opened his mouth to speak, but caught himself. "Did my appearance seem to change?"

"Uh, yeah. Why else would I freak out?"

Those hard eyes softened. "Ah. That. I'm sorry for scaring you. It wasn't intentional and it won't happen again."

"Sorry, I'm not betting my safety on a promise."

He sighed and scratched at the stubble that seemed as much a part of him as that scowl. "Jasper, when *She* takes control, are you aware?"

"Sometimes. *She* lets me watch and sometimes *She*'ll even listen to me, but I'm present. Is that what happened? Did Jordan take over for Jordy? Who are you right now?"

I stared at his proffered hand. There was no doubt in my mind that his strong calloused fingers could snap my neck with minimal effort, yet, I knew those same hands could just as easily cradled someone in pain and cared for them with the gentleness of a mother hen.

"Jordy," he said quietly. "Jordan has been close to the surface since we met. His interest in you is unexpected. It's out of character even for him."

"And you?"

Jordan — Jordy — smiled slightly and helped me to my feet. "Also uncharacteristic and unexpected. I haven't worked out my theory on this just yet."

She decided to get involved at the worst time. I felt *Her* prod something outside of me, something that responded with a hesitant curiosity. Our alter egos sniffed one another like two dogs being introduced.

I like this one. Stay with the beast. He will protect you at all costs.

Jordy guided me down one hallway after another until we arrived at the main gymnasium. I knew that because there was a sign telling me as much posted over the entrance. Mr. Brooding wasn't much of a help when it came to teaching me how to get around.

He opened the door and gestured with the flourished pride of a proud papa bear. "This is one of two places I go to relax. If you can't find me, there's a good chance I'm here."

"Uh-huh," I replied automatically. He'd lost my attention to the behemothic arena before us. Situated on a single floor, the gymnasium stretched across what must have been the footprint of the entire compound. The designer had forgone the usual series of rooms and instead created an open, welcoming space separated into functional areas. It was a playground for kids of all ages.

The weight "room" was delineated by a low guardrail that allowed one to keep an eye on the other sections. Across from us, open doors revealed small studios for yoga, Pilates and small classes.

Jordy cleared his throat. "This is the main facility. I have a few smaller training rooms that I use when I'm not in the mood to socialize or when I'm doing individual training."

"How many jobs do you have?"

A ghost of a smile flitted across his face. "Entirely too many. I'm not a personal trainer, if that's what you're implying. I only train my friends and those under my direct aegis. Honestly, I have neither the time nor the patience to work with anyone else."

Ouch.

I ducked my head to hide that stupid flush of embarrassment. "I'm sorry for adding to your workload."

"You're not." Jordy dropped his bag in front of a large slice of empty mat. "It's before dawn and I'm usually here at this time. I don't mind the company."

If I wasn't convinced that the man was either oblivious or indifferent to the world around him, I would have sworn that his ruddy complexion darkened with an embarrassed flush high on his cheeks.

"Oh," I said with enough curiosity to catch his eye. "Well, thanks. Can I be honest?"

125

"Sure." He reached his arms over his head in a deep stretch and yawned.

"Dakarai said that you're going to destroy me and find me lacking."

Jordy barked out a surprised laugh. "That asshole. He's just bitter because he couldn't keep up with me yesterday. I won't lie, Jasper. Training with me is going to be brutal. I'm not going to coddle you or give you so-called girly exercises. You'll keep up with me or you'll find someone else to train you."

I gulped and hoped that Jordy wasn't a coach of the Sue Sylvester ilk. "Do I get a learning curve?"

"Of course, silly. I'll make you a deal. Let's get through this assessment quickly. If you're not in horrible shape, I'll spring you from Quasimodo's Tower. We can run laps at the park."

§

"You're a devious, cruel man."

Jordy laughed. "You say the same thing every morning. And afternoon. I'm convinced you curse my name in your sleep."

"Spending time with you is bad for my health."

That was a lie. In six weeks, I'd replaced what little baby fat I'd had with rock-solid muscles. I was down to a nine minute mile and had been proclaimed ready for combat training. My body had never so looked or felt better.

"Mm-hmm. Keep telling yourself those lies. Are you excited about tomorrow?"

"Am I excited for the training you told me would be more brutal than anything I'd ever done? Or are you asking if I'm excited for you to punch me in the face?"

Jordy draped a sweaty arm over my sweatier shoulders and led me from the main gym. Unlike me, he ignored the people around us who gawked and gossiped about us. Most people treated him with deferential respect.

Me? I was the subject of speculation that had recently turned sordid. It was high school all over again. Although I'd asked Jordy to train in one of the private studios, he insisted that it was good for me to be around the other occupants.

I disagreed.

The Order was worse than a college dormitory. While most apartments had their own kitchens, the dining halls were always full. Families sat in groups. The older kids gathered in corners to play some sort of role playing game with cards and die. The younger ones jumped and screamed with excitement.

Every.

Friggin.

Night.

Dakarai's preference to stay in the QT, as we now called it, made a lot more sense. I joined him for most meals. Lately so had Jordy. They took turns creating stunning culinary masterpieces with vibrant flavors and scents that had me acting like Pavlov's dog. I took over cleaning up after meals, but it was a joke. They both cleaned as they cooked. My task amounted to little more than loading a dishwasher and waxing poetic about everything I'd eaten.

Likewise, I'd taken to avoiding crowds in favor of quieter, more enjoyable nooks and crannies, the inhospitable gymnasium being the only exception.

The morning's pleasantness came to an abrupt end as a group of teenagers sniggered and pointed.

"She's not his usual type," I heard a scrawny guy with glasses say. He poked his friend's side and pointed. "Do you know who she is?"

I knew that most people speculated about my identity and my relationship to some of the most powerful people in the Order. I'd heard every one of their theories before: I was someone's long lost sister, new support staff for the upper echelons, an orphan, an unsuspecting pawn, or Jordy's girlfriend.

Their words infuriated me. Apparently, I was someone needy and helpless.

Screw them. Or kill them. Whatever you decide, get over it. Time grows short.

She was back with smashing advice. Brilliant, darling, really. It blew my mind that *She* was fine with murder as long as it snapped me out of this temporary funk.

I seriously considered it when the little shits kept talking.

"I wonder how hard she has to *work* to keep his attention."

Jordy patted my shoulder and kissed my cheek. "Jasper, go on out. I'll catch up to you in a minute."

"What? Why? It's the same kids who've been talking crap about me all week. Dakarai told me to ignore them."

"Guess I didn't get the memo. Go." The word was soft, but the command was not. "You don't need to see this."

"See what?" Misdirection used to work with my parents and siblings. They got lost in my Socratic questions. By the time they figured out my game, they were so twisted around that they'd only remembered they'd been angry with me. "What is it that you don't want me to see?"

One of the teenagers in the group, a wannabe jock with budding muscles and acne, snorted. "She must have some mind control voodoo because she's not that pretty. She must have found a way to trap the big bad McAllister. Smug bitch."

Jordy blinked and the telltale change in eye color warned me that things were about to go terribly wrong. "Get out," said Jordan.

"No." *She* was no help because *She* liked the beast. We'd sparred a few times and it was like Christmas come early until he knocked us on our communal ass three consecutive times. "Jordan, don't do this. They're not worth it."

"I protect what is mine. Go."

He didn't wait for a response but instead turned from me and strode off toward the group.

Teen Jockstrap was either new or stupid because he squared his shoulders and smirked. His friends backed away, but he didn't care.

Jordan growled. "You don't look at her. You don't speak to her. Understand?"

Teen Jockstrap rolled his eyes. "Or what? You'll get in trouble if you touch me. My parents are in the Circle. Run along before I have you destroyed."

The water I was drinking spurted from my nose. The kid was so full of shit. I doubt he knew what the Circle was and I was positive his parents weren't in it.

"What, bitch?" The kid had a death wish. He raised his hands as if to invite me to fight him. The crowd gathering around us was silent, but he took the growing number as encouragement.

She was positively gleeful. If *She*'d taken control, *She* would have clapped her hands and bounced on *Her* toes. The idea of Jordan fighting someone over us was damn near orgasmic for both of us.

There was no warning. Jordan had the Teen Jockstrap pinned to the floor beneath him. Blood spurted through the air as the kid's face was pounded by those hammer-of-the-gods fists.

I looked around wildly. No one made a move to break up the fight. Adults covered the eyes of children, but it didn't help. The sickening sound of flesh being pounded and bone breaking were chilling enough.

"Jordy! Jordan!"

He paused for a moment. One of his massive hands flexed around the kid's neck. The other dripped with blood. "What?"

"Stop. It's over." I crept forward knowing that both Teen Jockstrap and I were both in mortal peril. Jordan was unpredictable, violent and, dear God, he was fast. He could kill us both before I'd have time to register that he moved. "Jordan."

"What?"

Gulping, I put my hand on his shoulder. "Hey. Hi. It's me. You recognize me, right? The one you're protecting?"

He'd just pulverized Teen Jockstrap's face, but he wasn't even breathing heavy. His face registered nothing other than mild annoyance with me. "I repeat: What do you want?"

She suggested that I continue with the physical contact because *She* was convinced that my voice was his anchor to reality. He just needed to understand that his charge was safe.

I tried to soften the fear in my voice. "I'd love it if you'd walk out with me. Someone promised me a Netflix movie marathon."

Jordy bit his lip and frowned. His eyes flickered between shades. "Not now."

"Please?"

Someone had apparently run outside and invited everyone see the "fight of the century." The collective body heat and morbid fascination pressed in from all sides. I didn't need *Her* to sense the probing energies, angry and pulsing, that were being directed at us.

One energy, stronger than the rest, sluiced through all the others. It was angry and it wanted to hurt me. Jordan's presence was the only reason it hadn't attacked.

I pressed into Jordan's side and tugged on his arm. There was no way to know if the energy was hostile or if it was even human. "Jordy," I whispered, "I need to get out of here. Can't you feel it? I don't need protection from this dipshit, but I'm afraid of whatever is coming toward us."

Jordy/Jordan shook his head like a wet dog. When he looked at me again, his eyes had returned to normal. He stood and frowned at the blood on his hands.

"He'll be fine," he announced to the crowd. "Just broken bones and some bruises. This? A warning to anyone who dares to misuse the name of the Order or the Circle."

"All that was a lesson?"

"Nope. The little shit has been testing the limits with me for a few weeks. He'll stop talking about you. I broke his jaw."

Jordy grabbed our bags and slung his arm around me once more. The crowd parted comically fast and I walked through it with my own personal Moses.

Instead of heading to the private gym, Jordy lead me back to Quasimodo's Tower. He talked about everything except what just happened. I learned the history behind every painting and photograph in the corridors that led toward quiet and safety. Except for the blood on his hands and my wariness, there was nothing unusual about the walk. The elevator still moved silently and the corridor was still obnoxiously red with cream accents.

Nothing had changed. Except...it had. Jordy had been in better control than he'd let on earlier. I'd seen him struggle with Jordan before and this wasn't it. That was Jordy making a statement and scaring people into following the rules. Jordan would have killed the lot of them.

Jordy took my hand in his. "If you don't have plans, would you like to go to breakfast? I'll spring you from the compound and take you to one of the better places around here."

131

CHAPTER 11

I pulled a knit cap over my head and yanked up the zipper of my new down coat. My other one had been shredded from my night in the woods and I didn't have anything else to combat the chill.

When I'd arrived in late September, it had been chilly, bordering on cold in the evenings. I hadn't the faintest clue of the temperature until Jordy returned with cold weather gear.

The sky was a flat gray, an improvement from the pewter canvas that had provided to the backdrop to nasty lightning storms the previous week. The temperature was ripe for a sleet storm. Even the drug dealers, whom Mikael had pointed out from the small window in his room, huddled together for warmth in front of the corner bodega.

Everything from the awnings of the stores to the streets signs was dingy and faded, giving the impression of a strange post-apocalyptic outpost in the middle of the modern world.

"Where are we going?" I asked.

Jordy lifted the hood of his sweater over his baseball cap and smiled. "Didn't I tell you that we'd go out for breakfast?"

I snorted. Jordy, for all his ferocity, was more clueless than most guys I knew. "That was a month ago."

"No way. Well, better late than never?" He slipped on a pair of fingerless gloves and took my hand as he led me out of the building.

The biting air was glorious. It reeked of burnt rubber and garbage masticated by the machines of a nearby recycling plant. At least I thought so based on the little research I'd done on recycling plants.

"Ooh, you know how to charm a girl."

"I don't charm girls. I don't do anything with *girls*."

I threw a pointed look to our hands.

He laughed. "This? You're not a girl. You haven't been outside in almost two months. One of your best survival tools is the ability to blend in with the crowd. You act as if you're a criminal."

"Last time I checked, I'm wanted for murder."

"What are you talking about? That was taken care of weeks ago. Watch it." Jordy steered me around a frozen pile of dog poop in the middle of the street. "Jasper, do you know today's date?"

"I don't even have a window, so it's only by the kindness of strangers I know whether it's day or night. The days are starting to blur together. Watch your step."

Jordy held back a gag as he jumped over the not quite frozen lake of excrement.

"Careful or you'll wake the Golgothan."

"Golgothan?"

My soul died a little at his lack of reaction. "Never mind. Where are we going?"

"To a local establishment that serves foods typically eaten in the morning hours."

The temperature dropped as the gray skies intensified. Jordy put my arm through his and shrugged. "I'm warmer than you."

"Hilarious and chivalrous. How'd I get so lucky?"

"What? Lucky to have such a bad ass trainer and protector? Yeah, you are. Do you think you can have a meal without freaking out?"

"Right. This is a training session."

The heart-shaped fantasy bubble burst into a gooey puddle somewhere in the vicinity of the frozen poop lake. We got along so well that it was easy to forget that I was merely his responsibility, his job, and certainly not his friend. I'd been a foolish, dreaming child for allowing myself to think that Jordy cared for me.

I couldn't think of anything to say so I held his hand and tried to take in as much as possible. I'd been sequestered for so long that I'd forgotten that I was in New York City, albeit in a crappy neighborhood, but the City nonetheless.

As we waited at the intersection of the main street and a freeway, Jordy pointed out the idiosyncratic landmarks of the area. The chop shops, junkyards, a drug den and a whore house took over a single city block. If there was such a place as a den of iniquity, then I'd found it. Every vice was on display in all its seedy glory.

Mothers and children bustled down the streets garbed in cheap winter jackets that were broken, mended and broken again. One child had a noticeable hole in his shoe. His mother took off her sneakers and traded with the grateful boy.

The near opulence of the Order's compound was a painful contrast to the streets around it. I hoped that they provided for the community. If I found out otherwise, I'd organize a food and coat drive. My bleeding heart couldn't take the suffering around us.

Jordy led me across the seven lanes of traffic. He stared down the owners of the cars who dared to inch closer to the crosswalk. My gut told me that I would have ended up a very dead Frogger if I'd attempted the crossing alone. Thanks to my protector my organs were intact and not under the wheels of those cars.

We turned down a side street and entered a restaurant with fogged windows. The place screamed "dive" with its chipped linoleum floors and wobbly tables. The two waitresses wore more makeup than I did on a good night out and clothes that were plastered to their curvy figures.

Jordy grinned at one of the waitresses and shooed me to a booth in the back. From what I could remember from my Spanish classes, I learned that he knew her well enough to ask about her family and tease her about something that made her blush. The waitress slapped his arm and sashayed into the kitchen. She called out that he needed to stop staring at her ass and instructed him to sit down with his friend.

She should have told him to sit down with his ward. I counted to ten and reminded myself to behave. It was my first outing and I refused to ruin it because I was pissed off.

Jordy snapped his fingers in front of my face. "Hey. Where'd you go? I've asked you the same question three times."

"Huh?"

"Freedom is getting to your head," he said with a healthy amount of sarcasm. "I asked if you spoke other languages."

I hoped that one day I wouldn't blush with embarrassment. It was out of control and made me appear younger and less experienced. "Three years of Spanish. That's it."

"It's a decent start."

"Is there a chill in here or is it just me?"

Jordy's face became a cool mask of indifference as he slid to the end of the booth. He positioned himself to see the entire restaurant. "I'm not feeling anything but I trust your instincts. Keep alert."

"So, ah, um, do you speak other languages?"

"I'm not a fan of the romance languages in general, but Spanish is a necessity. I'm also not doing business with the French these days. My Russian and German are passable, and my Farsi is atrocious."

The other pretty waitress came by with our menus. She listed the morning's specials in rapid fire Spanish while leaning on the table to show off her cleavage.

Hurt her. Kill her. Burn her and everything she holds dear. Destroy her.

I jumped up and asked for directions to the bathroom. My hands shook as I locked the door behind me and leaned against the small porcelain sink. This was the second time that *She* had encouraged me to, oh, murder someone.

"What the hell was that?"

My reflection in the stained mirror above the sink said nothing. The smirk on *Her* face made me twitch. I wished I could have reached through the mirror and choked *Her* psychotic ass.

"Oh, come on. Don't ignore me."

She threatens what is ours.

"Ours? Holy hell. Do you have a crush on him? Are you jealous?"

Outside, someone knocked lightly on the door.

"Jasper," Jordy asked softly. "Everything okay?"

I glared at the flickering image of a young woman with short black hair, hard features and flat eyes. It wasn't the first time *She* had played this game, but my defiance was brand spanking new. "You'd better behave."

Or what?

"Jasper?"

The growing protectiveness in Jordy's voice snapped me back to reality. *She* might have been staging a coup, but I refused to relinquish ownership of my body and consciousness. I couldn't, not when she threatened to kill someone over pettiness.

"We're so close," I begged *Her*. "Once we master what we need to know, we can go after the people who killed our family. Don't ruin it and get us tossed into the brig. Please."

She hovered on indecision for several long beats then nodded slightly. My evil imaginary twin made herself scarce.

"Yeah, I'm good. I'll be out in a second." My vanity kicked in. Without *Her* games, I could see the embarrassing mess I'd become on the blustery walk. I ran a hand through my wind-mussed hair. The little makeup I'd applied was intact, so I washed and dried my hands.

"Jasper? Do you need me to come in? TALK TO ME."

I opened the bathroom door and shook my head. "Jeez, dude. Can't I use the restroom without you listening? What's next? An ankle bracelet?"

Jordy's eyes were flat and his voice had a deeper resonance that chilled me to the bone. "Are you injured? Did anyone hurt you?"

"No and no. My full bladder isn't cause to sound the alarms. Jordan, listen to me."

He said nothing.

"Nothing happened. There's no maniacal killer waiting in the kitchen. Step back from the edge, Jordy." I caressed his cheek and smiled. "You're doing a great job at keeping me safe. The creatures that lie in the abyss of the bathroom trashcan are terrified."

He breathed through his nose slowly, deliberately, until he regained control. "Thank you." He kissed the back of my hand and led me back to our table. It was now covered in what must have been every dish on the menu. "I wasn't sure what you liked, so..." Jordy shrugged. "Here ya go."

"As long as it's edible, we're good. Beggars can't be choosy."

Cleavage came back and spoke in slow, deliberate English. "You are Jordy's little sister? Cousin?"

"No, I'm not." It was hard to maintain that polite chatter when *She* was dying to play or murder. *She* wasn't picky. Nor was *She* willing to wait much longer. I kicked Jordy under the table.

"Ow. What was..." He narrowed his eyes and threw a pointed look at my hands. They weren't glowing yet, but I suspect he knew it was a matter of time and discipline. "Nadia, this is my friend, Jasper. *Esto es nuestra primera cita. Le traje aquí porque ella quería tratar la mejor comida puertorriqueña en la ciudad. Estoy tratando de impresionarla."*

The woman snatched up our empty water glasses and stomped away, going over to the counter to refill them. Upon her return, she slammed the glasses in front of us, sloshing water onto our dishes. She told him off for bringing his girlfriend here after flirting with her for months.

I tried to ignore their heated argument and focused my attention on the fried goodness in front of me. The plate of fried eggs, cheese and salami called to me. I was a food junkie and this salty, greasy mess was my reward for months of steamed vegetables and portion control.

Jordy snorted with disbelief. "If you don't know the difference between flirting and getting ready to meet your family, then I can't help you." He held her gaze until Nadia shuffled into the back room.

"Great way to get me banned. Why did you tell her we were on a date?"

"Two people going out to enjoy a meal and pleasant conversation sounds like a date to me."

My temper begged to be released. I wanted to shout at him. It wasn't kind to suggest that we were on date. My last date had been a week before the explosion. I didn't miss the guy, but I did miss the thrill and butterflies that went along with it.

I shifted on the creaky seat and positioned myself diagonal from him. Pretending that my attention was focused on the food wasn't too much of a stretch. Ignoring him was more difficult. Once he picked up on my polite disinterest, he shrugged and ate in silence.

I kicked him. Rather, I tried to kick him but he caught my foot with one hand. "Let go of me."

"Stop trying to hurt me. It's an exercise in futility." He speared a sweet plantain and held it out to me. "Try it."

"Will you let my foot go? I want to finish this stupid exercise and go home."

He chuckled. "Honey, you failed the exercise twenty minutes ago. I know why you went to the restroom."

I was speechless.

"I'm having a meal with someone whose company I happen to enjoy. I fail to see why you're acting like I killed your puppy."

"You knew? You knew and you didn't help?"

"Nope. Try the damn plantain. It's a side dish, but I always take some home for dessert."

"Why?"

Two people with a complicated relationship was tricky on the best of days. Two people who had supernatural abilities and were pissed off with one another put everyone around us smack in the middle of a danger zone. My fingers tingled as I contemplated ways to hurt him.

"Because the plantains are tasty. I enjoy eating them. What is your goddamn problem?"

"You." I freed my ankle from his hand by holding up my right hand. I curled my fingers back and slowly raised the middle one. The tip was bright as an LED lightbulb. "You're my problem. Since we've arrived, you've toyed with the emotions of every woman here. I don't know what game you're playing, but I'm out."

I slid out of the booth and marched off with pride stiffening my spine. Jordy could have rotted in hell for all I cared. The personal boundaries were clear with everyone except him. Dakarai speculated that Jordy was unsure of how his efforts would be received. That Jordy was five years older concerned them both. Mikael, on the other hand, thought that Jordy wasn't sure what he wanted and didn't know how to behave.

My thoughts carried me back to the train station. I hesitated for a moment before finally descending the stairs.

§

The last time I'd been in Manhattan, which was the previous summer, Jude and I spent the day at Chelsea Piers. From the moment we'd arrived, everything had been a huge adventure. The batting cages were pathetic opponents. Rock climbing had been a breeze. We'd impressed on the basketball courts when we won three out of four games. My ball handling skills were bar none.

Just as we were deciding to go home, we had stumbled upon the parkour course. The sport seemed to have been made for us. Jude had used his ability to cushion our falls and to give us forward momentum. We'd known then it was cheating, but that only pushed us harder. I was lighter, faster, and more strategic. Jude was athletic grace personified. Our crowning achievement had been getting around the town square without touching the ground.

I'd been so lost in my thoughts that I'd ended up standing outside of Chelsea Piers. The parkour room didn't open for an hour, so I walked to a spot overlooking the Hudson River. It should have been tranquil, but the river's choppy waves and grayish water were better suited to a good brood.

My life had devolved into the shittiest and most depressing supernatural sitcom of all time. Girl blew up school. Girl's family died. Girl got kidnapped and had a bad case of Stockholm Syndrome. Hilarity ensued.

I weighed my options. Fleeing to Mexico and drinking Coronas on the beach would have been fabulous. But there was one tiny hiccup. I would've had to watch my back and prayed the boogieman never found me. My distant family and friends would have never taken me in, not after the murder charges.

The Order was my best chance of staying alive.

The gray skies turned stormy and, as I'd predicted, sleet began to pelt me from all directions. I got up and ran past the entrance to the parkour course straight to the taxi stand. I was starting to believe in signs and this screamed, "Get your ass home because danger is coming, dumbass."

Jordy was waiting outside when my cab pulled up to the Order's entrance. After he paid the driver, he offered me a hand and escorted me inside. I remained silent because I didn't know what to say or how to apologize for my tantrum.

Once we reached the Tower's elevator, he took my face in his hands and searched my expression for something. Whatever it was, he didn't find it. He let go and stared at the doors.

"I'm sorry," I said. "This morning was complicated and frustrating, but those were my issues. I shouldn't have argued with you."

His silence grated on my nerves. My biggest pet peeve was being ignored. Back in the day, a whole three months earlier, disregarding an apology was cause for a brawl. I'd once given Jude a black eye for avoiding me for two days. Unfortunately, I knew that pounding Jordy in the face was wishful thinking.

By the time we arrived at my door, I was glad to be rid of him. Jordy was an assassin with the emotional maturity of an eighteen year old. No wonder people speculated about him. Communication was not his strong suit.

Jordy cleared his throat. "Meet me downstairs tomorrow at five. We're going to try something new. If you're available, I'd like you to sit in on the advanced weapons class during the afternoon. I've considered moving you to a group setting instead of individual tutoring."

"Oh. Yeah, sure. Thanks." I opened the door and tried to smile. "Goodnight, Jordy."

"Jasper," he said, "don't worry about today. Like you said, it's complicated. We'll talk about it eventually."

I gave him a crisp salute. "Right. See ya bright and early, boss man."

§

Jordy's private gym was the perfect place to play. He'd amassed a collection of barriers, blocks, trampolines and swing ropes most trainers would have envied.

He must have known what I was doing, but he never brought it up. Perhaps he understood how important parkour had become to my emotional well-being. It might have been my reward for not complaining about the brutal hours I spent under his tutelage.

Friday nights were the best. The gym cleared out early and Jordy disappeared no later than ten at night. I'd spend a couple of hours bouncing off walls and perfecting my tumbles before dragging myself to bed.

§

My head pounded from the noise coming from Dakarai's apartment. He was hosting a dinner party for his friends. I hadn't been invited, not that I was bitter or anything. It was partially my fault. I'd retreated into myself after the disastrous breakfast with Jordy. Not even the lure of the holidays could budge me once I retired for the night.

It was New Year's Eve and the entire Order was one giant celebration. Dinner had included an early ball drop for the little ones and a chaperoned dance for the teens. Then there was the gala. From what little I'd gleaned, the Order threw a black tie affair for any adults who wanted to enjoy a snazzy end of the year. I told myself that I didn't want to celebrate the beginning of a new year without my family, that I didn't need friends to be happy, and that becoming a part of the community was a bad idea.

I didn't believe any of it.

My window of opportunity was dwindling. I'd counted the number of guests who went in and knew he was waiting for one more person. Only then could I safely sneak out of my room, down the elevators and into the least visited corner of the compound. I retied my trainers, checked my gym bag and tucked my hair under a ball cap.

Finally, the last person arrived and knocked on the door adjacent to mine.

"I'd wondered if you'd make it. I'm glad you're here," Dakarai said. I could imagine the boyish grin and energy he exuded.

"Sorry about that," Jordy said. "I've been running late all day. Is there still time?"

"Yes, yes. Of course."

Jordy cleared his throat. "Is she inside?"

"No. She avoids me outside of our work together. I'm sorry, my friend."

"I should check on her."

Dakarai barked out a laugh. "Let's put that particular problem aside for a few hours. I have more alcohol than should be allowed and it's not going to drink itself."

Problem?

Problem?

I'd been taking the time to get to know *Her* better and found our personalities melding together. Lately, I didn't know where she ended and I began. At that moment we wanted to blast a hole through the door and rage at them.

Unfortunately, you'd kill everyone if you decided to instigate a battle. We're not done here.

I waited until Jordy and Dakarai disappeared behind the door, counted to ten and sprinted down the hallway. The elevator doors were still open, and like a puppy who hadn't grown into its paws I slammed into the wall and bounced off of it, right into the panel of buttons.

The elevator descended to the gym level. My strut told my non-existent audience that I was a boss, not some little girl to mock. They should have been quaking at my feet. I could have killed them all and walked away without a scratch.

I threw open the hidden door to the training room and gagged. The musky smell of old jockstraps, unwashed towels and unsanitary equipment wafted into my nostrils and nested. This was Jordy's version of a mild diversionary tactic. He'd set up clearance for anyone who had his permission to use the space and if one didn't have the right thumbprint for the scanner, the smell would be the least of their worries.

The odor crawled into my mouth and liquefied in my veins. Thousands of fire ants burrowed into my skin, heating me from the inside and making me sweat drips of lava. The security pad was too far away. I'd be incapacitated or dead if I failed.

She woke up and a growl burst from my throat. We couldn't stop the fire ants, but we'd never go down without a fight. We rocked back and forth on our heels to gain momentum and flung our body at the wall.

Pain cut through me like a mesh net savages a block of cheese. I was dying. I knew it. I knew Jordy would be the end of me. The embarrassment was too much to handle. My body would be no more than a ruined lump of meat and bone and I'd have been taken out by the smell of teenage boys.

§

Sulfur burned my nose and yanked me out of oblivion. "My arms! Oh my God. Help me. Please God. Help me!"

I scratched at my body until I saw blood. The ants were still inside me. The liquid in my veins was going to fill my lungs and drown me from within. Unless I removed the poisons, I'd die.

"Someone woke up feisty."

"What? Who's there? I'll kill you!" The poisons were shutting down my organs and I was losing my senses. My vision had been reduced to an old movie theater projector. It was impossible for my brain to keep up with the onslaught of light and sound.

My attacker was nearby and I couldn't friggin' see.

"Ea...ow. Re..xy...sk... Put...the..st...over your...head. Breathe."

"Get away from me! I'll kill you!"

This time my foot found its mark on my would-be murderer's thigh. It was enough to knock him or her off balance long enough for me to scoop up the oxygen mask and tank and hightail it to the opposite corner. My hands sought the strings on either side of the mask and looped them into place. It could have been a trick, this tank of gas, but I'd run out of options. I sucked the air deep into my lungs. The fire ants and liquid stench receded as the air turned into liquid.

Of course the heat had been extinguished. The gas turned frigid in, my bloodstream, neutralizing everything in its way. I slumped over and stared at the ceiling.

For the first time I could remember, *She* wasn't even a shadow in my mind. I was alone, completely and utterly alone. No family, no friends, no potential for a real life. Nothing anchoring me to reality. I closed my eyes and saw my parents and sister. Livie smirked at my attire because only my sister had the ability to make death into a fashion critique. My mom and dad looked haggard. But they smiled widely, tears glistening in their eyes. Mom opened her arms and tried to bring me home.

Where's Jude?

Their voices were warped by whatever boundary separated us. My mom realized it first and began to scream and pantomime a single word.

Run.

§

I was ready the next time the sulfur hauled me out of whatever the hell had just happened. My attacker moved in closer and felt my forehead about the same time as my right fist connected with his or her jaw.

"Ow! Fuck! Goddammit! If I have a bruise you're going to pay in laps."

"Jordy?"

I opened my eyes and saw him standing above me. Jordy cradled his cheek and glowered. The sleeves of his white dress shirt were rolled up to his elbows and his tie was loose around his neck.

"Who are you? What do you want?"

"For fuck's sake, Jasper! How hard did you hit your head? And why the hell are you sneaking into my private training studio? Were you trying to get into my office?"

"Jordy doesn't wear suits. Jordy doesn't get hurt. Who are you?"

Jordy heaved his dashingly attired self into a chair. "I'm not playing games tonight. There are a million parties going on, one right across from your room, and you decided to break into my office instead."

My head throbbed, but a quick pat-down revealed nothing concerning. "I don't understand."

"I can't help you unless you use your big girl words to tell me what hurts." He rubbed his cheek again and smiled. "Holy hell, Jasper. That was a great punch. Your reaction time was stellar."

Nothing made sense. The room was identical to the one where I spent several hours a week. If I ignored the suit, I could entertain the idea that Jordy sat in front of me. But...

"Where the hell is your office? And what happened?"

"Can I examine you now? You gouged that arm like a pro."

I acquiesced and submitted myself to a quick and professional prodding. "What's going on? How long?"

"She speaks." He rose and dusted off his pants legs. "It's New Year's Eve. No one has permission to be anywhere except the designated areas. You were not cleared for this room."

"What? This was you? You did this to me?" I slapped the chivalrous hand he held out and jumped to my feet.

"Whoa, killer. Let's get you into a chair. We can talk while I monitor you. Fair warning," he said cheerfully. "I'm probably going to stick you with a needle."

The world kept going right round, right round like...crap. The rest of the song escaped me. "I'll kick you again."

"Go for it. You're not going to hurt me."

"Jerk."

"Never claimed otherwise. Did you truly believe that I was unaware of your nighttime Rocky sessions?"

"Yes. You never said anything."

He shrugged and Jordy the stranger who wasn't my friend reappeared. He took my pulse and stuck a thermometer in my mouth. "If you wanted my help or company, you would have asked. Since you didn't, I respected your space. That doesn't mean I don't keep an eye on you.

"Cameras?"

Jordy jerked his head once toward the back corner. "I had it set to turn off inside the gym. Only the hidden door, the antechamber and my office doors were monitored." His voice softened. "Why are you here?"

"Because it's my 'Rocky session'. What's the big deal? I do what I'm told and stay out of everyone's way. What did you do to me?"

"That's something else we need to discuss. But as to what happened? Nothing."

"Bullshit." I was on my last reserves of brain power and restraint. "Something happened."

"The canister released gas laced with a compound that was developed for this purpose." Jordy laid a hand on my shoulder. "You weren't supposed to be here. I never expected that you would be exposed."

Hell hath no fury like a woman who'd been drugged, choked, kidnapped and iced. Tiny fireflies danced underneath my skin, warming me from the inside out.

Power. Call on it. Claim it. Kill with it.

I perched myself on the edge of a weight rack. I took a few deep breaths. *She* might have been down to kill, but that was the difference between *Her* and me. I'd kill to protect myself, but senseless violence was abhorrent. If I crossed that line, I might as well have become the owner of the Wraith Bordello.

Yet, embracing the power — and *Her* — was more appealing than this lamb-to-slaughter shtick that had plagued me for so long. My voice was no longer my own. Nor was it *Hers*. Cold, calculated rage infused every syllable. "What did you do to me?"

Jordy raised his open hands in front of him and took a step backward. "Want to dial that back a notch, Sparky? I'm not invincible. If you go boom, Jordy goes bye bye."

I sneered. The power, whatever it was, responded to my thoughts and flowed to my fingertips. "Jordy goes where I tell him to go. I won't ask again. What did you do to me?

"The gas contains a compound we created here. Jasper, I need you to remember that you were never meant to be exposed."

Months of training and observing Jordy finally paid off. I noticed the shift in body movement that meant he was preparing for a fight. I'd already done the surveillance. The smooth walls offered no real purchase, so they couldn't be used in a fight. Nor could the room's only door as it was the only barrier between us and the poisonous antechamber.

I tracked his cool, assessing eyes as they moved around the gym. When his gaze settled on the weight rack, I knew that we'd come to the same conclusion. The weights would have to do.

I knew that if it came down to it, Jordy would do whatever was necessary to subdue me, but he wouldn't hurt me more than necessary. Unfortunately, I couldn't say the same thing. I'd destroy him and keep destroying everyone in my path until the rage subsided.

"Jasper, you're off-kilter and on a hair trigger. Remember that. We laced the gas with a compound that mimics the effects of a bad LSD trip without the addiction or long-lasting damage."

"You drugged me with LSD."

"Yes, I did. This isn't the only room in the compound that I've rigged with an anti-theft system. I'm sorry that you suffered through this, but I won't apologize for my security methods."

Who booby traps their office with LSD gas? What kind of cold calculation did that require?

How can we become just like him?

She might have been insane, but it appeared as if I was joining the party. The idea of deliberate violence didn't repel me. I needed it. I craved it. I'd die without it. The hunger for power gnawed at my insides, begging for a relief I couldn't provide. "Teach us. Me."

Jordy lowered his hands and stood straighter. "Be specific."

"Don't teach me how to use a weapon. Make me into the weapon. Show me how to turn off the emotions."

"No."

"No?"

"No. I won't make you into a weapon. I'll teach you the mechanics of how to kill. I can teach you how to torture. But I won't make you into anything. That's not my choice. You decide how it shapes you."

One of the most important lessons I'd learned from my time with the Circle was that control over thoughts and emotions was everything. In this heightened state, Jordy's gentle rejection smacked of disappointment and revulsion. I wasn't good enough, strong enough or worthy of his guidance. I was a child, a student, who was incapable of knowing what I needed.

They were wrong. The power that had been concentrated in my fingertips flowed through my veins like molten lava, tearing me apart, reshaping me and making me indestructible. My skin was aglow with pure energy and light. I was power incarnate.

"I wasn't asking. You will teach me, even if I have to summon the beast himself."

Jordy's eyes shuttered. His face lost all traces of emotion as he rose to his full height. "You do not command me. You do not summon me. I will teach you nothing."

"I command all. I am Vishnu and Shiva and Shakti. I am Asha Vahishta and Ma'at. I am Datin. I exist in the dawn and the dusk. The Vespers and the beast exist to mete out justice as I deem necessary. You will teach me."

"I will not."

A sense of calm washed over me as I spoke. "Then you will die."

§

I lost control.

The power within me roared through my body and exploded outward with the force of a nuclear bomb. I was the conduit and the waves of energy. I destroyed and created.

It seduced me, teased me, and promised pleasure and pain, everything and nothing. It promised to ease my burden and return the powers that were not mine. Equilibrium.

It was beautiful.

"Jasper!"

The guttural scream pierced my perfect cocoon and threatened to bring me back to the imperfection and imbalance. Rough hands grabbed at the body I'd been so close to shedding. Arms wrapped around me. The voice grew louder. It shouted, demanded, begged and prayed for my return. It begged for mercy for itself and for the others. It told stories of friendship and love.

My body fought corporeality but the beast was stronger. Its grasp was solid no matter how much I struggled. It absorbed every strike and was unfazed by kicks and bites.

The beast held me close and whispered in my ear.

"This is going to hurt. I'm sorry."

Pain radiated through my skull. My vision faded.

I was gone.

CHAPTER 12

Consciousness slapped me out of the cocoon of darkness and shackled me to my body. I braced myself for the inevitable waves of pain. There was no possible scenario in which I had escaped from the explosion unscathed. I couldn't bring myself to open my eyes and look at my charred flesh and broken limbs. If I did, the explosion would have been real and I would have caused destruction and injury.

Voices surrounded me.

And you really don't remember? Was it something that he said? Are the voices in your head? Calling Jasper!

She had officially claimed the top spot on my shit list. Whatever happened earlier could have been prevented if she'd been with me. We could have subdued the rage. This was her fault.

Oh, Jasper. Don't be such a spoilsport. Admit that you liked the power. You wanted it to consume you and bring you to oblivion.

"Her raw power is unparalleled. You could have been decimated. Based on the damage, you should have been a burnt corpse."

Jordy groaned as he lowered himself onto my bed. "Do you think she shielded me? Is there any record of that kind of ability? I need to go back to make sure there wasn't any damage outside of the room."

"Do what you think is best. However, it might be a good idea to wait until she wakes," Dakarai said. "Jasper has begun to navigate uncharted waters. Her abilities are manifesting too fast. She is dangerous."

"Damn. I'd hoped...it doesn't matter anymore. I have to suspend her training with me and limit our interactions. You know why."

Dakarai hummed his agreement. "The High Council will want to place her in containment."

"Not going to happen. I'll go to war with High Council over this. Jas is volatile already. If she's imprisoned, there's no telling what she'll do."

I swallowed, prying my tongue from the roof of my mouth, and forced my eyes open. "Don't talk about me like I'm not here. Where am I?"

Dakarai reached for my hand and smiled. "Ah, there you are. I wondered when you'd join the conversation, you nosy eavesdropper."

"Couldn't help it. Eyes wouldn't open. Why won't my arms move?"

Jordy and Dakarai exchanged apprehensive looks.

"I can't move my legs." For the first time, I noticed that a blanket covered my body and rested beneath my chin. "Oh shit. Please don't tell me you had to Robocop my body. Please tell me I'm not a cyborg."

Mikael walked into the room holding a bag of something that smelled delicious and a tray of coffee. "How's she doing?"

"Mikael! Am I a cyborg? Did I lose half my body? What the hell is going on? Where am I?"

He smiled ruefully. "It is wonderful to see you awake, Milaya. You gave us quiet a scare. I will answer your questions on the condition that you allow me to help you eat. I've seen you become ravenous after an exhibition of power."

"Huh?"

"My visions." Mikael lifted a cup of water to my face and put the straw against my lips. "Drink."

The water was perfect. It soothed my parched throat and put something in my aching stomach. "Thank you. Will you tell me what's happening? Where am I?"

He shooed Jordy off of the bed and sat down. "You are in our infirmary."

"You make it sound like a school's nursing station," Jordy snapped. "It's a high level and fully equipped medical center created to handle things like this."

That explained the ammonia smell and awful florescent lights. "I'm in a hospital. Why?"

Mikael squeezed my ankle reassuringly. "Your explosion was violent and life-threatening. Thankfully, you are unscathed. Jordy suffered minor injuries. The gym is destroyed."

I took in Jordy's appearance. He sported a nasty deep gash above his left eye and his right hand was in a splint. "Jordy? I'm sorry. I'm so sorry."

"You owe me a new suit. It was custom-made."

"I'll buy you ten suits." I struggled to move my limbs. "For cripes sake, why can't I move? Jordy?"

Dakarai shooed Mikael and Jordy to the corner of the room. He stepped forward and peeled my blanket off slowly. My ankles, wrists and midsection were locked into place by thick restraints.

"You could have killed Jordy. I don't know why he has so few injuries and I'm astounded that the building hasn't collapsed. The High Council wants answers and I have none. Until you exhibit control over your emotions and powers, we can't leave you unsupervised. This is the best I can offer."

"You think I'm some sort of monster. I don't know what to tell you. Maybe I am. Goddammit, Jordy. Get your ass over here so I can make sure I didn't burn a hole through you. Please."

Dakarai assented and offered Jordy a chair next to me. "Control yourself."

My eyes tried to take in every inch of Jordy. His face and arms bore streaks of soot and plaster. The gash above his eye had been stitched, but it looked like it would need another set if he expected it to heal properly.

"How are you?"

"I've had better days." Jordy moved his chair closer and lowered his voice. "Jasper, I know this is hard, but I promise you that this is for the best. Mikael and Dakarai will take great care of you."

"What do you mean? What about you?" I pursed my lips. "Cecilia and Danny?"

The big man's shoulders sagged. "No, not me. I'm here to check on you and to say goodbye. Once I leave, I don't know when I'll see you again."

I liked Mikael. I was fond of Dakarai. But I'd come to rely on Jordy's presence in my life. Even when I shut everyone out, he never pushed me. It was as if he understood that his silent companionship was enough. I couldn't lose that too. "Don't leave me. Please, Jordy. Don't leave. I'm so sorry I hurt you and I'll rebuild the gym myself. Just tell me what to do."

"Oh, Jas, honey." He smiled wistfully. "It's not about that. I don't care about the gym. That's a weekend project. And I don't care about my injuries. But—"

"Then what's it about? I'll fix whatever's wrong. If you leave, then I'll have lost someone else." I broke down and cried, embarrassed and hurting. The hollow ache was akin to how I felt about losing my family, Jude especially. Jordy was a part of my life and he was tearing me apart again. "Please?"

"You're too emotional. There's no place in my life or work for that kind of behavior." Jordy pushed back his chair and stood. "I suggest you figure out a time to work out in the gym with one of your chaperones. You'll be fine with the routines you have now. Your weapons training is suspended indefinitely."

Jordy stuck his left hand in his pocket. "Be well and be smart, Jasper. I'm counting on you." He reached out to touch my face, but pulled back. "Goodbye."

§

Darkness filled my room as dusk became night. Boredom threatened to drive me mad enough to scream until someone came to check on me. At least I'd have company and something new to think about. It occurred to me a few hours ago that there was no ambient noise. Aside from the echo of heels clacking on the linoleum floor, the only sounds were the incessant beeping from my heart rate monitor. If this was an infirmary, I should have heard something, anything, by now.

I'd begun to suspect that this was my new prison.

There would be no conditional release. When I was too tired to go on, I'd let myself return to that place in the light and that time. I'd leave this all behind.

§

"Wake up, buttercup. We have much to do and little time."

I grunted and rolled over on my side. I was weary in the way marathoners felt around the twentieth mile, when they'd hit the proverbial wall and felt the weight of the last several hours. It was the make or break moment — they had to push through or give up. Whomever was in my bedroom could stay or leave for all I cared. I was going to get my rest.

"Jasper, it's time to get up."

I was about to object to the cheerfully insistent voice but the coarseness and cheap feel of the pillowcase warned me that something was off. *My* bed engulfed me and kept me cocooned with soft sheets that smelled faintly like lemon. This mattress was thin and flimsy, allowing the metal springs to dig into my already aching back. It was an itchy, pain inflicting cage.

The problem was that I couldn't remember why I was imprisoned. All I knew was that I no longer trusted anyone. Jordy was gone. Daniel and Cecilia were gone, not that it was any great loss. Danny still loathed me and Cecilia was a decent shopping companion but nothing more.

"Go away," I mumbled as I hugged the Styrofoam pillow that had gone flat from too many heads seeking and probably not finding comfort. "Don't wanna."

Dakarai's voice took on a resonance that vibrated through my being. "Child, quit your foolish stubbornness. Unless your desire is to remain confined indefinitely, you must demonstrate control."

I cracked open an eyelid and stared at my mentor. For the first time since we'd met some months ago, Dakarai looked tired and frazzled. Gone were the cashmere sweaters and purposely obnoxious sneakers. A well-loved hooded sweatshirt and jeans with paint splatters had taken their places. His normally bald head was covered in a dark brown fuzz. Dakarai hadn't slept because someone needed to make sure I didn't lose my temper. He likely hadn't left this room in the bowels of the Order's compound.

"The only way I'm getting up is if there's a shower, breakfast, and my own bed in my immediate future."

Dakarai smiled. "You will have the shower and breakfast, but the bed must wait. It is too dangerous to teach you how to use your abilities right now. Truthfully," he said, "I haven't figured out how to teach you how to master each ability. Guiding you on how to use all three in concert is inconceivable at this point."

I yawned and sat up against the protests of creaking joints and tight muscles. Then it hit me. Someone had removed my restraints. I whooped for joy. Freedom! No more rope burn! Peeing in something other than a bed pan! Oh, the little joys in life.

"How long was I asleep?"

"Just about thirty-six hours. But don't give it a second thought. You're awake and we can begin the next phase of your training."

"When can we leave? Can I use a bathroom? Thirty-six hours is killer on the bladder."

"Of course." Dakarai held my hands as I swung my legs over the side of the bed and tested them. My newly sculpted calves were seriously challenged by the effects of inertia; still, they trembled and would have held but my ankles had another plan. They explicitly told me to go screw myself and gave out.

Dakarai caught me a split second before I had an up-close-and-personal meeting with the floor, which was great considering the layer of grime. I knew I'd have nightmares about the origins of those rust colored sticky puddles and smears of ash. Suddenly, my need for the bathroom was even more pressing. I was going to relieve myself and throw up. The order was unimportant.

I hated anyone seeing me this weak. Not too long ago, I'd been dangerous enough for restraints and isolation. Now, I was a pitiful thing that needed to be carried and placed on the toilet.

Dakarai was nothing if not respectful and kind. He settled me on the porcelain throne and backed out of the bathroom. As soon as the door closed, I sighed with relief, as did my bladder. For a moment, my life was simple and good. Then I stood and met my reflection in the mirror.

Holy hell in a hand basket.

Not even after a week of stomach poisoning had I looked this bad. My greasy tangled hair was the best of it. Dark circles under my eyes were the most prominent feature on a face that was oily, pimply and haggard. I lifted an arm and immediately wished I hadn't because I reeked.

Poor Dakarai had been putting up with this for the last two days. And I'd just probably hit him with major dragon breath. Every ounce of me wanted to crawl into fetal position until something changed. But that wasn't an option. Dakarai was speaking to me through the door, asking if I was okay and if I needed assistance.

Having him place me on the toilet had been embarrassing enough. If I were going to regain my equilibrium, I needed to brush my teeth without interference.

"I understand," he said, his tone indicating that he didn't, in fact, understand. "But please be quick about it. There are matters that require our immediate attention."

The simple pleasure of having a clean mouth and a washed face infused me with the confidence to take the next steps in this bat shit crazy adventure. I staggered back through the door and into Dakarai's arms. He slipped an arm under my shoulders and helped me walk back to bed where I found a pair of leggings and a t-shirt.

"Thank you. I'll feel human again once I shower. Can we leave now?"

Dakarai sighed. "In a moment. We are waiting on Mikael to return with —"

"Always with the summoning," Mikael said dryly. He walked into the room pushing a wheelchair. "I am better than your Beetlejuice, da? Jasper! It's wonderful to see you awake."

"A wheelchair," I said numbly, "You're making me leave in a wheelchair?"

"Da, Milaya. We must also restrain you for the time being. Just until we return you to your rooms."

It wasn't worth the tears, so I remained silent as I dressed with my back turned to them and allowed them to use the thick ropes to bind my hands, legs and chest.

§

It occurred to me as I towel dried my hair that normalcy was now a thing of the past. This was uncharted territory for all of us, so expectations were useless. I dressed in a practical pair of jeans and a warm long-sleeved shirt and tried to convince myself that staying awake was the best course of action. One last look in the mirror confirmed that my appearance was as close to normal as I could hope.

Mikael and Dakarai spoke in hushed voices in my small living area. It sounded ominous. I coughed loudly to give them time to wrap up their conversation. They both smiled and told me I looked refreshed. Mikael bustled around my kitchenette and served me a plate of eggs, bacon and grapes.

"Sorry. I am not sure what you like to eat. Try?" Mikael patted my shoulder then took a huge step backward. I ate in silence, hoping they'd continue their conversation. Not for the first time that day, I was sorely disappointed.

"Is this going to be a thing? You two gawking at me while I do the mundane? Because I should warn you right now that I take a really long time giving myself pedicures. You might want to get coffee for those nights."

Mikael diverted his gaze and rubbed a hand over his mouth to hide his growing smile. Dakarai, however, scowled.

"Humor does not have a place in your training. Not anymore. You must commit yourself fully to these studies." He raised his voice as his words jumbled together. "Jasper, I don't know what will happen to you if you don't gain control."

"Do you know about the boy?" Mikael crossed his arms. "Dakarai, did you not tell her?"

My breakfast was on its way to a second appearance. There was a boy? I didn't know anyone except the Circle members and I hadn't seen anyone but them in several days.

"What boy? What didn't anyone tell me?"

Dakarai and Mikael exchanged the same looks little boys share when they're debating who would speak on behalf of their guilty friends. Mikael sliced his head to the side.

I was fairly certain that was his way of saying "not it."

Dakarai harrumphed. "Coward."

"I never claimed otherwise, my friend. So?"

"Will one of you start talking? Who is this boy? What happened?"

I recognized their apprehension. It was the same fear they had shown when they'd revealed my restraints. Right. I was the ticking time bomb. "Don't worry. I'm calm."

Dakarai took a few fortifying breaths. "We didn't tell you earlier because you were distraught enough over Jordy. He wasn't the only person injured."

"What? Where? Who? Are they okay?"

"There was a young boy, Ismael. He'd wandered downstairs in search of the children's indoor playground. Ismael was walking past the gym door when you lost control. The door blew outward." Dakarai stopped and hung his head.

"No. Oh, god. Please tell me he's okay. Can I see him? His parents? What can I do?"

Mikael shook his head. "I'm sorry. Ismael died on impact."

CHAPTER 13

Somewhere within the complex the funeral of Ismael Cordova had just begun. I was told that funerals within the Order were formal affairs complete with specific rituals. Everyone within the compound had been invited except me.

A cacophony of bells rose from the lowest levels of the Order and filled Quasimodo's Tower with an awful reverberation. It was the saddest piece of music I'd ever heard. The high and low notes sounded like a mother and father's wails for their dead child. It was the sound of unimaginable heartache being expressed through the only means it had.

Ismael's family had been told that their son's death had been a terrible accident, a freak explosion caused by a faulty hydraulics system within the walls. A few minor incidents had been staged within that area to create the appearance of a larger malfunction. The High Council and the Circle didn't want anyone to suspect that a person was behind Ismael's death.

Mikael had told me that the Cordovas were planning to leave the Order after they wrapped up their affairs in New York. They'd decided that they'd rather take their chances in the outside world, especially now that their son was gone.

A little boy was dead because I lacked self-control. A family was torn apart and ripped from their friends and home because I'd lost my temper. I was the Grim

Reaper. I'd killed my family. I had probably killed people at the police station back home.

In order to keep my role in the accident a secret, the Circle agreed to confine me to the Tower and the facilities attached to it indefinitely. The only spaces that were off limits to the inquisition were my bedroom and bathroom. To the rest of the Order, I was gone: either a hazy memory or no one at all.

No one blamed me directly, but we all knew that Ismael would have been alive if it hadn't been for me. I assumed that was why Jordy refused to see me or respond to messages. I tried to see him, but they'd taken to locking my door from the outside.

Earlier I'd heard Jordy's voice outside of Dakarai's rooms. I begged him to talk to me, to at least update me on his injuries. I asked when we could train again.

He walked away without responding.

So I waited.

Hours went by without anyone coming to visit. I was going crazy. After my attempts at reading yet another barely intelligible tome from Dakarai proved futile, I tried writing in my journal.

Dear diary,

I am a psychotic bitch and a child killer. Only I have split personalities and I'm not sure which one was guilty of that particular crime. I also injured one of my only ~~friends pals training buddies~~ regular companions and he's no longer talking to me. Did I mention I killed a child? Yours truly, Jasper

"Fuck that." I hurled the leather bound journal across the room. Grim satisfaction flooded me when it upended the lamp and caused it to shatter into a million pieces.

My ears perked up as I heard the elevator open at the far end of the corridor. They were back. It was a small comfort to know that I was no longer alone.

I resumed my perch next to the door that led into the shared hallway and closed my eyes.

Dakarai sighed with the weariness of Atlas himself. "We will not discuss this in front of Jasper."

"Da, da. I understand, but I must speak with her."

"Right now?" I imagined the disbelief etched on Jordy's face matched his tone. "Why?"

Mikael made an impatient sound. "She has been alone for hours with her thoughts. I cannot erase what happened, but one of us should try to ease her mind. Since you will not—"

Jordy growled. "It's a dead horse. Do your job or drop it."

"I suggest," Dakarai said, raising his voice above the others, "that we each return to our corners and take some time to think about everything. Mikael, we can see Jasper at dinnertime."

"Fine."

"Do you want to say anything to her?"

"Do I want to talk to her? Of course. Will I? No. There's too much at risk right now. I can't do my job if I'm..." Jordy exhaled deeply. "You understand. Tell her I...never mind. Call me tomorrow."

§

My dreams resembled a horror movie. I was the hidden menace, the girl next door who begged for help until almost everyone was dead. I was the girl who knifed that last survivor in the back and laughed. Each scene was worse than the last and it played on a constant loop.

The paranoia and high emotions caused by the LSD fog raged through my system. I screamed as I trashed the gym, but it wasn't enough. I turned my back to Jordy and focused that white hot energy at the door behind me, I stood over Ismael's his mangled body and walked away.

I saw myself choosing to unleash the entirety of my power and creating a blast that leveled the better part of Manhattan. Thousands lay dead at my feet while I walked around and pilfered their belongings. I walked

163

into Nordstrom's and clapped with the joy of a woman set free in a department store with no limits. The pooling bodily fluids were an excuse to buy as many new boots as I pleased.

Alone in the meadow behind my parents' home, I cursed them for pawning me off to strangers. The rage built in my chest. I cried out in fury and thrust my hands toward my unsuspecting family. My laugh echoed the detritus of my parents' home as it rained down around me.

The last dream was so horrific that I fought my way to consciousness. My voice was hoarse from screaming in my sleep. I was soaked with sweat and close to vomiting. After I stripped and tossed my sheets into the hamper, I turned on my shower. The spray was viciously cold as I scrubbed myself raw. I couldn't have stopped if I'd wanted because the loathing and guilt were sticky layers that went deep into my skin.

Too wired and too cold to go back to bed, I curled up on my couch and began to wonder if this was my punishment. It was easy to imagine the High Council passing a sentence of solitary confinement with Dakarai as my jailer and Mikael as my secondary handler. They'd wait for me to go insane and kill myself.

It seemed like a fair sentence for my crimes.

§

The world woke slowly. The elevator at the end of the corridor whined as its gears readied for the first trip of the day. Across the hall, I heard Dakarai wake and turn on his television to a political talk show while he puttered around his apartment. He sung to himself as he did whatever it was he did first thing in the morning. It may have not been company, but it was soothing enough to lull me into a dreamless sleep.

§

Mikael laughed so hard that juice spurted from his nostrils. He wrapped his arms around his middle and slid to the floor from his perch on my small couch.

"But it's so, so bad. I didn't realize that old American movies were so awful."

"Flash Gordon was one of my dad's favorites. We watched it all the time."

"Your father must have had fascinating tastes. Do you know of other bad movies? If you make me a list, I will purchase the titles for our library."

"Our library?"

Mikael gave me a toothy grin. "Yes, ours."

Mikael had been my constant companion over the last week. Once we'd gotten past the initial awkwardness, it had become apparent that we were destined to be friends. Our natures and humor complemented each other. There was nary a lull in conversation and those few were filled with comfortable silence. Mostly, we laughed.

"You must be plotting shenanigans. What's your game, pal?"

"Your rooms are bigger than mine and you have been given a better television. We will have our movie nights here. It only makes sense to keep everything in one place."

I wanted to pinch his red cheeks. Mikael's tragic upbringing hadn't allowed him the comfort of physical touch or affection. Now, as an adult, he was too shy and embarrassed to ask for the simple pleasure. There was little I could have done to erase his past, but I was determined to ease his pain in the present.

"See? Shenanigans. You're lucky that I like you so much."

"Yes, Milaya. It is my luck indeed." He leaned into the hand that ruffled his hair and smiled to himself. "It's getting late and you need your sleep."

My stomach rolled as Mikael stood and stretched. He didn't need to elaborate. Our little vacation from the world was over. Whatever precautions necessary to ensure I didn't kill anyone else had been taken and it was time for me to resume my studies.

"When?"

"Dakarai and I will come for you just before dusk." Mikael's smile did nothing to mask the sadness in his eyes. The mischievous little boy was gone and the somber man, my guide and mentor, had returned.

I nodded and walked him to the door. "Before dusk."

"It's an important time of day." He grasped my shoulders. "You know this. Why?"

I searched my mental card catalog for important times of day and came up blank. I knew I was looking in the wrong section. Dusk.

Something clicked.

"Vespers service."

CHAPTER 14

Dakarai led me Mikael and me into a small meditation room located on the bottom level of our Tower. He said nothing as I took in the plain space. The Order was a fan of anything ornate, so the unadorned red walls, fat wax candles, and low pillows seemed out of place.

The only object of note was the shrine in the back corner. On it rested three statuettes. The two on the sides were archetypal renderings of the Judeo-Christian God and Devil.

It was the center image that sent ice through my veins. A replica of the image I had seen in the High Council's chambers watched me from beneath the bodiless hooded cape. The tattered hem was carved to give the appearance of an eternal wind. The message was clear.

No apocalypse, earthly or heavenly, would move this being. It was as eternal as the deities we'd long worshiped and it would endure. Its children and our mission would endure.

The strangest outcome of the New Year's Eve tragedy was directly related to my senses. *She* had gone all but dormant. *She* was angry that a new entity had encroached upon my mind. It was as silent as it was massive, taking root in every part of my brain and claiming a portion of my soul.

I could sense people from a distance, especially those familiar to me. I knew when Dakarai awoke each day, not because I heard him, but because there was an imperceptible shift in my awareness. I knew when he had visitors before they exited the elevator. Mikael, who lived on another floor, had become just as palpable a presence in my mind.

My new abilities weren't confined to being their personal locater. I sensed everyone nearby. Their identity or signature just wasn't as clear. I'd had a vague sense of when Jordy was making repairs in his gym and office. Danny and Cecilia were weaker signals, barely a blip on the horizon.

They felt different. Some felt inherently good and appeared in different shades of white on my mental landscape. And while no one registered as inherently bad, some, like Danny, felt malevolent and appeared darker than most.

Dakarai, Jordy, and Mikael, however, didn't register as any color. I had my suspicions, but wasn't quite ready to voice them or face the ramifications.

Mikael tapped my shoulder. "Focus. What do you feel?"

I took a few calming breaths and closed my eyes. This room had a signature distinct from anything I'd experienced. In the hallway, I'd felt the pressure of a thousand beings press against the edges of my awareness. They disappeared from my consciousness the moment I stepped inside.

"Nothing," I whispered, "absolutely nothing."

Dakarai smiled. "Neutral ground. It's the perfect place for us to try my newest idea."

"As long as it doesn't end with my death, I'm game."

§

Beyond the threshold lay a stone tunnel. It sloped gently for a couple hundred yards before it curved out of sight.

I had a gut feeling that it led to a chamber deep underground. I was certain that I'd find the answers to my questions there.

I was completely and utterly positive that I didn't want to find out. My experiences in the High Council's chamber had all but sated my desire to traverse secret tunnels and hang out in caves. Whatever creatures lay below could suck a big toe if they'd anticipated getting their hands on me again.

What were they thinking taking me somewhere underground? If their fears were correct, an uncontrolled explosion would be nearly as dangerous. We needed a plan B, one that included a cabin at the edge of some woods. Ideally, I'd be near a large body of water, but I'd accept a nice lake. I'd live alone and the monotony would be broken by visits from Dakarai and Mikael. They'd bring everything I'd order online, fresh food and supplies. And when they found the people who killed my parents, they'd hand them over and let me have at them. Hell, I'd be open to being the executioner on the lake.

Anything was preferable to going underground.

As if I had a choice.

I took a deep breath, squared my shoulders, and strode forward as if I was the biggest, baddest monster to walk those halls. Mikael and Dakarai followed a few beats behind.

Unlike the trip to the High Council's chambers, there was nothing foreboding or threatening about our descent. No dark creatures of the night or magic attacked us as we descended a dizzying circular staircase. Even the wraiths stayed away.

Less than ten minutes later, the tunnel ended at an oak door, a twin to the one above us.

Dakarai came up to my side and smiled. "Welcome, sister."

§

Dakarai invited Mikael to join us on the low cushions in the middle of the room and lit a single candle.

"Meditation."

I groaned. Since my arrival, I'd learned every form of meditation from Dakarai. The goal had been to teach me how to find my center of calm whenever *She* decided to join the party. It hadn't worked.

"Today, we will try to focus on the connection between your emotional state and the raw power inside of you. If you can remain calm we can begin teaching you to manipulate that power safely."

"Will this help?"

Dakarai rubbed his forehead and muttered his doubts under his breath. "We won't know unless we try. Shall we?"

Mikael patted my knee with a kind smile. "You're in good hands. The good news is if it doesn't work, you'll be able to check it off your list."

The adage "it can't hurt" no longer applied to me. If it didn't work, I'd likely kill my only two friends and cause structural damage to the compound. If it did and I could learn the kind of control Jude and Livie had over their powers, there was a strong possibility of regaining my freedom.

"Okay. I'm ready. How are we doing this?"

Dakarai smiled. "Trataka. Candle flame meditation. In our previous sessions, we've worked on mindfulness. Tell me the core principles."

School was in session.

"By focusing on the present, my current task, I can learn to shut out the noise around me. The goal is to be in the moment at all times."

"Has this technique worked for you in other situations?"

I thought for a long moment. "At the gym," I said, "I block out the noise from the machines and the voices from everyone else. My attention is on my form and my body's performance. It's cut down on injuries."

Mikael smiled. "Excellent example, sestra. You told me you meditate at night."

"Yes. When my brain is on overload, I use the breathing techniques to quiet the monkey mind."

"Good. Trataka will bring your focus away from your breath and will focus your attention on just one thing - the flame."

Dakarai must have read the confusion on my face. He smiled slightly. "The flame is an external manifestation of the power within you — your energy, Jude's manipulation of the wind, and Olivia's control over thoughts and memories. Your task is to identify the source within you and remain mindful of it at all times. As you sit with that power, you will learn how to control it because it will be an extension of yourself, not an invasive supernatural squatter."

I snickered as I imagined my consciousness standing next to *Her* on a picket line outside the building where my squatter currently resided. We held signs that said, "Go back to where you came from!" and "Eminent Domain does not apply to our body!"

She threw rocks at one of the slimy tentacles descending from one of the highest windows and missed. We briefly considered a rocket launcher, but decided against anything that could cause permanent damage to the building itself.

Mikael snapped his fingers in front of my face. "Where did you go?"

"Away from this lesson." Dakarai's disapproval made me feel like I was ten years old. "How can we teach you control if you go off on mental side trips?"

I ducked my head in shame and willed away images of the building and invasive tentacles. "Okay, okay. I'm back and ready."

Dakarai let out a weary sigh. "That's fine for now. As I said, as you gain control internally, your relationship with your abilities will transform from parasitic to symbiotic."

"That means it will no longer take over as it pleases. There will be cooperation and trust," Mikael said.

"Yeah, thanks. I figured that part out." I winced at his hurt expression. "Sorry. I'm just anxious."

He nodded and closed his eyes.

Dakarai's patience was wearing thin. He glared at us and spoke louder. "You'll learn to summon those abilities at will. Watch."

His eyes returned to the flame and remained silent as the tension flowed from his body. He lifted his right hand slowly and wiggled his fingers.

The overhead lights in the room flickered on and off several times until he closed his hand in a fist. Then he directed his hand toward the empty pillow to his right. Like a puppet with strings, it rose and hovered two feet above the ground. Without warning, the pillow was thrown across the room and exploded into a mess of feathers and stuffing.

Gone were the humor and gentleness from Dakarai's expression. His features had hardened and made him look like a predator. A killer.

I was intoxicated.

"This is child's play, a mere taste of my abilities. Shall we explore yours?"

"Yes."

Dakarai's hypnotic voice enveloped me. "Close your eyes. Sit with your spine straight and relax your muscles. Take five deep breaths. Feel the air enter and exit your lungs and find that comfortable breath."

I adjusted my posture and focused on my breath until I found the space between each inhalation and exhalation.

"Now, open your eyes slowly. Allow your gaze to come to the flame. Ignore the wick. Keep your eyes trained on the flame itself. Let it occupy all of your focus. When your mind wanders, acknowledge the thought and put it away. Focus on nothing but the flame."

My peripheral vision began to disappear and soon all I could see were gradients of light that flickered and frolicked with joy. It was the kind of light I associated with evenings, the moment when day fades into night. It was beautiful. I wanted to merge with it and remain in this place forever.

As soon as the thought formed, an invisible force pulled me away and threw me into the void. I screamed. I begged and tried to barter pieces of my soul. I offered deals to the devil and made promises to God. They remained silent and allowed me to be dragged away from the one place I'd been happy.

The void disappeared and a city began to form in the distance. Around me, men and women walked along dusty roads, too intent on their destination to notice my arrival. The sun's intensity evaporated any hint of moisture. Sweat disappeared from my skin almost instantaneously and left a layer of dried and cracked salt. I wanted to crawl into the shade and wait for this experience to end.

Across the road, however, I spied a boy no older than ten staring at me. He had deep chestnut skin, eyes that seemed too big for his body, and a mischievous grin. He stuck his tongue out at me and ran into the market.

I ran after him. As the only person seemed to be seeing me, I figured he probably knew who or what could send me home. He weaved through the rows of stalls with practiced ease. Every hundred yards or so, he paused to turn, point and laugh at me. As soon as I got within shouting distance, he dashed away.

I zigzagged around women in long dresses and beautiful hijabs who examined the wares of various stalls and men who laughed as they shared their meals. The boy was nowhere to be seen. I pushed my way to the edge of the market and leaned against a building to catch my breath.

This area wasn't safe. The women here were different than those in the market. They were hard and angry. They shouted at the men in the stalls and brandished weapons until their prices were met.

The men scared me just as much as the women. They gave off a predatory vibe. They stalked the women and weaker men, pulling them into dark corners and committing unspeakable acts. Victims walked out dazed, bloody and broken, if they walked out at all.

The boy screamed nearby. I chased after the sound and froze at the mouth of an alley.

The boy was being beaten by men with sticks and leather straps. He sobbed as a foot connected with his ribs. The men were going to kill him.

I tried to run into the alley, but something rooted me in place. A deep male voice whispered in my ear.

"You can do nothing to help him. Watch, Jasper, and see your fate."

The boy's cries transformed into howls as he wrapped his thin arms around himself and curled into a ball. His attackers, those sick fucks, exalted in his pain and redoubled their attack. Each strike was more violent than the last, spraying the child's blood on their clothes and faces.

Helpless and broken, the boy stilled. The men cried out in surprise and bumped into one another as they scrambled away from him. For the first time since the attacks had intensified, I saw him. His eyes, once playful, were a glassy white. He pushed himself to his knees, flung his arms out to his sides and lets out a scream of hatred and defiance.

White light exploded from within the boy with the force of a bomb. Its destruction passed over and around me, the intense light overwhelming my vision. The boy's screams transformed into sobs of abject terror.

The bonds that had immobilized me earlier loosened their hold. I grabbed onto the wall next to me and used it to guide and steady me as I crawled toward him. My hand touched a hot, sticky puddle. I raised it to my face and smelled rust. Someone's blood dripped through my fingers. My stomach roiled but I kept moving. The boy needed me.

My vision returned. I glanced around once and vomited. The boy stood in a circle of destruction, drenched in the blood of his enemies. Their bodies had been reduced to large chunks of charred flesh that radiated out from him in a perfect circle.

The boy's sightless eyes found mine. His lips formed a single word.

"Run."

CHAPTER 15

The boy lifted a skinny, trembling arm and pointed at me.

"Run," he screamed. "Run!"

My feet propel me backward until I reach what used to be the end of the alley. The boy spared me one last glance before curling into himself and let out an agonizing wail. Armageddon had arrived. The market had been flattened and scorched to the ground. The smell of blood, burnt skin and death clogged my nose and clung to me like a second skin. It was too much.

I ran.

The market was a scene from a horror movie. Everyone around me was either dead or dying. They'd been hit by the blast before they could register the danger and died mid-sentence. Old men in the middle of a chess game were gone. The vendors and the wares they'd been hawking were nothing but ashes.

The knowledge that they hadn't suffered allowed me to keep moving forward through the rubble. Beyond the center of the market, the landscape changed. Damaged buildings had become makeshift shelters. Those whole enough to walk picked through the bodies and carried away the barely living. Women sobbed over the bodies of their loved ones and children huddled and rocked in groups.

Nothing I'd seen prepared me for the children. Just beyond the buildings was a playground that had been impacted by the blast. Mesmerized by the gruesome sight before me, I stood in front of a blackened set of swings. The bodies must have fallen where they stood. Children and toddlers had been cut down in the middle of some game that involved running. They were petrified mid-stride.

One of the smallest bodies twitched at the outskirts of the game. The child's long dress had partially melted into her bubbling, raw skin. Her hair was nearly gone. She spoke in her native language, but I understood her perfectly. She begged me to make the pain go away. I fell to my knees and gathered her in my arms as she gasped her final breaths.

I bowed my head and sobbed for the hundreds, maybe thousands, of people killed by that uncontrolled explosion. Mostly, I cried for the children. How many children had cried for someone to hold them and ease the transition to the beyond? How many had seen their friends and families die?

"Dakarai," I screamed, "is this the lesson? Is this what you wanted me to see? Do you believe that I am destruction? You're wrong! I control the flame!"

I laid the girl's broken body on the ground, closed her eyelids, and offered a prayer for her soul. Viscera and other bloody gunk clung to me, but I didn't brush it off. It felt like a desecration of the memory of the newly dead.

My entire being flooded with rage until my vision was distorted by red as dark as the blood on my hands. The power inside that little boy had murdered these people. He'd been too young to control it. Worse, he'd been left to live with the consequences.

The voice had prophesized that my fate would be the same. Screw fate. I refused to be controlled. With a roar of defiance, I called the flames to me and stepped out of this nightmare.

§

Someone must have picked me up and carried me to my room because when my eyes opened and I let out a scream, I was tucked beneath my warm comforter. I yanked it off, expecting to find my ruined and bloodied clothes, but I was in a clean pair of pajamas. The blood covering my arms was gone.

I sprung out of bed and attacked my clothes hamper. The last several hours couldn't have been a dream. I needed to prove that I wasn't crazy and my clothes were likely the only evidence I could put my hands on to prove that I'd experienced something too terrible to put into words. Piles rose around me while I sorted my clothes by item as I searched.

I found nothing. Growling with frustration, I turned to my small closet and ripped pants and dresses from their hangers. I ripped out the drawers in my dresser and crawled under my bed.

My clothes were gone.

The realization that it had been nothing more than a vivid nightmare did nothing to comfort me. My memories of the market were slowly fading, but the boy remained. I saw him bleeding in the alley surrounded by gore. I felt the last shuddering breath of the little girl I'd held in my arms. The faint odor of death still clung to my nostrils.

Nothing made sense. How could have something that had seemed so real turn out to be a nightmare? Why did reality feel so wrong? I didn't dare check my reflection in the mirror in case the monster inside appeared. Sleep was an impossibility. Conveying my dream to someone was too daunting to consider. Out of ideas, I climbed into bed and pulled the covers to my chin.

Hours later, heavy footsteps crossed the hallway and paused in front of my door. Dakarai knocked softly and let himself in without waiting for an answer.

"Jasper?"

"Hi," I whispered from beneath the pillows. "Dakarai, I need help. There's something wrong with me and I can't fix it."

The mattress shifted as he sat on my bed. "The wrongness isn't in you. The massacre you witnessed was real. It occurred eighteen years ago."

I popped up so fast that my pillow flew into his face. "What? How do you know? It was real?"

He gave me an imperceptible nod. "It was reported as a terrorist bomb. There were no witnesses to claim otherwise. Only a handful of people knew the truth. Of those, two remain among the living."

My head hurt too much to interpret his cryptic language. "Explain."

"You pushed your way into my mind. That was my memory." He smiled faintly. "All these years, I wondered about the strange looking woman at the end of the alley. If she'd survived. Now I know."

"Huh?"

"I am that little boy."

§

Dakarai and I settled into opposite sides of my couch and said nothing for a long time. My tea had long cooled and Dakarai seemed to be in a light sleep. I took the opportunity to study him and tried to reconcile the man clutching a pillow to his chest with the little boy.

The scar on Dakarai's neck was identical to the gash created by the man with the whip. I knew that if he removed his shirt, I'd find remnants of the boy's wounds.

That made sense. I saw a younger version of Dakarai. What didn't make sense was how it happened. With the exception of the rare dreams I shared with my brother, I'd never connected with anyone. I'd never been inside Jude's memories.

Yet, Dakarai swore that I'd not only seen what happened, but I'd also been present in his reality. Was time travel real? Where was my body during that time? How did I end up in bed?

"You're thinking too loud," Dakarai said. "Please relax."

"How are you relaxed?"

He opened one eye and glanced at me. "Who says I am relaxed? On the contrary, I am sifting through everything I've learned to find an explanation."

"More tea?" I walked to my small stove and waited for the kettle to heat. "Are you hungry?"

"Thank you, but no. My stomach has a hard time settling on the rare occasions I revisit those memories. You want an explanation."

When the kettle whistled, I prepared my tea and returned to the couch. "Yes."

Dakarai sighed with the weariness of a man who longed for oblivion. "I do not understand how this happened. It must be a side effect of your mixed abilities."

"Will you tell me?"

He held the pillow tighter. "Yes. As a child, I lived in Ethiopia, in a city called Addis Ababa. My parents and I lived in the business district most of the year. I spent summers with my grandmother and my mother's people. They called me a wild child. I refused to wear shoes because I believed them to be an unnecessary inconvenience. From sunrise to sunset, I was allowed to roam free."

I smiled at the memory of the boy who stuck his tongue out and laughed. "You were happy."

"I was indeed a happy child, at least until that day. The men had seen me before, seen me glow and steal things without touching anything. Telekinesis wasn't a word that was known to me, but the action was as natural as breathing. I was young enough that the men thought they could beat it out of me or, if they couldn't, kill me and dispose of the demon."

The cruelty was breathtaking. Grown men decided to hunt and kill a child because he was different. I wanted to comfort him but there were no words to erase that pain. I touched his hand and hoped he understood that I wasn't afraid.

Dakarai frowned for a moment. He appeared confused about the meaning behind the gesture but squeezed my hand nonetheless. "Before, I could summon and control small amounts of energy. My cousins urged me to make little fires — children's games. But the pain unlocked something inside of me that day. I didn't understand why the men were so angry. I wanted the men to stop hitting me and to go away. A small part of me wanted them to receive a harsh spanking. It was the first time I had exploded with such violence."

The destruction of that market and the deaths of all those people was the work of a seven year old who had barely come into his abilities. He'd only wanted the pain to stop. I wanted to vomit.

"There was a woman in the alley with me. I told her to run because I didn't want to hurt her. The power was building again and even then my concern was for your safety."

"What happened after?"

A ghost of a smile flitted across his face. "If this had been a natural phenomenon, scientists would have called it aftershocks. I emitted small bursts but none were bigger than the circumference of my body. By the time I'd been found, stories of the demon boy had spread. Thankfully, someone within the Order had seen me in their visions, so a small group was already searching for me. They were the ones who took me away from my home."

My heart broke for the skinny little boy, broken and bleeding, turned out by his family and ripped away from everything he'd ever known. "Did you see your family again?"

"No. One of my uncles had been the one to inform the men about the demon boy and led them to me. He was killed in the explosion. My family did not want me and, as far as I know, no one has ever looked for me. They were glad to hand me over to the Order."

I had a new plan. I'd find my family's murderers, kill them, and jump on a plane to Ethiopia. No matter how long it took, I planned to find every one of Dakarai's family members, torture and kill them. I wanted them to beg for death.

Dakarai's hand on my arm snapped me from my violent daydream. "Jasper, come back. Breathe with me."

"Oh," I said with a sheepish grin. "Sorry. I got carried away in my thoughts."

"You're glowing."

I cursed my luminescent skin and focused on my breathing. The rage wanted an outlet but my willpower was too strong. I imagined shoving the violence and power into a metal lock box. The box was then put into a larger metal box, which fit into a wooden crate. I covered that with a Plexiglas box and wrapped it in Teflon. With effort, I dropped the whole damn thing into an imaginary ocean. When it sank, I dusted my hands with satisfaction and opened my eyes.

"Did it work?"

Dakarai broke out into laughter. He pulled me across the couch and hugged me until I couldn't breathe.

"Dude," I choked out. "Dying here."

"Dude," he teased. "You did it."

CHAPTER 16

Mikael hurled yet another dodgeball at my head. "For someone so tough, you run from a rubber ball like a scared little child."

"Ow! Cut it out!" The next ball struck my thigh. "Asshole! I get the point. See, still not getting angry."

"We are not even close to done, Milaya." He laughed and threw another stinking red rubber ball. "Did you not play this game as a child?"

I snarled at him. "Yeah, but there was only one ball and I had a team. Stop it."

"Maintain that Zen attitude and catch them. Then we will see."

The ball moved across the room in slow motion. It was headed directly at my face. I thought about moving but time sped up just in time for it to smash into my nose and knock me on my ass. I fell backward and slammed my head against the floor. Clutching my nose, I staggered to my feet.

"Time out! I think you broke my nose!"

Mikael walked over to examine me. He clucked as he pushed and prodded. "I feel nothing. Shake it off and get ready."

I expected to get angry, to feel the need to hurt Mikael, but the urge never came. Instead, I felt pathetic and wanted to hide somewhere no one would see me blubber. My nose still ached and my head throbbed. But it was Mikael's lack of concern that hurt most.

He resumed his position and launched three balls in quick succession. "Stop crying and start catching."

Only one made contact. It grazed my right shoulder and continued to sail past me. "Stop it. I'm done for the day."

"No. We will rest after you stop allowing yourself to get injured." He lowered his voice. "Please start catching. My arms are getting heavy."

"I don't want to play anymore."

Mikael stormed over and shoved me against the wall. "Do you think I enjoy trying to hurt you? Do you think I find pleasure in seeing you bleed? This isn't a game, Jasper."

"What the hell are we doing," I yelled.

"We are in a safe place where the worst that can happen is a bloody nose. What happens when someone wants to hurt you? What if someone is trying to hurt me? Could you save me? Or would you destroy at least one of the five boroughs?"

Mikael was stronger than I imagined. His hands pinned me against the wall and no amount of kicking or writhing budged him. "How do dodgeballs help?"

"The ball is roughly the size of a man's head. If you become angry, you need to direct your energy at your target without risking the lives of bystanders. "He regained some of his humor and smiled. "Since I am your favorite person, I am an ideal candidate."

I stopped struggling. These people were out of their minds. They'd shipped me to an off-site location with Mikael. Someone thought throwing things at me was a great idea. And Mikael came willingly. Idiots, all of them.

"What is wrong with you?"

He let go of my shoulders and stepped back. "Nothing is wrong with me. I trust you and believe that you won't hurt me. We will stay here until you believe the same."

"Can we take a break?" Fatigue threatened to take me down. I considered stretching out on the mat and trying to catch a few hours of sleep. It would have been pointless because Mikael would have kept launching my rubber nemeses at my face until I got with the program.

"Sure. I brought you a peanut butter and jelly sandwich." Mikael sat down gingerly. "My head has been hurting for days. Do you have any remedies?"

I took the sandwich and a bottle of water from him. "Is it the visions?"

"Yes. The frequency has increased. Something is coming, Jasper. We need you to be ready for it."

"We? Why can't I stay here where I'm not a danger to anyone? What danger?"

Mikael grimaced. "I can't see the danger. I see friends and colleagues dying. The blood of children is everywhere. The balance will be destroyed if our children die."

"What children?"

He whimpered and curled into a ball. "It never stops. The children. I cannot see their faces, but their little bodies are mangled and discarded. Whatever forces seek to destroy us are near. We need you, Jasper. I need you."

I put my arm around his shoulders and stroked his hair until he relaxed and the tears subsided. "It's okay, Mikael. Don't cry anymore. You can throw those stupid things at me until your arms won't move. I won't let you down. No one else will die because of me."

§

"Yeah!" I pumped a fist as the last dodgeball exploded into a mess of rubber and sand. "We did it!"

Mikael dusted his shoulders and grinned. "I shouldn't have worried. I knew you wouldn't misjudge and hit my face."

Once I'd mastered the art of staying cool in the midst of a bombardment, our focus had shifted to letting out small, controlled bursts of energy, similar to what I'd done as a child. Soon enough, I was destroying anything and anything Mikael threw at me.

"Oh, get over it. I only hit you once and it was just a tiny bit." I smothered a grin as he pointed to his left shoulder. "You're fine."

He plopped down next to me with a groan. "My arm aches."

"You should have switched arms occasionally."

"I can't throw with my left arm. Are you ready to go home?"

"Yes, yes, yes. I don't enjoy sleeping on stinky workout mats and I'm tired of these four walls. There's something about the echoes at night that creeps me out."

Mikael agreed. Nights had found us next to each other in sleeping bags. We'd pretended that the noises hadn't bothered us, but it was still a lie. Neither of us planned to sleep in cavernous places anytime soon.

He changed the topic to our favorite subject: food. Our shared weakness was spending too much of the Order's money on deliveries from every restaurant within a five mile radius. We were both starving, so he waxed poetic about the meals he'd order and the obscene amount of food we'd eat during movie night. This was serious business for Mikael. He was sweet as pie but turned into a surly teddy bear when his stomach was empty. He had a craving for Italian and I wanted Vietnamese. We settled on Mexican.

As we packed up, I voiced a nagging concern. "They've been watching us the entire time. Who?"

"Does it bother you?"

I shrugged and began to pack my belongings. "It's not surprising, but it sucks to be treated like a feral animal. So?"

"Charles and Miriam from the High Council, Danny, and Jordy. There might be others."

"Fantastic. Hey, Jordy," I shouted. "Stop being an asshole."

"Milaya, please don't do this. I know it has been difficult to lose a friend. He has his reasons."

"Do you know those reasons?"

He shook his head. "Trust his judgment and try to understand he's doing what he believes is right."

"Yeah, I know. It still hurts. Ugh, I wish there was a silver lining. I get how lab rats feel. All this work for no payoff."

Mikael shouldered his pack and grinned. "You forget that lab rats get a treat once the experiment is complete."

I clapped my hands together. "Presents? Gimme, gimme, gimme!"

"Nope. You'll have to wait until we get home. I promise it will be worth the wait."

§

Freedom.

I asked Mikael to explain it twice. Then I asked him to say it again because I couldn't believe it was true. The powers that be were easing my restrictions. While I wasn't granted full access to the compound, the Tower was mine again. My bedroom doors no longer locked from the outside. I had access to all the facilities including the nicer gyms and the Order's libraries.

My training with Dakarai was scheduled to resume the following Monday. Cecilia and Mikael were charged with educating me on the history of the Order and showing me the lineage of the direct line. Someone from the security team had been assigned to me for weapons training and hand-to-hand combat drills.

Hell, even Danny had gotten on board. I was to shadow him as he managed the administrative side of the Order. More importantly, he intended to introduce me to the data collection team. They analyzed trends from police blotters and leads on major crimes.

The High Council had agreed to tutor me on the unsavory side of maintaining the balance. They'd show me how the tough decisions were made and explain the rationale.

The rituals and training were nearly complete. I'd been inducted as a full member of the Order. I was the sixth member of the Circle.

PART 4

CHAPTER 17

Dakarai and Mikael waited for me to say something about the sheet of paper in my hand. It was a weekly schedule with chunks of time carved out for training each day. Those days began in the early hours of the morning and continued through quitting time for the rest of the world. The evenings were mine to do what I pleased.

"It's, um, thorough."

"It provides the most amount of training in a short amount of time."

Mikael gave me a timid smile. "I will join you, if you don't mind. I didn't go to a proper high school. The experience might be fun."

"You're insane. I don't know of anyone who wants to go back to high school, including me. But," I said when I saw his disappointment and embarrassment, "I think we can make an exception for my Netflix and no chill best buddy."

With a grateful smile, he pointed to the schedule. "It's busy, but you'll have sufficient time for a midday nap and you might make it to bed on time occasionally."

"Mikael," Dakarai said gently. "High school isn't exciting. No one will burst into song and there will be no dance numbers."

I rolled my eyes. Dakarai had taken to watching sappy teen movies and had recently come across High School Musical. He was tickled by the music and the groovy dance moves. I was tickled by his use of the term "groovy dance moves."

"It's okay, Mikael. We'll make up our own dance routines and we won't let Dakarai play with us."

We broke out into laughter. They thought I was being supportive and funny. What they didn't know was that I'd created a playlist of potential songs in the space of our conversation. High school part deux didn't seem so terrible with Mikael in tow.

§

The Order's library was beautiful in the same way pugs were adorable. Despite the googly eyes and ever-present lolling tongue, I'd never turned down a snuggle with those puppies and their fat rolls. Imperfections be damned.

It was believed that the Order's original collection once existed levels beneath the incomparable Library of Alexandria. Those precious records of our history and rituals had been toted across the globe as the Order struggled to establish a home base. Legend had it that sometime in the fifteen hundreds a member who was particularly skilled in magic had created a secret location that could only be accessed by the High Council and the Circle.

What resulted was an immense cavern that reflected years of hodgepodge decorating. To the uninitiated eye, the library was a lesson in chaos. Papyrus scrolls lay next to a modern coffee table book. Near the section on serial killers was an ancient Roman amphitheater that had seen better days. I was all for the older-than-the-gods look, but I wasn't cool with sitting on moss and vines just to watch Mikael belt out show tunes. Dakarai had a special affection for the replica of the Buddhist temple, while Cecilia found comfort in the era of card catalogs and an understanding of the Dewey Decimal System.

I'd found my temporal home beneath the arches of Hagia Sophia. Three weeks ago, I'd spent almost twelve hours beneath one of its semi-domes. When I wasn't reading, I stretched out on the floor and traced my fingers across the tiny pieces that created a stunning mosaic.

Most days, however, I spent two hours with Mikael and Cecilia learning about the controversy of Il Separatio's existence. Talking Head had warned me that the topic strayed from the traditional path of recorded history. What he hadn't mentioned was that I'd have to read through early suppositions and conjectures of pre-history. The book of Genesis and the Big Bang Theory barely scratched the surface.

I was convinced I was allergic to the section on Catholicism. I'd developed a nasty case of hives the last time Cecilia had me retrieve the original copy of the Council of Nicea. The topic itself was fascinating. I hadn't realized that politics played such a significant role in the creation of the Bible. I'd surmised that my allergies were related to the intrigue and nonsense.

At the moment, I was knee-deep in the suppression of extraneous books and gospels and how it shaped the course of human perception of the world. My desk was buried under books on the mythos of superheroes in popular culture. The story of man kept playing out through the hero's journey of every single supernatural story I'd ever read. Even the idolization of historical figures followed the great Joseph Campbell's model.

I asked Mikael, who was engrossed in the history of American baseball, if he'd be willing to help me draw out graphs and models of my theory. He looked at me as if I was crazy, but agreed.

Cecilia had little patience for my sidetracks. "What is your obsession with the irrelevant?"

That stung. "I hate to point out the obvious but this place is new to me. I have so many questions."

"Write them down and we'll get to them eventually."

I bit the inside of my cheek until I tasted blood. There was no use to argue with her. Cecilia's tentative friendship had all but disappeared after New Year's Eve. Danny and Cecilia were among those who had fought for my permanent imprisonment and had been bitterly disappointed when they were overruled. But they were good soldiers in this war and had resumed my training with little complaint to the High Council.

"Fantastic," I said with a smile so fake that it belonged on a Beverly Hills reality show. "Can't wait. I'll just go back to the rituals of ancient civilizations."

"Good. While you're muttering about me under your breath, consider what those rituals were trying to accomplish. Why is it important that we return to the seeds of humanity?"

Behind me, Mikael's book thumped closed. I could have sworn that I heard his voice in my head.

"Don't get rattled. You know this."

I looked up and grinned. "Stability. Equilibrium. Holy shit."

"You're almost there," Cecilia said. If I didn't know better, I'd have thought pride flickered in her eyes.

"The ancients thought they were appeasing wrathful gods so they'd be blessed. But they really just wanted to balance the scales. Crops were necessary to make sure their people didn't starve to death. Even prayers before battle asked for their safe return. They only needed to be greater to keep their people safe."

Cecilia waved her hand in a circular motion, urging me to continue. She insisted that I was almost there, so close to whatever she wanted me to learn.

"Wealth was a tool to help civilizations flourish. Moving away from the nomadic life gave tribes a chance to have a stable food source and home." An unsettling thought occurred to me. "Does this mean that prayers to the deities are useless?"

"No," Mikael said quietly. "Some say man's nature is violent and greedy. To a certain extent that is true. But humanity as a whole leans toward justice."

"The arc of the moral universe is long but it bends toward justice," I said. "Isn't morality a social construct?"

Mikael leaned back in his chair and stared at the ceiling as he spoke. "The Order believes that morals and ethics exist in a neutral category. Murder is a perfect example. Ending a life is never *good*, no matter how just the reason. But if that one death saves a million lives, how can it be deemed a *bad* action. True morality and ethics are derived from universal truths that are designed to ensure the propagation of the species."

"So the Vespers are moral creatures?"

Cecilia let out a sharp laugh. "No, not even close. As beings outside the flow of moral good and moral bad, we're completely ambiguous. We're charged with stopping the actions that will set in motion changes in humanity that will disrupt the balance."

"And how—"

She interrupted me again. "That's a discussion for Dakarai since it touches on the mystical aspects of our work. Your homework is to summarize the Vespers mass in the Catholic Church."

I bit back a snarl as I stuffed my laptop into my battered messenger bag. Cecilia had taken this mutual dislike to a new level. While I had access to the library, she made it all but impossible to find the dank pathway that led to its oak doors. Nor had she provided me with the means to enter. With the primary librarian out on maternity leave, Cecilia held the keys to the kingdom.

Mikael patted my shoulder. "You're doing well. If Danny is alive at the end of your hour, I will make banana splits on our next movie night."

"I can't make any guarantees, but I'll try. You always pick the perfect bribes."

§

The command center resided on the second floor of the main building. On my first visit, I marveled at how it resembled the NASA control center in every space movie I'd seen. Danny had rolled his eyes, but hadn't corrected me. Instead, he introduced me to the head of the various teams.

I'd never admit it to anyone but Mikael, but I loved my apprenticeship with Danny. He was a great teacher and always explained unfamiliar jargon and data collection methods. We met with a group of statisticians, epidemiologists, and crime analysts weekly to examine the data from the ten thousand foot view. Once the data was compiled and layered, trends emerged.

A string of child abductions had occurred at roughly the same time a prominent world leader disappeared. Within the same week, one of the largest banks in a South American country had been robbed and an industrial city had seen its residents flee. The group had consulted with someone on the ground who'd heard rumors of satanic rituals. The current theory was that the town had been evacuated and taken over by a group with enough funding to house a large operation. The few details of the ritual implied that the children were being used as human sacrifices.

Danny asked for records of eyewitness accounts or news stories. The only firsthand documentation involved the missing children, who had all come from the same village. He felt more intelligence was needed and said he planned on asking Jordy to deploy some of his mysterious field team to the location.

At the end of the meeting, Danny pulled me aside. "Do you think this merits an investigation?"

I blinked rapidly. It was the first time he'd asked me for my subjective input. "I, uh, I think so."

"That's not a good enough answer. Is it worth sending our guys or contractors to South America to investigate what could be nothing more than coincidence? You have to think about the Order as a whole. I've allocated staff time to continue working on this. That means they can't work on anything else, which could possibly set back other projects. We fly private, so

I have to consult with my budget guy to properly allocate the funds that are used for fuel, staff, and maintenance. Our guys are good and could sleep in trees for a month, but it's not necessary. If we're going incognito, then credit cards stay in the wallet. How much cash should they bring? Who gets the cash from our accounts and brings it to them? Who's responsible on the ground?"

My mind was spinning from the sheer amount of thought that went into making what had seemed like an easy decision. Kids were being abducted and possibly being used as human sacrifices. That was categorically bad, so we had to do something.

My hand quickly cramped from trying to jot down notes fast enough to keep up with his train of thought. If I hadn't been so wrapped up in the whole maintaining the cosmic balance gig, I would have begged for a job.

"So?"

I glanced up. "So?"

"Let's say the decision is yours and you have to make the call right now. Do we send our people?"

The circumstantial evidence was compelling. When the different layers of data had been compiled, I'd been positive that we needed to get our SWAT team equivalent on a plane pronto. Yet, no one had seen these mysterious forces or knew anything concrete.

I shook my head slowly. "No. We need more data. If Jordy has local contacts, we should deploy them to do reconnaissance of the town. Since we have a private plane, we can get our team there quickly. Right?"

Danny smiled. "Yes. Go on."

"I don't think the entire team needs to stay on top of this either. In terms of the workload here, is it possible to identify a few key people and assign them to a special task group? The rest can continue their regular assignments."

"Nice job!" Danny squeezed my shoulder and flashed a genuinely proud smile. "The task group is a great idea. Give me a list of names first thing tomorrow.

Do you want to accompany me to the meeting with Jordy?"

The dratted heat returned to my cheeks. Jordy's abandonment was no secret. My devastation wasn't either. I tried to play it off and shrugged. "I don't want to intrude or slow you down with questions."

"You won't." Danny stared at me while I looked at anything but him. "Next time."

"Thanks for the opportunity. I've just—"

"Don't say anything. Sometimes things get more complicated than you expected. You've got a pass for this meeting. Next time, you're with me."

"Got it." At the end of my shift, I thanked Danny for letting me get so involved.

He patted my hand. "I never thought I'd say this. You're intelligent, rational and sharp. I thought you'd be overwhelmed by the administrative details, but you're rolling with it. I'm impressed. Keep it up and I might let you intern for me one day. See you tomorrow."

CHAPTER 18

Sweat dripped into my face as I dodged the next blow from Joshua. My new trainer was less of an instructor and more of a brawler. He fought dirty and in this sub-basement gym, he was a god. It was evident in the force of his blows and the flatness in his eyes.

"Josh, can we take a break? I'm exhausted."

He lunged at me with the force of someone trying to take down a feral beast, cursing me under his breath. His fist would have connected with my face, but I ducked and threw a well-aimed shot at his right kidney. Stunned, he fell to one knee and glared. "You rest when you die."

Whoa. Someone had gotten up on the wrong side of bed. Joshua must have skipped his coffee too. He was normally awful, but this was different. As he staggered to his feet, I understood. The anger and annoyance had been drained by my insistence on staying conscious. What had taken its place was terrifying.

Joshua bared his teeth and sneered. "No more playing, little Jasper. I'm going to destroy you and let you live in pain. It's going to be beautiful." His eyes revealed nothing but lust for my blood and pain.

Something nefarious was afoot. A man didn't just swing from teaching someone to fight to wanting to kill them without cause. Other than the jab to jaw, I was innocent.

I scanned the room for weapons or anything that could incapacitate him long enough to hightail it out of there. Thankfully, we were in the perfect place. The gym was laden with equipment that could do serious damage in the right hands.

Joshua's gaze followed mine and I could tell he knew my plan. He growled and charged me again. Damn, that man was accurate. His next move was faster, more painful. Dropping to a crouch, he charged me and lifted me off the ground.

Shit. Shit. Shit.

I was going to die because my instructor probably needed a girlfriend and a night off. I chuckled at my wit until time sped up again and the force of his blow sent me sailing across the room. The padded mats on the floor did nothing to soften my fall. It rattled my bones and shook my brain inside of the skull.

My lungs wheezed and cried for help as I rolled over and crab-walked backward to get away. The sweat coating my body dripped down my arms and wet my palms. The condensation between the mat and my hand refused to cooperate and I fell backward.

Joshua bared his teeth and pounced. Straddling my lap, he cuffed my hands together with one hand and pummeled my ribs and stomach with unparalleled viciousness. I cried out and begged him to stop. I hollered that I'd walk away and never speak of it again.

"Shut up, stupid bitch," he spat. "No one wants you around. You'd be dead if it wasn't for your freakish powers. Die."

Well, then.

In a desperate attempt to free myself, I bucked my hips, but he held firm. My flailing arms did nothing but irritate him. Joshua spat in my face and slapped me with an open palm.

"Get off! Dammit, Joshua. I'm not kid—"

Joshua interrupted me by wrapping his hands around my throat and applying pressure. "Stubborn bitch. Why won't you just die?"

"Aack...can't...don't...why..." I weighed the benefits of unconsciousness. Sure, he could kill me, but I wouldn't feel it.

"Fuck it. I'm going to enjoy watching you suffer."

I didn't remember him moving, but in the blink of an eye, my head slammed against the floor. I got real up and close and personal with the mat as he slammed me down again. And again. Lights danced behind my eyes in vivid reds and yellows. The rattling in my skull roiled my stomach. When I heaved and coughed, blood splattered us.

Joshua reared back and thwacked the side of my head just above my ear. I screamed and tried to block my sanguine and busted face, but he continued to rain down blows anywhere he could reach.

"Josh...gotta...gonna...don't kill me," I wheezed. "Begging you."

He laughed and dismounted.

I gasped and curled into myself, positive that a series of kicks and stomps were imminent. Blood and tears mingled in my eyes. It was impossible to see.

It didn't matter. I was choking again. Joshua had grabbed the back of my collar and yanked backward. Satisfied with his hold, the asshole dragged me across the gym. I struggled to find purchase on the mat but my hands were slick.

I went down hard.

Jordy once told me that during a fight, there would be a moment where I'd question my judgment. My fight or flight instinct would stutter and allow me to decide my fate. If I chose flight, I might as well give up and die.

Fuck that. No one put Jasper in a corner.

I raised my hands above my head and let gravity do the work. My arms slipped out with ease. With my hands free, I ripped the collar and ducked out.

For a precious few seconds, Joshua was oblivious to my escape. I tumbled away and landed in a crouch. Using my forearm to wipe the blood out of my eyes, I let out a guttural scream and charged.

Joshua's eyes darted between me and the empty shirt in his hand. He froze in his confusion. Good. It was time to change things up.

I tackled him and slammed him against the wood paneled wall. He lost his footing. The force of the blow rattled his head. When he slumped, I dove and pinned him beneath me.

My mind went blissfully blank. Without the burden of emotions, my strikes were efficient and savage. I attacked his face with the same intensity he'd used on me. He'd suffer as much as he'd inflicted.

His jaw, nose and chin cracked under the assault. He howled with pain, raising his arms to shield himself.

No biggie.

My attention moved to his torso with a series of well-aimed jabs and hooks until we both heard the sickening crack of a rib bone. He screamed again.

Not enough. Never enough.

Panting, I stood and stared at him for a moment. I smiled, reared back and stomped the inside of his bent leg. The knee separated from its socket with the audible tearing of muscles and crunching of bones.

He rolled over to protect himself, screaming and threatening me. He and his friends were going to slit my throat and desecrate my body as the life drained from me.

Subduing him and causing pain had been my goal until now. I was going to kill the sick bastard.

"You piece of shit asshole jerk face." I wrapped my left hand around as much of his neck as I could reach and squeezed.

Joshua gurgled and flailed.

"May you suffer a thousand deaths and I hope all of them end with a spike up your ass, you sick rapist." I prepared to shatter his face and roared.

"Jasper!" Jordy grabbed my arm, tearing me away and pushing me behind him. "Not like this. Not yet. Stop fighting me!"

I tremble with rage and willed myself to keep in those angry tears. "No! He has to die! He said he was going to slit my throat and rape me!"

Jordy's eyes shuttered and the man was gone. "You should have blasted his legs off and cauterized the wounds. Don't worry, though. You'll have your fun soon enough."

I nodded and stepped back. Jordan promised me violence. That was good enough for me. I was content to watch him work.

He leaned over Joshua and spoke in a conversational tone. "You had me fooled. Shame on me. I might have let you live but you touched mine. Jasper, how bad?"

"Me or him?"

"Him."

"Broken ribs. I'm fairly sure I separated the knee from the rest of the body and I might have fractured the bone. A concussion for sure. A few kidney punches."

Jordan snorted. "That's my girl. Good work." He wrapped his left hand around Joshua's neck and lifted him off the ground in one fluid movement. "You thought you'd kill a little girl? How'd that pan out for you?"

"Jordy, man. Please." Joshua was a sniveling punk. "I was following orders. You understand that."

"Kill him."

"Wait." He backed Joshua into the wall and held him a good four feet above the ground. Joshua's lower leg was just a sack of meat stretching the skin in unnatural ways. He'd begun to resemble one of those action figures that was on its last legs, stretched out beyond recognition and useless.

Jordan flexed his fingers until Joshua slapped at him wildly as if he had a sliver of a chance to escape.

"You know how this plays out," Jordan said quietly. "If you want it to be quick, start talking."

Joshua struggled but the pain from his injuries had drained his energy. He slapped Jordan's hand again. "I'll talk."

"Jasper, get me resistance bands, a chair and your favorite toy. Now."

It would have been uncivilized to clap and jump up and down with glee. I stared at the men for another beat and then ran to the corner of the boxing area. The items Jordan requested were things I used in my daily workouts. I had a feeling this show was for me, bless that man-beast.

Joshua was in tears when I returned with the requested items and a kettle bell.

"Can I help?"

"Easy, tiger. Watch and learn." The resistance bands secured Joshua to the chair and put consistent pressure on his injuries. "You have one chance. I ask. You answer. If I'm not satisfied, she gets one swing at you with her kettle bell per question. The only rule is that she can't kill you."

"Please don't kill me. I trained her just like you wanted. Jordy, you know me. Don't do this."

Jordan arched a brow, stepped back and gestured for me to swing. "Make it count."

I wrapped my hands around the handle and swung my arm back and forth until the momentum carried me forward. The kettle bell hit his uninjured knee and shattered it.

"Do not speak unless you are answering a direct question."

Joshua's head bobbed in acknowledgment.

"Good. Yes or no. Are you working alone?"

"No."

"Are there others in the compound?"

"Yes."

"Do you have orders to hurt the civilians? The children?"

"No. Injure a few to scare the rest into staying at the east end."

"Who are you hunting?"

Joshua's lips curled into a sneer. "You don't get it. This was just a message, a precursor. We know who you are and we will not stop. We will use the blood of your most powerful and your innocents to summon forces you can't imagine. The world will be remade in our image. I want you to watch, Jordy. I want you live with the memories of the blood flowing from her soiled and mangled body."

"See what I mean?"

Jordan said nothing.

Sighing, I picked up the line of interrogation. "What innocents are you talking about?" I knew if I approached him, nothing but the hands of God, the Devil, and the Annonnimus One would be able to stop me.

"You'll find out soon enough. Their blood is on your hands, little girl."

Jordan straightened and took a step back. "Lovely sentiment. Here's my counteroffer. I will rip the throats out of anyone who gets in my way. She will do much worse. When you're all in Hell remember to mention my name to the guy in charge. He can thank me later."

"Thank you," I whispered as I slipped my hand into his.

"My vow to protect you has never faltered." Jordan reached for the handgun strapped to his leg and handed it to me. "Careful. It's loaded. This is the Kimber that you used at the range. I modified it for your grip and added a laser sight."

I almost drooled. "Thank you."

"I need you to follow my instructions to the letter." He waited until I gave a small nod of agreement. "See my duffel bag in the corner? Open it. Inside you'll find a smaller bag with your name on it. Strap on the harnesses and load up."

"What about him?"

Jordan snarled. "He's my problem now. I ignored my instincts and he nearly killed you."

"Okay, boss." I stood on my toes and kissed his cheek. Jordan closed his eyes and smiled. "I trust you."

"Go on. Consider it an early birthday present."

I marveled at my lack of concern for Joshua. Jordan was going to kill him and I'd just given my blessing.

Inside his black bag, Jordy had indeed put aside a small backpack, upon which he'd placed a removable sticker with my name. It was heavier than I expected. I unzipped it cautiously and squealed.

It was a killer's dream. Another Kimber, two Colt 1911s, a 9 millimeter baby Glock and an assortment of wicked knives. Each one was tailored to my hands and preferences. I looked over at him and melted a little at his smile. There had to have been something pathological about us, but I was okay with it. This was what I was meant to do.

Joshua was a broken and bloody mess. His sobs did nothing to ruin the moment.

"Keep going."

I reached into the bag and pulled out ankle, shoulder and belt holsters. Each pocket was labeled with the appropriate weapon.

Shit. I didn't have a shirt because that jerk had tried to choke me with mine. "I don't have…"

"Figured. Change of clothes. Quickly now."

As promised, cargo pants with extra pockets, a long-sleeved shirt, socks and sturdy boots awaited me. Modesty had disappeared somewhere between the description of my impending death and the loss of my shirt. I didn't care if anyone saw me naked at this point.

Jordan spoke to Joshua in a low voice that didn't travel. He didn't strike our prisoner nor did he seem to threaten him. But Joshua was more terrified than ever. Although he'd stopped crying, he had the look of a man awaiting a horrific death. We all knew it was the truth. It was just a matter of time.

I snapped on the last of my harnesses and slipped on the backpack. "I'm ready."

"Stand at the door. Don't walk beyond it and don't look back." Jordan's attention returned to Joshua. He stood, dusted off his pants and removed his beloved Glock, the first handgun he'd ever purchased legally and which he had subsequently modified.

We both knew I wouldn't fully comply. I walked over to the door and peeked over my shoulder.

Jordan lifted the gun and held it securely in both hands. "May the afterlife balance the scales and return to you all the pain you've inflicted on others."

Joshua's head rocked back in an explosion of blood and brain matter as the crack of the shot echoed in the gymnasium.

Jordan flipped on the gun's safety, stored it back in the holster and walked over to me. When he took my face in his hands, Jordy's eyes stared back.

"Did he hurt you anywhere else?"

"No."

He nodded, grabbed my hand and tugged me behind him. "When we leave, if you hear anything, shoot at it. Aim to kill."

"What the hell is going on?"

"Shit has hit the proverbial fan and it's worse than we imagined."

§

Jordy led me into a small utility closet and promptly sat down with a sigh. He patted the spot on the ground next to him. "No point in holding up the wall. We're going to be here for a while. Besides, we need to talk."

"I'm fine."

I was so far from fine. In mere moments I'd gone from elation and the gratification of exacted vengeance to horror at my actions. Sure, Jordy had pulled the trigger, but I was the one who'd beaten Joshua into submission and I would have killed him. Sitting next to Jordy and talking it all over with him didn't exactly promise to be my idea of a good time.

Jordy said nothing as he leaned back against the wall and extended his hand.

"Has everywhere else been cleared?"

"Yes. I'm sorry it took so long to find you, but no one told me you were missing. The security feed was compromised and you didn't have a workout scheduled. I thought you were safe in the Tower. Sit down." He gritted his teeth. "Please, Jasper."

I shook my head. Tears threatened to spill and if Jordy extended any kindness I'd lose my composure. Once we'd accounted for every last person in the compound and we figured out a plan, then I'd consider breaking down. Too much was at stake.

"It's fine. If I'd known someone was going to try to murder me today, I probably wouldn't have gotten out of bed."

"Like I said, we're not going anywhere." Jordy removed his hooded sweatshirt and dangled it. "I'll let you wear this if you sit down."

My lips twitched. Jordy looked nearly as bad as I felt. Speckles of blood dotted his face. If I squinted, the drops might have passed for freckles, cute little strawberry dots that danced over the bridge of his nose. He looked haggard. Any other man would have curled up and at least called for a time out. Jordy? The purple lump on his temple, split lip and blood-smeared limbs were a minor nuisance to him. Only his eyes gave away the massive grief and exhaustion that threatened to overwhelm him.

I plucked the sweatshirt from his hand and did a little happy dance. The chill in my bones faded and left me feeling slightly less shitty. "That's some major body heat."

"Mm-hmm."

"Why are we going to be here a while? And I know that it's bad timing and probably in poor taste, but would you walk me through everything? When else are you going to find such a perfect moment to teach me about crisis management?"

"Please?" Jordy held out his hand again.

"I don't want to talk about it. Him."

"We won't. Anything else off limits?"

"No." I slipped my hand into his and lowered myself to the ground. The sweatshirt pooled around me like a macabre circus tent, big enough to fit another person comfortably. I zipped it up and folded the sleeves until my hands were visible. "Thank you."

"Always. Whatever I have is yours."

That would have been great but everything I'd seen pointed toward an austere life with few vices. My holiday list hadn't included oversized men's gym clothes or Jordy's pop music collection. Sitting under the flickering lights that emanated from the computer equipment around us, Jordy seemed more alone than ever. It may have been a paltry inheritance, but he wanted me to have it.

"Don't make promises like that," I warned. "One day I'm going to hold you to it. You'll be miserable without your...have you ever owned a teddy bear?"

He snorted and scratched the back of his right hand. "More than one. I didn't spring from the womb fully formed."

"Nuh-uh. You're too," I paused and bit my lip, struggling to come up with the right word to describe the old soul with the bizarre tastes of someone much younger. "I can't imagine you as a little boy."

"I wasn't too different. Shorter, not as fast, and hardheaded. I slept with a teddy bear at night. When we get out of this and have rested for a few weeks, I might introduce you to one I've held onto for years."

My jaw dropped. If I needed to cast the bad guy in a movie, Jordy would have been at the top of my list. "Oh my God. Either we're actually friends or you're so convinced that we're going to die, you'll say anything to motivate me."

"We're friends," he allowed. "That's never changed."

Why dear God, Devil, and Annonnimus dude who told me to read a book? Did the man have a death wish? The months I'd spent feeling awful over the death of a little boy and the loss of our friendship had been tortuous. I wanted to scream and shake him. Friends, in my book, didn't abandon you without an explanation. Friends, however, dropped the subject when emotions were too close to the surface.

"What happened to your arm?"

Dark red syrup pooled in the crook of his elbow. It oozed toward his hand with the urgency of the first blob of ketchup from a new glass container. Based on the amount of dried rust powdering his forearm, it was a miracle he was alive.

"Oh. That. It's nothing." He used the hem of his black t-shirt to blot away the worst of it. "It's healing already."

"Hook a girl up with that adamantium."

Jordy grinned. "I've always been more of a Beast guy. He wore cool glasses and he hung upside down."

"Glasses? Hanging upside down? What are you—?"

My shriek was cut off by Jordy's hand clamping over my mouth. He moved us into the shadows of the deepest corner and whispered urgently. "Someone is here. Keep quiet and don't move."

He eased his hand away and nodded his approval at my wide-eyed silence. In a brilliant spark of foresight, Jordy had reloaded all of our weapons the moment we'd entered the utility closet. I'd thought it was simply paranoia at the time, but it was smart thinking. Although he'd cleared the area, he suffered no illusions that it would stay empty.

That meant either someone was still here or there were more coming. More innocents were at risk. I pressed my lips to his ears. "Not leaving your side. You made me promise."

Jordy shushed me again. The networking equipment was loud enough to mask small movements.

It wouldn't mask conversation or the sounds of either of us bumping the walls.

The footsteps grew closer. Our would-be attacker opened one of the classrooms doors that was badly in need of a little WD-40. It screeched horribly as the metal pieces ground against one another. Right now, it was better than a fire alarm and a GPS device combined.

The man swore loudly. He had no need of stealth since the sound had given away his position.

In the dark, Jordy bared his teeth in a ferocious grin. He'd known the doors were squeaky and had purposely done nothing about it. The trap was about to snap down on that little mouse.

That sneaky bastard was a genius.

Freddy, on the other hand, wasn't. He flung open every door he passed, cursing more vilely with each empty room. I could feel his rage pulsing toward us and prayed that he didn't find us. There was no chance of him being subdued.

One, two. Freddy's coming for Jasper.

"Going to end this. Stay here." Jordy kissed my forehead. "If something happens to me, shoot everything in sight. Go to the command center and don't let anyone else into the room. Find Dakarai."

Not today, buddy. I refused to say goodbye or contemplate the horror of seeing the life fade from his eyes. He'd just admitted that we were friends! The universe got no take-backs on that kind of relationship progress. Letting go of him was not an option.

I exhaled and leaned into him, taking and giving the small comfort of physical contact. "Oh, don't be such a drama queen. You said someone betrayed us. Let's go ahead and blame that person instead. Better yet, let's kill the dirt bag together."

"Someone needs a new nickname. Tiger? Champ?"

"You can't leave."

Jordy wrapped his arms around me and dropped his head on my shoulder. "Don't do this to me, not now.

I need warrior Jasper, not the one who likes my sweaty hugs and eats my post-workout snacks."

"And you don't get to be hardheaded about this, not after..." I closed my eyes and bit back a sob. "Earlier. What you did."

"Fine." Jordy returned to his position watching the door. After a few moments, he raised a hand and signaled for me to move deeper into the corner. Freddy was one room away.

One, two. Freddy's coming for Jasper.

We lifted our weapons and trained them on the door. The knob whined as Freddy turned it clockwise. I took a deep breath and held it, ready to exhale when it was time to pull the trigger. Jordy's face had gone blank, but the wheels were turning beneath the surface. He'd probably mapped out every scenario while I'd contemplated filching his sweatshirt permanently.

A sliver of light appeared.

"Psst."

What the hell kind of assassin said, "Psst"? That guy was clown town and we were the goddamn League of Assassins.

"J?" Freddy waited a beat. "Jordy? There's blood on the knob. Are you okay?"

Jordy was gone and with him, all traces of compassion. His features hardened as he aimed in the general direction of the person's head. He said nothing and waited.

"J, don't shoot. It's Hugo. Josh told me that he was down here with Jasper."

Bingo. Definitely a bad guy.

Jordan coughed weakly and groaned. "Hugo, thank God. I thought I was going to bleed to death down here. I can't walk without help."

"And Jasper?"

The door opened wider but not enough to give either of us a clear shot. Hugo wasn't stupid, but he was desperate and filled with a sick glee that saturated the air. If he killed Jordy, nothing would be beyond his reach.

"Who the fuck do you think did this to me?" Jordy coughed and spat. "Ah, fuck. That's a lot of blood."

Hugo exhaled with relief. "Sorry about that. Had to make sure that you were al—"

The cracking sound of a shot being fired should have drowned out the explosion of the right side of Hugo's face. But all I heard and saw was the flesh being torn and bone shattering on both sides of his skull. Brain matter and blood rained down in sickly reddish and gray chunks.

I swallowed down the bile and lowered my weapon. "He would have hurt you. He wanted to kill you," I said quietly.

Jordy stowed his gun. His expression was bleak as he plopped backward and tugged me onto his lap. "It was too soon. I didn't want you to —"

"Neither did I, but I'd do it again in a heartbeat. A million times if it meant keeping you safe."

I shut my eyes and buried my face as my body trembled from the force of the sobs that wanted to explode. Just like Hugo's head had exploded when I'd decided to put a bullet in it.

"You made the right call. He mentioned Joshua in the present tense, so he saw the body and lied or hadn't found Joshua yet and lied."

"He would have killed you. I protect mine."

PART 5

CHAPTER 19

I retreated to the corner and huddled against the wall as I tried to erase the images of Hugo's body from my mind. The bullet had pierced the bone between the bridge of his nose and eye socket and had made a mess on its way out. After I'd finished crying, I explained to Jordy that I wasn't upset that I'd killed him. I wasn't even upset that I'd taken a life. I was angry that these monsters had come into my home, again, and threatened to destroy the people closest to me. I hated them and I wanted to lash out at something. Anything.

Jordy squatted in front of me and squeezed my shoulder. "Hey. I took care of everything and cleared the next few hallways. Can you walk?"

"Did he have any information on him? A business card?"

"No. Do I need to carry you? I need to make one more stop before we can get out of here." He brushed a traitorous tear from my cheek. "It's almost over. We're almost there."

"It's been hours."

"Honey," he said carefully. "It's been less than an hour. I know you're exhausted, but we have to keep moving. I need to make sure you're safe and people are waiting on me. There are decisions that need to be made that can't be done over the phone."

I climbed to my feet and tested my legs. "Good to go, boss."

"Don't. Just don't act like nothing happened. It only makes it worse."

"What do you want me to say? That I wish I'd shot him until every magazine was empty? That I wish I'd done that with Joshua? Hugo was going to hurt you, Jordy. That's not happening on my watch."

Jordy chuckled and guided me away from yet another one of my bloody scenes. "I'm yours to protect now? Last time I checked, you'd demoted me to that stupid asshole jerk face."

"Last time I checked, you were a stupid jerk face who loves to ruin a moment. Jordy?"

Jordy slowed and jerked his head toward a door on our right. "Circuit breakers. It's grimy in there. Never mind. Just don't...I don't know. Don't eat anything off the floor."

"You're adorable," I drawled. "Want to remind me not to pick my nose and eat the boogers?"

We walked into the dank room and spun around slowly. It almost dark, with the only illumination there being what little was coming off the dials, buttons and gauges of the aisles of computer equipment. The floor showed years of neglect. What must have been dirt and grime had been stepped on so often that it had turned into muck.

"Like I said, don't eat anything." Jordy frowned as a light bulb went off in his brain. "Wait, did you actually do that? Eat your..."

Jordy leaned a hand against the wall to steady himself as the first heave wracked his body.

"Jordy?"

He mumbled something from behind the hand he'd clamped over his mouth and gagged like I'd served him a plate of said boogers. The next wave of nausea hit him harder, doubling him over as he spat.

"Ugh. Disgusting. Don't ever talk about that in front of me again. Come on." He reached into his bag and pulled out a mini bottle of mouthwash and one of those tongue Swiffer things.

Seeing him brush his teeth while opening a laptop near one of the main computer stations was too much. He was covered in blood but brushing his teeth was too important to delay. He finished quickly and then turned his attention to a program I didn't recognize.

"What are we looking at, boss?"

He scowled at me, perfect teeth and minty fresh breath. "What? I'm checking the security system's programming. What is so goddamn funny?"

I erupted into giggles. Not the maniac's cackle from earlier. It was the peal of laughter of someone who'd been tickled too hard and was about to wet themselves. The sight of him walking down the aisle and setting up with the toothbrush hanging from the corner of his mouth was so incongruous with the situation. It was ludicrous.

"You," I gasped. "You're...blood...mouthwash!"

"Shut up." Jordy's face was redder than a ripe tomato. He diverted his gaze. "Do you want to learn or not?"

"Of course I want to learn. Will you answer a question first? About everything?"

"I'm searching through the programming line by line to see if I can find the command. Whomever did this was good." He pointed to a row of words and symbols strung together. "This is what the code should say."

"Can you find it?"

"Don't know, but I have to try if we want to regain control of the building. Let me think."

Giggling aside, this was an eye opening experience. Jordy typed rapid-fire commands that should have been able to reboot the security system override from there. The program had other ideas.

I scooted over next to him. The interface was unfamiliar. "Did you check your TCP/IP settings?"

"What?" Jordy glowered. "Of course I checked the TCP/IP settings. They inserted a virus, a line of code that automatically attacked the system. Unfortunately, it's time for help desk option number two: doing a manual reset of the entire program and power cycling the whole goddamn building."

"Isn't it a fifteen second blip?"

He rubbed his eyes and exhaled. "It's a million different connections in a compound denser than most city blocks. It's phones, hospital equipment. Pick a worse scenario. What if—?"

The what-if game had become my constant companion since the death of my family. I'd only directly killed one person. Jordy had killed hundreds if the stories were to be believed. He'd just thrown on the weight of responsibility for every last person and pet in the compound. Jordy knew the cost and would have taken on the guilt everyone else felt.

I moved next to him and dropped my arm around his shoulders. He stiffened at the touch. It could have been the stench of gym clothes, sweat, blood, and brain chunks. It could have been his discomfort at my familiarity.

"Hey. Stop that. How many people are alive because of everything you've done today? If Joshua and Hugo were telling the truth, they're not here to torch the place."

Jordy exhaled and typed in a few more commands. "Found it. But I don't know how to remove it. If I reset the entire network, we'll lose some of the established protocols."

"Is that a big deal?"

"Months of work and personal time dedicated to learning something I have no natural aptitude for will go down the drain. Certain alarms won't work. There's a slight chance I'll royally screw up any device connected to the network. So, yeah, big deal."

"Ah. What can I do to help?"

"Nothing at the moment. Sit down with me."

I rolled my eyes and pointed out the obvious fact that there was only one chair and his butt was firmly planted. Jordy solved that problem by pulling me around and sitting me on his right thigh. One hand continued to peck out commands while the other held me in place.

"This is so unprofessional."

"Ask me if I give a shit. Take the keyboard and follow my instructions. You'll learn faster if you're doing it yourself."

"It's not working."

"Fuck. It was a long shot. I'm wiping everything and power cycling the building."

Perching on his lap was the single most uncomfortable position I'd ever tolerated. Yoga had nothing on trying to evenly distribute my weight while not sitting down hard enough for him to feel my actual weight.

"What can I do?"

He shook his head with frustration. "Stupid people don't listen to anything I say. Fuck it. We're going down in 3. 2. And 1. This is going to be the longest thirty seconds of my life."

"Jordy, if I somehow manage to live through this, we're going to find a quiet place to talk. I'm going to scream at you until I lose my voice. Then I'll do some text-to-speech thing on my phone. I'm probably going to throw things at you."

His eyes remained on the countdown on his cell phone. "If? Not an option. You haven't trained this hard to roll over like some spineless chump. What do we say to death? Not today."

"Are you seriously quoting George R.R. Martin? Right now?"

"Hold on." Jordy held his breath as the power came back. He watched data scroll on the screen. "Come on, come on, come on. Please let this work."

"The power came on. That's a good sign. Right?"

His eyebrows furrowed even deeper than usual, making him look like a kid trying to play a villain. He hushed me and switched to another program that showed him the layout of the building. The instant that first room lit up, he exhaled with relief and smiled. "It's promising. The power is coming back right away. Now we wait."

"For?"

Jordy entered a command that zoomed in to a classroom. "Right now it says zero out of three. If any of the devices fail to reset, we'll see a red dot on the layout."

"I hadn't realized you manage the technology end of security."

"I don't have a natural aptitude for networking or programming. Hell, I don't like or enjoy this work, so we have someone to handle it. Since the intruders hacked the system, we can't ignore the possibility that he's involved. I've learned enough to keep things going in case of an emergency."

In my previous life as a popular high school student I'd been an organizer. Jordy made my exacting lists and plans look like child's play. He'd taken on a complicated field of study for the minute chance that something like this could happen. He was in charge of the security force, an instructor, the director of the armory and apparently monitored the entire building's power and network connectivity.

I was a lazy lima bean. I bet he had twelve jobs by the time he was my age.

"What else are you monitoring?"

"Indoor and outdoor cameras, the alarm system, and the sprinkler system. I'd like to run reports to see if anyone tried to access our networks. It would be great if someone could review security footage. I don't have the time."

Jordy flipped between windows rapidly, giving the illusion of watching an old television with static. The screen stayed in focus less than a second before it switched to the next image. I closed my eyes and tried to fight off the headache it was already giving me. But I couldn't keep them closed for long because I was too curious.

"Wait, wait. Go back a screen." I pointed to a cluster of three black dots that appeared on the image of the layout. "What are those dots? And why are they moving?"

"Sonofabitch." Jordy stabbed at his phone. He typed furiously as he waited for someone to answer.

"Jordy? Thank goodness."

"Dakarai. Three cars are being taken from the garage as we speak. The garage doors haven't gone back online yet. Get someone to track them."

Dakarai shouted to someone in the command center. "Done. I'm running downstairs to see if I can find anything."

"Stay put. We'll be there soon enough."

"Jasper is well? Has she been injured? Where is Joshua?"

Jordy growled. "Yes, yes, and dead. I expect a full report when I get there. Make sure that happens?"

"Yes, of course. What else?"

"Medical."

"Fine."

I frowned and poked his arm, hoping for a quick translation of their abbreviated conversation, but Jordy ignored me. There was something vaguely guilty with the way he averted his gaze. "The other thing we discussed?"

Dakarai sighed. "Already handled."

"Bad?"

"Not great. I'll explain when you arrive. Hurry."

§

At first glance, it appeared that the command center was in total chaos. It was packed with the remainder of

Jordy's men, some of the High Council members, and a few of the injured.

"I need to find Mikael."

"Last I heard, he'd gotten down here early on, so he's fine. Dakarai too." Jordy hesitated, then pulled me into another of his bone-shattering hugs. "Don't leave this room without me."

"Sure thing, boss," I wheezed. "Please stop breaking my bones. I may have a bad ass tolerance for pain, but even I have limits."

He chuckled as he stepped back. "Agreed. Try not get the shit kicked out of you. It makes my job easier."

"If I recall correctly, I'd inflicted plenty of damage. Thanks for the kettle bell, by the way. There was something perversely satisfying about it."

He spotted Mikael across the room and asked him to keep an eye on me. For my protection, of course. Someone needed to make sure their favorite brawler was well rested for the main event. Jordy chucked my chin and was swallowed by the remaining men in his security team and the logistics folks.

Sighing, I shifted my attention away from him to Mikael and the rest of the command center. I'd been wrong. The room was organized chaos. Someone had sorted those who had taken shelter into logical units.

The children had been directed to play in an empty corner, but they were mostly silent. Whatever they'd seen had been too much for their brains to handle. They were shutting out the world and trying to process the last few hours. The smallest of them huddled next to their siblings or temporary sitter, their expressions vacant. A few of the oldest children had streaks of blood on them and competed to tell the best story of their heroism.

At least the bravado of teenagers was still intact. The world was allowed to move again.

As bone-chilling as the children had appeared, the injured were the worst. Nurses provided the best care possible in this unsanitary environment, but it couldn't have been enough. Survivors were morphing into casualties. A little girl, no older than seven or eight, saw me watching and smiled. Her head was wrapped in bandages and her right eye was shrouded by gauze and tape.

I had to turn away. It was only a matter of time before grief threatened to overwhelm me. A few feet away, a couple leaned against the wall and held one another. I recognized them from the dining hall. They went with their children on Fridays. Their teenage son sat on the floor with his knees pulled to his chest. He stared ahead, seemingly unaware of his surroundings. When a nurse offered him water, it was clear that he'd disappeared into whatever images played in his head.

"Their daughter, Yana, she didn't make it," Mikael said. "She was…injured in the stampede when the assailants took a teacher hostage."

My stomach dropped. "Is the teacher…?"

Mikael wrapped me in a comforting hug. He sagged against me as tears spilled down his cheeks. "She's gone. Those bastards. They hurt the children. Yana was a good girl. Smart. Kind. They hurt her."

"Shh."

"Don't tell me it's going to be okay. It's not."

I stilled and pulled back enough to see his face. "Have the visions changed?"

"It's constant, Milaya. My head feels like it's about to explode from the death and sorrow."

"Mikael, what have you seen? I'll take care of your headaches, but I need you to focus while you're still conscious."

He averted his gaze. When he spoke, it was barely audible. "Tangentials. Private moments. Death. But nothing makes sense except how this will end. You're surrounded by light. So much death." Mikael shook his head. "And you?"

"Did you hear," I whispered, "they found closed circuit television footage of the compound's entrances and exits. Ooh, I wish I could be there when they find Joshua with a bullet in his head."

"What are you talking about?" He stared at me, horrified, as he took in the blood on my arms and face. "What happened to you?"

"Shh! You're going to scare folks. If it makes you feel any better, not all of it is mine. That traitor bastard got what was coming to him."

"You killed Joshua?" Mikael shuddered. "I think I saw that in a vision earlier. It was just a flicker. But I saw Jordy with you."

"He showed up at the end. When I told him," I paused and took a deep breath. "About the attack and the dirty shots, he asked to do the honors. I'm not ready to talk about it yet. Grab a seat and rest your head on a desk. You need your rest and nature calls. Gotta go."

Mikael's hand tightened around mine for a moment. His face scrunched up as he held back tears. Exhaling, he let go and directed me to the women's restroom. "Clean up while you're there. You're mildly terrifying when you wake up. This is much, much worse."

I snorted and flipped him off as I walked away.

§

Inside, the space was surprisingly large for a single stall room. There was enough room for at least four other toilets and a couple of sinks.

No matter. I had to clean up and rejoin the action. I'd be damned if someone was going to sideline me.

"Holy shit snacks," I said to my reflection. "You're straight out of a horror movie."

I stripped off my new clothes and tossed them onto the changing table. My entire body was covered with smears of blood. It was a miracle Jordan hadn't tried to murder a small village. I leaned toward the mirror to take in the worst of the damage. There were a few cuts and bruises on the inside of my mouth that were going to hurt when healing. The blue and purple lumps on the right side of my face wouldn't be much of a picnic either.

I frowned and turned my head to survey the rest of the damage. My head felt tender, which shouldn't have been a surprise given everything that transpired. I'd have been shocked if I didn't have a major concussion.

It was only a matter of time before I looked like I'd just auditioned for the Blue Man Group. There was no helping the imminent swelling and bruising, but I harbored hope that I'd look less ghastly. The children had been traumatized enough.

The process was slow. I swiped two handfuls of paper towels and dunked them under the sink's faucet. I pressed one to my cheek and massaged in slow circles, as I did with my morning face wash. Instead of removing the blood, I only made the smear worse.

There was no way I'd have maintained my small grip on reality if I had to walk around in dead Joshua's blood. Images of him on top of me, his cold eyes as he beat me, and the gleeful lust that had overcome him as he described his plans for me hit me with the force of a Mack truck. I ran to the toilet and heaved. My wet hands left bloody imprints as I held onto the porcelain throne.

More blood. Dead guy's blood. I hadn't pulled the trigger, but I'd broken him and signed off on his death. My stomach rolled. Everything I'd eaten expelled itself. I slumped against the wall, shivering and exhausted.

The intruders had attacked me and mine. That alone signed their death warrants. Putting them out of play in the cosmic balance was a bonus. It was time for them to pay for their transgressions against the Order and my family.

Suddenly, I didn't need Mikael to see the future. No matter how hard I fought, they had something that would destroy me. Someone I loved was going to die at their hands. I was going to kill everyone.

CHAPTER 20

I found Mikael pacing next to the restroom door. The mother hen instinct in this one was strong. He smiled with relief as he took in my appearance.

"I was worried. There was so much blood."

"Like I said, most of it wasn't mine." I sighed. "Joshua was thorough. My body is covered in bruises. I'm dreading tomorrow."

Mikael cursed and prayed that Joshua would suffer a thousand excruciating deaths. He wished that he'd been the one to kill the traitor and briefly considered emptying a magazine in his dead body for fun. He was tired of the endless cycle of death and war.

I took a step back and saw that Mikael was strapped to the gills. He had nearly as many weapons as Jordy and all looked wicked. "You can't leave," I blurted. "You'll get hurt and I don't want you to die."

"I'm not useless, Jasper. I've gone on missions and survived. We can't leave too many qualified people behind."

"We need trained folks to stay. What if they return?"

Mikael crossed his arms and glowered. "That's already been handled. I'm going whether you like it or not. Try not to kill me."

I stared in disbelief as Mikael stormed away. The darkness that had always lay beneath the surface had taken over. Those monsters had attacked his home, hurt me and killed children. The holy trinity of offenses.

For a moment, I almost pitied Joshua's friends. Jordy's team had a reputation for being more skilled and lethal than secret factions of the armed forces. With Mikael, Dakarai, and me bringing our enhanced abilities and rage, these monsters had no chance of survival. Not in the face of a team who'd made annihilation their sole purpose.

Dakarai. Shit. I hadn't spoken with him yet and had no idea if he had been injured. I pushed through the crowd of adults who were moving toward the area designated for the security team.

"Excuse me, pardon me, coming through," I called as I wiggled through the press of bodies. "Sorry! I'm needed at the table!"

It was as if I didn't exist. No one responded to my entreaties and ignored my shoves and elbows. Had I turned into a ghost or some other entity? Were my friends the only ones who'd see me? Could ghosts kill?

I gave up after a large man refused to move out of my way. I might have been amused any other day. But at that moment, I was livid. The only way down was shitty, but I was out of options. I pushed my way to the periphery and exhaled as I dropped to my hands and knees and crawled under the row of work stations.

It was disgusting. Danny should have been ashamed at the grime that had made the brown carpet flat and slick. I resigned myself to the fact that I'd have to bleach my hands if I expected to avoid whatever plague had sprouted on the petri dish masquerading as a carpet when I fell off the end of the platform and onto the next work station.

My shoulder exploded with a million sharp needles of pain. I refused to cry out and gritted my teeth until the worst of it passed. Then I rolled back onto my hands and knees. If anyone in the crowd noticed, they'd decided to ignore this as well. My fingers dug into the carpet and found nothing but the same shiny layer of germs.

"Jasper!" Jordy's voice carried across the entire command center. "Has anyone seen Jasper? She's um, short with black hair. Probably looks banged up?"

I froze as the heat of a hundred eyes turned on me in all my glory. I'd nearly made it across this work station, but my butt was still up in the air and visible on one side and my embarrassed face poked out of the other.

"Hi," I said weakly.

"If you see her, make sure she gets down here."

I dropped my head, positive that my embarrassment couldn't have gotten worse. But I'd forgotten that there were children still hanging out in the command center. Children were evil little jerks who ratted me out.

"She's under the table," a little boy wearing a pair of overalls with a train embroidered on the pocket called out. "Mommy said we can't crawl under the tables. She's gonna be in trouble."

Jordy replied with exaggerated patience and a smile in his voice. "That's right, buddy. There's no crawling under the table. Think you can be my assistant?"

The boy jumped up and down and whooped the way only a six year old could manage. He shouted that he was Scary Jordy's assistant because he was a big boy and so cool.

Even I had to laugh at his exuberance as he pulled my hand and "helped" me get to my feet. Once he was convinced I was steady and hadn't gotten get any new owies, he dragged me through the crowd of highly amused adults with the air of a seasoned medic.

"Out of the way! We're gonna see Scary Jordy! He wants to see his friend. It's my job! Move please!"

The child, who introduced himself as Matthew, parted the sea of adults with impressive authority. By the time we arrived at the table, not even Jordy could keep a straight face.

"Mr. Jordy, I did it! I brought Ms. Jasper down here to you. Are you gonna yell at her now?"

Jordy knelt in front of the boy and put a hand on his shoulder. "You did a great job, Matthew. I couldn't have found Jasper without you. When all this craziness is over I'm taking you out for ice cream."

Matthew's face lit up with hero worship. "Yes, Mr. Jordy. Can I still help? Now?"

"Definitely. It's a big job," he warned. "Do you think you're ready for a big boy job?"

"Uh-huh."

"Good. I want you to stay with the kids. They can go to the bathroom or to see their parents, but this area is off limits. If you see someone, tell them very nicely that we're having a meeting."

"I can do that. Thank you Mr. Jordy." Matthew took a deep breath and threw himself into Jordy's arms. He hugged Scary Jordy tightly and promised to do a good job.

Stunned and red faced, Jordy hugged him back. He stood and picked up Matthew. "Everyone see this guy? He's super cool and he's my helper. He's going to stay here and watch over things for me."

He gave the boy a smacking kiss on the cheek and sent him on his way before turning back to his assembled team. His body shook with the effort of trying not to laugh.

"Right, now that we've secured this place thanks to my buddy over there, let's go over what we know. Has anyone been able to check the security footage?"

The answer came in the form of a heart-rending yowl. "She's gone! They took Cecilia and her third-graders. They're all gone."

§

The war room, er, table, fell silent as Danny sobbed and ranted. He'd been reviewing the security footage when he came across the single camera feed that pointed to the playground across the street.

Cecilia had been substitute teaching for the third graders for the week, something she did often. Since it was a beautiful day, she'd taken them to the playground for some fresh air. The video zoomed in and caught Cecilia laughing breathlessly as she chased her students in a game of freeze tag.

Two black vans screeched to a halt in front of the park's only entrance. Men wearing black fatigues, hats and masks that hid their lower faces descended upon the playground. Cecilia gathered the children behind her and tried to reason with the disguised men, her hands gesturing wildly. She pressed the children into a corner and threw out her hands to protect them. As she tapped into her abilities and gathered the blinding energy in her hands, a small bullet struck the side of her neck. She dropped to the floor unconscious.

The children sobbed as their teacher was picked up and thrown over a man's shoulder. One brave boy kicked and punched Cecilia's captor until the man cuffed the side of his head and knocked him out. At his gesture, the rest of the men shot the youngsters and hauled them away.

The entire assault and kidnapping took three minutes. Twelve children and one adult disappeared this morning and no one was the wiser. Breaking in and messing with our security feeds had been a diversionary tactic. My gut told me that they knew exactly who to grab and had access to the logs each teacher updated in between classes. The innocents had been selected and claimed.

Danny's bloodshot eyes landed on me. "You. This is your fault. You're the reason everything has gone wrong." He threw himself across the table and grabbed the front of my shirt with one hand and my shoulder holster with the other. His strength, fueled with grief and rage, surprised me. He surprised everyone.

Danny had used his leverage to slam my face into the table. Stars exploded behind my eyelids as my brain rattled around in my skull. The pain was unbearable, worse than the hundreds of other times my head had been used to dimple a surface. It robbed me of air as efficiently as a well-aimed punch.

I flailed and smacked his arms, tried to poke his eyes out, and considered breaking his nose. He was too strong and I was too dazed to do more than anger him. When my face hit the table, I lay there, unable to move or speak. Blood spewed from my nose and bile or whatever was left in my stomach oozed out of my mouth.

Around me, the men recovered from their shock and tackled Danny. It took the efforts of two men to pry his hands off of me and another two to restrain him. My one good eye opened enough to grant me access to the shit show.

The madness had taken over Danny's soul. He'd do anything to save Cecilia, including killing me or delivering me alive to whomever was behind the attack. He thrashed against the restraints and kicked or head-butted anyone who came too close.

Dakarai grunted and stepped back, his hand clapped over his jaw. His stunned expression was akin to that of a child whose hand had just been swatted for the first time. It screamed hurt and betrayal. He staggered to a nearby seat and watched his sometimes-friend battle for his freedom.

Danny and I locked eyes as I pushed myself off the table and wiped the drool from my face with clumsy hands. His eyes bulged and he redoubled his efforts to get to me, every muscle straining and his neck nothing more than a band of tight, corded muscles slick with sweat. Danny grimaced and howled as he yanked one hand free of the restraints.

He'd broken his thumb to slip his hand free.

The scene devolved further as the children ran around, unsure if more fun would be had seeing the fight up close or shouting support and jeers. Of the healthy adults who'd gathered nearby, a handful let out their own cries of defiance. The woman whose daughter, Yana, had been killed climbed onto a wobbly table. Her eyes were wild with grief as she lifted an unsteady arm and pointed at me.

"Jasper is the problem," she roared to her companions in desperation. It was my fault the compound had been raided and the deaths that occurred today could have been prevented. The only chance of saving the children was to hand me over.

Oh shit.

"Enough!" Jordy whistled sharply. "This is over! Mikael, bring the injured to me. The rest of you, back up or I will personally end you." He threw his hands in the air. "What the fuck is wrong with you? We've lost loved ones and it hurts. It's awful and there's nothing I can do to make it better. Neither will killing Jasper. This is over."

Mikael scooped me up and carried me toward the makeshift trauma center. "Hey. How's the head?"

"Been better."

He froze and nearly dropped me.

"What? Why are you staring at me?"

Shaken, he lowered me onto the cot nearest Jordy and grabbed him. "Her speech. She responds, but it is incoherent."

Jordy pinched the bridge of his nose, took a deep breath and bellowed. "Silence!"

Not even the children dared disobey. They returned to their corner of our world and awaited further instructions. Matthew regained his composure and whispered that Mr. Jordy was going to get really scary and yell at them if they didn't shush.

The adults stopped abruptly.

"This is over. Rubios," Jordy said to a stocky man with battle scars visible on his neck and arms, "move the evacuees to the dining hall. The injured can go to the nearest sterile room. The little guys, like my buddy Matthew? Have someone cord off a space for them to nap or play quietly. See if someone can't get games for them."

"On it."

Jordy's face appeared above me. "Jasper, can you hear me? I want you to pull my finger for yes."

I tried to scowl at the silly joke, but I was too tired. "Coffee? Soda?"

"Say that again. You're angry? I know that, sweetie. We'll deal with that later. I don't have a sofa for you."

"No," I said, taking care to enunciate slowly. "I'm tired. Gimme caffeine."

Dakarai reappeared with a cold bottle of water, a straw and a handful of pills. "One day you must teach me how to start a riot."

"Ha, ha. Caffeine."

"I'm sorry. No one will give you anything until you've been examined by the medical staff."

Jordy's leg jiggled. "It's a concussion. She'll be sore but nothing has been damaged."

"Only my pride."

They both let out surprised laughs.

Mikael showed up with a pissed off nurse in tow. She was one of the angry ones and told us that she'd fix me up enough to make it through the hostage exchange.

There wasn't a spot on my body that didn't hurt. I was tired of the pain and of the guilt heaped on me. They were right. Those twelve innocent kids and poor Cecilia were in danger as long as I remained here. An exchange was the only solution.

"You'll fix her up to the best of your capabilities or —"

I groaned and forced myself into a sitting position. "Stop. She's right. Just need to look okay enough to get through this. Unless there's a superhero power that lets me heal myself, let her work. Don't argue. Not your choice."

"Fuck that. It's my goddamn choice whether you like it or not. Protect does not mean hand over to some sick fucks. You heard what they're planning to do to you. I'm not letting that happen." Jordy glared at me the way he did right before a punch came flying toward my face. "Not your choice, so don't bother trying to change my mind."

The nurse muttered all sorts of unflattering things about how unfair it was for Jordy to save his girlfriend while Cecilia had to die.

"I'm not his girlfriend!"

"Seriously? That's your response?"

"No." Frustration threatened to boil over. "Point is that no one is choosing me over anyone. I'm going with them, Nurse Hatchett. Do you think I wanted this? I'd trade my life for theirs a thousand times over. You have no reason to believe me, but I won't return without them, no matter how long it takes."

"Well said." Dakarai's approval bolstered me more than the pills currently being shoved down my throat. "Get her a can of pop while you're at it."

"Now," I said with renewed vigor. "Do we know where they are? Did the cars stop moving?"

§

I leaned against the wall of the conference room and willed the Percocet and caffeine pills in my system to kick in. It probably wasn't the best idea, but it was the most practical. I needed to be sharp, which meant the pain needed to disappear. Adrenaline would take care of some of it, but I was relying on good ol' Percocet to handle the rest.

Earlier in the day, I'd gotten the impression that Jordy's team of super assassins numbered in the thirties. Only ten joined us.

Nine men and one woman sat at the conference table, oblivious to our presence. Perhaps it was the comfort and faith they had in their team. Maybe it was an utter disdain of people like us. Hell, maybe they just didn't care because this crisis was just another day for them.

Dakarai sidled up to me and leaned against the cheap pressed wood panel. His face mirrored the exhaustion of everyone in the room, but there was something deeper in his expression. Resignation. "I must tell you something before Jordy arrives. Promise me you won't overreact."

"Why does everyone keep saying that? Have you seen me overreact today?"

"No, you haven't. However, I am not convinced that's the most appropriate response. Having a breakdown would not be unexpected or judged. It happens to the best of us."

What was with everyone telling me how to react? I was comfortable with my responses. My judgment wasn't clouded. On the contrary, my senses and thoughts were sharper than ever. I was what I needed to become, what everyone had hoped — their greatest weapon.

"Dude, I'm fine. I'm saving the dramatics for afterward."

Dakarai smiled with understanding. "I am remaining behind. It's too dangerous for both of us to unleash the full extent of our abilities in the same space."

"We need you. I need you to walk me through everything."

"Jasper, we both know that you no longer need my guidance." He kissed my forehead with the tenderness of a big brother and parental figure combined. "You don't listen to me anyway."

"Hey," I said with mock indignation. "I'm the epitome of the ideal padawan."

"You're no longer a padawan. The student has become the master."

"Can I change your mind?"

Dakarai shook his head. "No more than I can change yours. Take care of them for me. Mikael will be more useful than you imagine, but he still needs protection. And Jordy needs you to remain safe. He will not rest until he believes that the threat is gone. You must keep him grounded and sane."

"Do I need them?"

"You never needed any of us. Nonetheless, we found each other and it would shatter us if you didn't return home."

Damn him. I'd never wanted to care about anyone after my family died. Yet, those three annoying, stubborn, emotionally bumbling oafs had become the dearest parts of my life. I'd walk through fire if it meant sparing them an ounce of pain.

My eyes flew to his and asked the unspoken question. He tilted his head in acknowledgment. "They will need you. After. Promise me you'll take care of them?"

Jordy's appearance ended our conversation with the grace of a serrated knife. He had a stack of folders in his arms, which he promptly dropped on the table. It struck me as a bad time to give in to the maudlin feelings so close to the surface, so I refrained from tackling him with a hug.

He pulled his chair from under the table and slid it toward me, his expression daring me to refuse. It was a small gesture, the most he'd do in a room full of his employees, so I didn't have the heart to turn him down. I lowered myself into the cushioned seat and bit back a sigh of relief.

"Right. I'm going to make this quick. We've located the vehicles outside of a warehouse in Brooklyn. It's less than ideal because of the proximity to the housing projects." He sighed. "In your packets, you'll find a layout of the facility with points of ingress and egress. You'll also find your assignments. Look everything over. We'll reconvene in five and we're rolling out at 21:00. Go."

§

Dakarai knelt in front of me. "Remember everything we've taught you. I have faith."

"Faith in what?"

"You," he said. "You'll do what is right and you will protect what is yours. I ask one favor."

I scooted to the edge of my seat and wrapped my arms around him tightly. "Anything."

"What I'm about to suggest is based on years of research and prayer. I don't ask you to believe anything, only that you follow my instructions. It may be the only way to save us all."

Ice water sluiced through my veins. "I'm listening."

CHAPTER 21

I grunted as I hefted another bag of ammunition into the back of our black SUV. The trunk resembled the armory of a small country preparing for a small insurrection. It wasn't enough though, I was thinking. But of course without a head count, it was impossible to know the extent of what we were facing.

My corporeal body and I had become well acquainted the last several weeks, so when she screamed that I was a masochist, I was inclined to agree. Each bruise had taken on a life and personality of its own. The ribbon of purple covering my spine threatened to give out before I could make it inside the car. Although my right knee wholeheartedly agreed, the left one was holding out for a miracle named Percocet and the goddess Caffeine. Neither body nor mind approved of those things called nerve endings and pain receptors. They were as unnecessary as a gall bladder and infinitely more debilitating.

"Out of the way," Jordy said. He hefted the remaining two bags into the trunk. "Get inside. We need to talk."

Dammit. Nothing good, in the history of all humankind, had ever proceeded those words. I'd hoped that we'd have a quiet moment before we walked into the madness, but that seemed unlikely. "What?"

The toe of his boot slapped against the asphalt floor. He sighed. "I'm tired, Jas. It's going to be a hell of a long night, so just say whatever is on your mind."

"Yeah." I blew out a breath. It was just a string of words that would likely be forgotten before we left the garage. Shame heated my face. I'd navigated my way through similar conversations with Dakarai and Mikael. I stared at the ground and spoke in a quiet voice. "Thank you for everything. You didn't have to invest so much time into teaching and training me. I can't imagine how you found the time to sleep with so many responsibilities."

"I'm organized. What are you doing?"

Audacity became me. I patted his cheek and grinned. "Hasn't anyone ever told you that you'd find out sooner if you just listened?"

"Too many times. So?" Jordy gently tilted my chin upward until I met his gaze. "Don't you dare."

"Chill out. I'm the one who's supposed to save the world, which means I'm entitled. Hush." We gazed at one another and I tried to communicate what I'd never say out loud with my eyes. I hoped his reddening face meant that the message had been received.

"Fine. Talk."

"You've been good to me in your way, even when you knocked me out. Twice."

"Stop."

"Jordy," I said over his protests, "promise me something. Two things."

"No. I'm not doing this."

"Promise me that when this is over, you'll take care of Mikael. You'll need one another." I covered his mouth when he began to speak again. "And promise me that you'll remember that you're a good man, Jordy McAllister. You're loved and you're worthy of being loved."

Jordy tugged me into his arms and held me tightly. "I hate you," he whispered into my hair. "Please. I'm begging you. Stop talking. You don't get to waltz into my life, drive me batshit crazy, assault me, and make me care about you. Don't lose hope, honey. Not just yet."

"I'm not hopeless."

"You're not helpless either," he retorted. "Don't act like a victim of circumstance and fate. Nothing is written in stone."

"The shackles of circumstance and fate no longer apply to me."

He glowered. "What does that mean?"

"What it's supposed to mean. You'll see when the time comes."

§

Mikael settled into the backseat of the vehicle and slapped my arm. "What happened?"

"Nothing happened, doofus. I needed a moment like we had earlier."

He sighed heavily. "Did it help?"

"No. Nothing will make this easier. He doesn't know, Mikael, and I'd like to keep it that way. We all need Jordy to be on his game. This will ruin it."

"I wonder why."

Jordy slid into the driver's seat. "What do you wonder?"

I glared at Mikael with a thousand threats we both knew I'd never realize. "He wonders why I'm walking around with a pill bottle. I've already said I'm leaving it in the car. Did you want to talk about something?"

He pressed a finger to his lips and pointed to the lights above the center console. Quicker than I thought possible, he removed the cover and tore out a flat disk that resembled a button. It turned into dust between his fingers. "Listening devices. I wouldn't care, except we need to discuss something that only Dakarai and I know. We've been sitting on it for a week now."

"You cannot keep information from the Circle," Mikael said. "Why would you violate that oath?"

"Because those who administered the oath had broken a much more sacred vow. Charles, Miriam and Ian are missing."

"Oh shit," I breathed. "No, no, no. This is worst case scenario. Five alarm fire. Right?"

Mikael grabbed his head and groaned. "Shadows and anonymity are no place for the greed that lies in their hearts. They would venture into the dark to become gods among men."

"Fuck." As an afterthought, I patted Mikael's leg. His face was ashen and his hands trembled with the weight of another vision of death. I passed over a bottle of water and ibuprofen. He passed on the Percocet. I shrugged. "Your loss. Back to my original point. Fuck."

"In a nutshell." Jordy tapped his fingers on the steering wheel. "It's not unheard of for someone to become disillusioned and leave the Order. High Council members retire and are replaced. They don't disappear and go completely off the grid. We're walking into one of two unenviable situations. Either they've been kidnapped and are part of the sacrifice or—"

Mikael kicked the back of Jordy's seat. "Please, let's hear the better of the two scenarios."

"I'd bet that our plans will be derailed by someone we least expect. And if you kick my seat again, you're going to find yourself without a foot. Not in the mood, Mikael." Jordy reached behind him with one hand and managed to untie the laces of one of Mikael's boots. "I call a shenanigans truce for the next twenty-four hours."

"Fine. It's time for me to explain the disillusionment." Mikael leaned forward in his seat. "I am sorry, Milaya, but we lied to you."

I snorted. "Color me surprised. I'll muster up some righteous anger later. Tell me what's going on."

Jordy took my hand. "Remember your first meeting with the High Council?"

"Duh."

"We lied when we said that the Annonnimus One doesn't speak. Mikael, Dakarai and I have all had visions and conversations with the big guy. So have some of the High Council members. We are bound by powers, magic, whatever you want to call it, and cannot reveal this information to anyone. This is a failsafe. I'm shattering the glass on the fire box."

"Why?"

"What if you served an entity who was selective of those with whom he communicated? If you're not one of those chosen? Would you become bitter with the knowledge that you're good, but not good enough? We wanted to guide you through the process and work on your direct connection, but the binding, well, bound us."

"Is that what you think this is? A revolt? Why would they —" I broke off with understanding. "They want to be heard. If they absorb the abilities of those who have that existing connection, they'll be more powerful than we can imagine."

"Blood sacrifice has always been a way for humans to communicate with those beyond our perception of the world. Demons, gods, whatever. I've done extensive research on the topic. Everyone thought I was losing my mind," Mikael said, his mouth drawn into a sad smile, "again."

"Okay. What's the point of this?"

"Many cultures believe that the blood contains the soul and wisdom of a person. It's important that the blood flow from someone important and from the innocents. Cecilia is of the Circle and one of the direct lines. She may not be physically powerful, but her blood is the repository of the wisdom of the ages. The High Council and the Circle are the only ones aware of her importance."

Jordy grimaced. "We're left with two options. If we can't save Cecilia, then we must collect and destroy her blood."

"How do you destroy blood that powerful?"

"Fire. The hottest, most destructive fire conceivable."

Sonofabitch.

Images flashed before my eyes. My siblings and I stood before an altar drenched in blood. Three unique abilities balanced each other in the destruction. Livie compelled those presiding over the ritual to collect the blood and bring it to us. Jude created a wind tunnel around us to keep us safe. My soul energy burned bright as I destroyed the sacred blood. In the last moments, hands clasped together, the wind became a maelstrom that contained the final expulsion of energy. Blinding light surrounded us, exploded through us.

Although I knew it was wrong to speak poorly of the dead, I was pissed off. "Screw you guys for dying and leaving me to clean up the mess. Typical. Jerks."

§

Exhaustion was a bitch who hated me. My eyes refused to open, so I curled up in the front seat while Jordy drove us through Brooklyn.

"Is she asleep," Mikael whispered.

"Yes. She needs to recharge. I need time to come up with a new plan or six. She's going to wait until my back is turned, sneak off, and do something stupid. I can't protect her if she goes rogue."

"Jasper was never meant to be contained. We have to have faith in her instincts and hope that she has a shred of self-preservation remaining." Mikael sighed. "She's young and innocent."

"No, she's not," Jordy said. "Jasper lost her innocence today. I refuse to let her die out of some misguided desire to atone."

Mikael hummed in agreement. "Have you told her? Time is short, my friend."

"She's cute. I'd bet that if she had a blanket, it would stop somewhere around her eyes. What if…"

The car rolled to a smooth stop.

"No, I haven't told her. There's no point."

"It's the end of the world, brat. What better time is there to confess?"

Whatever they meant, it was clear that Jordy didn't want to talk about it.

He shook my leg gently. "Hey, sleepyhead. How are you feeling?"

"Good." My body still matched the colors of the rainbow if they'd been dunked in oil and left out in the rain. The bruises began to sing in rounds. First came the arms.

Jasper sucks.
She got beat up.
She didn't fight back.
Hurrah!

The legs followed, and by the time we reached my head, I had an impressive four-part acapella.

"Time for some caffeine. You can take half a Percocet now. Carry another in your pocket. But that's it."

"Got it. We're here?"

"Yeah. Everyone is in position."

"Half a mile perimeter? How do we keep them from slipping through the wide cracks?"

"Not my department. Something about a neutralizing net that turns idiots into babbling idiots. The average person will grow sleepy and find the nearest place to nap. People with abilities will lose them until we remove the nets." Jordy turned in his seat to speak to Mikael and me. "Once we exit the car, things are going to happen at rapid-fire speed. The only way all three of us go home is if you listen to me."

Mikael grunted. "The plan where I stay in a corner until everything is over?"

"The one where you comfort the rescued children and use your considerable strength and knowledge to protect them." Jordy's knee began to jiggle again. "Jasper, you know the deal. You stick to my ass like a shadow. The goal is get in and get out as fast as possible with minimal injuries and no fatalities."

"I know. I won't leave your side."

The lies were spilling from my lips with greater ease. I gave him the same expression as I had Dakarai and Mikael, but he appeared unfazed. "You'll try. Save me the trouble. Stay with me."

I needed Jordy to get me close enough to the ones in charge. Once I was within shouting distance, I'd run. It wasn't fair or kind, but it was necessary. I couldn't risk the most powerful member of our team. He was the key to everyone getting out alive.

"Chill out, boss. I've got it. Stay close and don't shoot yourself in the head."

Jordy rolled his eyes. "Things are going to happen fast and you're not going to be in the best control of your faculties. Be smart. Follow the rules. Jas, recite the rules."

"Are you...?" I paused and blew out a breath. "Okay, okay. Treat the weapon as if it's live and ready to fire. Don't point it anything I'm not prepared to kill. Keep my finger off the trigger until I'm ready and my sights are on the target. Situational awareness. Make sure I know what's behind."

"Good job. Time to go."

CHAPTER 22

The rubber soles of our boots made almost no sound as we approached the building in teams of twos and threes. Jordy, Mikael and I took off for the northwest corner and held outside the exit door. Thanks to some early reconnaissance, we knew that the doors were unlocked. That was the good news.

I tried some slow, deliberate breathing but I could only focus on the worst case scenarios. We were facing an unknown number of soldiers and cult members alike. These were people who sent in military-grade security experts to kidnap a woman and twelve children, terrify the Order's members, and capture me. I was less concerned about the soldiers than I was with the crazy devotees who may or may not have special abilities. Soldiers were fairly predictable. Crazy people in the midst of human sacrifice? Not so much.

"On my command," Jordy murmured into his headset. "Go."

Mikael and I clicked the safeties into the off positions on our weapons and pointed them downward. "We've got this," he whispered.

Sweat dripped down my spine as Jordy opened the first door. He stepped inside and swept his weapon in a thirty-ish degree angle around the room. I followed him, turning left instead of right, and swept my section.

Mikael took up the rear and ensured no one was behind us.

Jordy nodded to us. "Status."

Rubios was the first to respond. "Clear."

"Clear."

"Clear."

"Roger that. Stack up."

Nothing could have prepared me for the abject terror I felt while waiting to hear from the other teams. Nor could I have known that my body would respond before my brain processed. The man said to stack up, so I positioned myself behind him and got ready to clear the next section.

We were slapped with the disgusting scent of blood and carcasses as we made our way to the chilly staircase. It was enough to make anyone gag, but my recent brush with murder and mayhem had given me some immunity. Mikael wasn't so lucky. He gagged and retched until his stomach was empty.

Jordy was furious. The sound echoed both ways on the staircase. We might have just given up our single advantage, the element of surprise. He ground out a single word. "Slaughterhouse."

Fan-friggin-tastic.

I couldn't wait to get my hands on those assholes. They'd chosen a location that could easily cover up their activities. Unless someone knew what they needed to find, a search would be useless. If we didn't wrap this up immediately, we were all dead and no one would know where the bodies were buried. Literally.

We took the stairs going up to the second floor. It was too quiet. The only sounds were the echoes of our footsteps. There was none of the expected chanting or screaming. Something felt wrong.

Jordy ordered an abrupt stop and signaled us to listen. On the other side of the flimsy metal door came practiced and measured steps. The door burst open and a man dressed in fatigues moved into the small alcove with his gun drawn.

Time came to a screeching halt.

Jordy drove his hands forward, knocking the gunman's hand down and to the side. In a quick series of movements, he disarmed the man and brought the muzzle down on his head twice in quick succession. Dazed, the man fell against the wall and hunched over.

"Jas. Now."

Ever the teacher, Jordy had disabled the man enough for me to attack. I grabbed his head and gave him a wicked knee to the face, smashing his nose into a mess of blood and cartilage. Infuriated, bleeding, and desperate, he reached for my throat.

My mind went blank as his bloody fingers scrabbled to find purchase on my neck. I knew I should have moved, ducked, struck him. Something.

Jordy made the decision for me. He placed the gun at the man's temple and fired once, tugging me aside as the body slumped. "What did I tell you?" he hissed. "Don't wait for your abilities to kick in or to decide you want to brawl. Shoot, goddammit. Mikael, you too."

"Yeah, yeah. Sorry. Got it." We grabbed weapons and ammunition from the body, sticking whatever we could in pockets and holsters. He was armed to the teeth, forcing us to assume that the rest would be equally ready to kill.

"Status."

"Clear."

"Clear."

The fourth team, comprised of the woman, Aurelia, and her partner John, wasn't responding.

"Status. Reli, John. Status. Over." Jordy swore in the silence. "Rubios, how far away are you from their position?"

The line crackled. "Found a room with...ah, fuck. We cleared the room. All fatalities."

"Fuck. How many? Cause of death?"

"Two children. Slit throats. They suffered."

Joshua hadn't lied. The innocents were being slaughtered before the main event. This was just the opening act.

Jordy sensed my urgency. "New orders. Shoot to kill. Once the hostages are removed, I want the biggest show of force you can manage. Over."

"Copy that."

"Copy."

"Copy."

Mikael gave my shoulder a comforting squeeze, the slightest pressure to let me know that he was there and had my back. In front of us, Jordy examined the rusted elevated walkway. He cursed and gestured for us to look. The path wrapped around the periphery of the main slaughtering room and gave us a direct line of sight.

Beneath us was an altar of three dark and heavy stones. The legs sported graffiti of the ancient and mystical kind. Clad in a simple pink dress, a little girl lay bound and gagged on the top slab. Her hair and face were smeared with the same ruby liquid that coated the altar. She moved her head from side to side, desperate to find someone who would save her from the same fate as the two dead children that had been kicked off the platform and discarded.

We raised our weapons and aimed at the man sharpening the edges of a curved ritual knife. As we pulled the triggers the man, seemingly guided by preternatural instinct, whirled around and dragged the blade across the girl's throat.

The bullets whizzed by the murderer as the child gurgled and bled out.

Oh, dear God.

§

Hell broke loose.

The cult's rent-a-cops trained their weapons on us and opened fire.

So great was my fury that I didn't bother to duck. I pushed Jordy away and aimed.

Pow.

The first round clipped a heavily armed man in the shoulder. Mikael's bullet, however, found its home between his eyes. We found a rhythm quickly enough. I selected a victim and squeezed the trigger.

The recoil shot up my arms and shook my frame. In the second it took me to recover, Mikael fired twice. Body shot, head shot. We were merciless.

One of the doors along the west wall of the elevated path opened with a bang. I squeezed off two shots that pulverized the side of his face. "I'm out. Reloading!"

I reached across my body and snatched a magazine while my other hand hit the release valve. Using my palm, I shoved the new cartridge, racked the slide and took aim. The weapon had become an extension of me, exacting vengeance and putting down those animals masquerading as human beings.

"East and North walkways cleared."

"West cleared," I said brusquely, having no real interest in broadcasting my progress. The fury raging inside needed an outlet. It cried for violence and destruction of its own making. When the familiar warmth of energy and power flowed through my limbs, I was ready.

Mikael dispatched the attackers on the south wall and disappeared without a second glance in my direction, whispering back to inform me that he was going to the children, the ones who were still alive and penned into human-sized kennels.

At least I had Jordy watching my back.

Crap.

Jordy had already hit the ground floor and was grappling with a giant of a man with red hair. Despite the twelve inch disadvantage, Jordy was inflicting major damage. The giant grunted and curled into himself to protect his vital organs, making the fatal mistake of leaving him open to the killing move that snapped his neck. In an instant, the beast reared its head and cut down everyone in his path. Jordy or Jordan, whoever was in control, attacked with brutal efficiency.

Rubios, Houlihan, and a few others joined the close combat. John screamed. One of the giant men wrapped his hand around his neck and slammed him against the wall. John struggled to get a decent hold, but the giant had a much longer reach.

I exhaled through my nose and fired. The bullet ripped through his chest somewhere above the heart. It wasn't enough. The giant turned toward me, grinned, and shoved his gun in John's mouth. He pulled the trigger and laughed. Without bothering to wipe the gore from his face, he pressed a hand to the seeping wound and shot in my direction.

"No more!" Mikael roared. He took aim and put three bullets into the man's head. Children screamed and pointed at another man charging them. Mikael and I fired at the same time and struck him in the chest from both sides.

"Mikael, go!"

He nodded briefly and worked with Aurelia to free the children. They hightailed it out of there, hopefully off toward one of the waiting vans.

I jogged down the stairs, sweat dripping into my eyes. Cecilia was still missing.

And those asshole cult priests? They hadn't fled because they were too busy collecting the spilled blood and packing up their supplies. The youngest, a towheaded man in his twenties, stepped on the bodies in an effort to avoid getting hit.

Humanity deserved better than the slaughter of children and the desperate grabs for selfish gains. Our enemies deserved no better than the suffering they dealt to others.

The carnage and screams around me faded as I strode forward. The soldiers deserved a death meted out by their kind. Those who used the blood of innocents for their gain deserved something far worse.

Me.

§

I transformed into something greater than myself as I stepped over the dead. The energy pulsing in my veins flowed to my fingertips on command as five acolytes surrounded me. I laughed savagely.

"Run away while you can."

One of the robed lackeys tossed the words back at me. He bared his teeth and lunged. Pure energy shot from my hand, hitting the center of his chest. Like an angry beast, he shook off the blow and came for me again.

They needed to quit while they were ahead. I threw my arm out and laughed as his body was engulfed in flames.

Two of his friends rushed to his side and tried to smother the fire. To my left, another raised a gun and pointed. I raised my other hand directed the energy into his body. He screamed and writhed as his organs boiled in fiery blood.

"Who's next," I screamed. Four acolytes pressed closer and chanted a containment spell, as if the power inside me could be contained. Their words grew in confidence and volume with each step. The way they looked, they were giving in to the visions of being the ones to subdue me, fueling their heady dose of blood lust.

Unfortunately, mine was stronger. I released a surge of energy that knocked them down, laughing when I saw the reason for their inability to rise. Their heads had been ripped off and popped like grapes while their bodies still twitched.

"Jasper, no!" Jordy bounded across the room and tackled me, protecting my body from a spray of bullets. "Are you okay? Talk to me!"

"Get *off*. Must kill."

"Fuck." He slapped my cheek. "Listen to me. You have to snap out of it before the rage consumes you."

"They must pay."

He scrambled to his feet, grabbed my hand and ran toward a low wall. "Yeah, no shit. Stay here and try not to blow up anything important. You know. Like me."

I snatched his gun and reloaded it for him. "Don't move. This needs to end."

§

Cecilia's scream rent the air. "Help me, please. It's Charles! Charles said he's going to slit my throat!" She sobbed as two more robed figures picked up her legs and torso and tied her to the altar.

I peeked over the wall and saw our team overtaking the cult's joke of a security team. All that remained was to free Cecilia and destroy the items used in the sacrifice. Needless to say, I'd fulfill Dakarai's request and torch the place on my way out.

Hurt. Torture. Maim. Take from them what they've taken from us. Make them beg for death.

"Jas," Jordy said. He shook my arm and snapped his fingers in front of my face. "Get your shit together. If you can't, stay here and don't move."

What Jordy hadn't yet understood was that he had no role to play in these last moments. Worse, he had no influence on my decisions. I knelt down and held his face in my hands. "I couldn't tell you my plans earlier because I needed confirmation. Jordy, In case this doesn't work, I wanted to say goodbye."

His eyes grew wide. "No. Jasper, no. You can't. You don't—"

"Dying is not on my agenda, so cross your fingers and hope I'm not wrong. But...I wish for you a long and happy life. You deserve it." I hesitated then pressed my lips to his. "Thank you for everything."

"I'm begging you not to do this. There has to be another way. And what is wrong with you? Kissing me now? Talk about terrible fucking timing! Stay and fight with me. Together."

Shaking my head, I stood and released him. I spoke the words of compulsion that Dakarai had taught me earlier in the day and infused it with the ability to bend others to my will. "Protect yourself at all costs. Don't leave until it's safe."

He roared and thrashed against my gentle command. "No! What are you doing? Don't sacrifice yourself. Don't leave me!"

"Never, silly man. You couldn't get rid of me if you tried. Be good, Jordy."

It was grief, both mine and his, that nearly caused me to run back to his side. But the knowledge that I was the only one who could permanently end this threat propelled me. I squared my shoulders and allowed the entirety of my abilities to take over.

"Charles," I bellowed. "Stop this madness. Free her and end this peacefully."

"Child, you are in far over your head. Call off your dogs and I will allow them to leave. Even Cecilia."

I lifted a brow. "This isn't a negotiation. Untie Cecilia and I promise that you will be given a fair trial within the Order and permission to live out your days in comfortable solitude."

"This isn't a negotiation," he mocked. "Miriam, Ian, for cripes sake, hold her down!"

Ian reared back and smashed his fist into Cecilia's temple. "She's down. Miriam, a little help please?"

Unlike the two men, Miriam remained silent. There was something profoundly wrong with the situation. Charles and Ian had demonstrated violence, while she merely had watched. When we first met, I'd wondered if she was the seductive power behind their actions. Her curious stare and the way she idly caressed Cecilia's throat confirmed it.

"Miriam, tell your dogs to back down."

She frowned slightly. "That's impossible. What we aim to do will allow everyone to have insight and power.

253

We'll free everyone from the bonds of cosmic equilibrium and the world will play out the final battle between light and dark."

I snorted. "Armageddon? You're an end-of-days looney? Jesus, people. Give it up."

Charles lifted his arm and made a come-hither gesture. Hundreds of stomping feet drew closer. "You are a foolish little girl. We have been protecting a myth, a fairy tale. Il Separatio doesn't speak to anyone, if he even exists. We are tired of protecting a cause that inhibits human development and progress."

"Look around you, Jasper," Ian said, his voice wrapping around me like unctuous tentacles. "These people are willing to die for our cause."

When I laughed, I had to admit I sounded unhinged. "Your people are ready to die. Do they know you're unwilling to offer the same sacrifice? That's what makes you weak."

"It is your weakness as well, child."

"That's where you're wrong." I smiled crookedly. "You've sealed your death warrants. Any last words?"

"Stupid bitch," Charles spat. "I should have killed you with the rest of your pathetic and weak family. Our new world has no room for pathetic, whining children."

My legs gave out. "You?"

His soot black eyes were emotionless. "Yes, me," he taunted. "Your precious Circle were devastated when they learned of your loss. They insisted on bringing you into the fold and teaching you. They thought they needed you."

I staggered to my feet and glowered. "May your death be equal to your life. May the suffering you wrought come back to you a thousand fold."

The world narrowed down to the pinpricks of energy beneath my skin and the presence of Charles and his cult. He ordered the acolytes to restrain me, the traitor of humanity.

The primordial need for justice would be denied no longer. I closed my eyes and screamed as the pulsing beneath my skin erupted with the force of a nuclear bomb.

Epilogue

Journal: Winter 2016

It's been three months since I last saw you and I'm slowly going crazy. After ... well, after, it was a madhouse. When the smoke cleared, the slaughterhouse had been decimated. Our people, including Cecilia, were unharmed.

The Order is in chaos. Members from around the world have been flocking to headquarters. Danny's analysts were right. What happened in Brooklyn was just one of many incidents. Unfortunately, they didn't have you, so our numbers are diminished.

Rebuilding has been a nightmare. The influx of new people has caused us to reevaluate our usage of space. A new family residential wing is being created in the east building. Since we wrecked the command center, I promised Danny a complete renovation. Between the new space and having Cecilia back, he's content.

We've managed to conceal the roles Charles, Ian and Miriam played, but I suspect it won't last for long. The Circle has assumed leadership and Dakarai is boss. It shouldn't surprise you that he was made for the role.

Mikael.

Poor guy hasn't stopped crying. His visions are constant, and while he doesn't tell us what he sees, it's horrific enough that he won't speak to anyone other than me.

I don't cry often. It's just not in my nature. But when I think back to that night, to when you said goodbye, I lose it. Imagine me curled up under a blanket in bed with my teddy bear. Sometimes it's the only way I sleep.

My free time is spent digging for clues and chasing down leads. Charles had a fat bank account that was being padded by funds he siphoned from the Order. He was involved in shady shit. If you hadn't incinerated his body, I'd have had him revived just so I could kill him myself. I still can't figure out what Miriam and Ian were getting from all of this.

At the request of almost everyone, I've moved out of my room and into an apartment in Quasimodo's Tower. Dakarai told me that more than a few people wanted to confine me since I'm Scary Jordy.

Insert Jasper-like eye roll here. There's no way anyone can confine me, supernatural or otherwise. They know I'm here at my choosing.

It's not so bad. I have a small, one-bedroom apartment on one of the underground levels and have access to a small gym and a library. Food magically appears in my fridge.

Mikael comes by a few times a week, and when he's not in a trance or crying, we play board games and watch television.

I thought about leaving. Packed my bags and everything. But I can't. I don't know where I'd go and I'm afraid I'd become that bad person I came here to escape.

I miss you so much. Half the time, I expect you to show up with coffee at five. Sometimes, when I'm working out, I laugh out loud because I remember how you whined about this thing or the other, then how you mastered it. How your face lit up when you finally ducked a punch. And the way you cheered and hugged me when you hit me in the stomach. I wasn't faking, by the way. That shit hurt like a mother.

I never told you how much you mean to me. After so many years of building a wall around myself, I looked at you and I felt. I didn't have a chance, not with the way you just kept at it. Badgering me, smiling, grumbling and pushing back. You weren't scared of me and you didn't treat me like a monster. You liked me as a person, as a man.

I'm sorry I didn't hug you and tell you that you're the best thing in my life. I hope you know that.

Everyone thinks I'm crazy. I keep telling them that you're not gone. You're just ... someplace else. I can't explain it, but I know you're not dead. Sometimes, at night, I can feel you in my room. Creepy ghost, like you promised.

They say it's wishful thinking. That I can't let go and am creating a narrative in my mind that keeps you with me. I know they're wrong.

I'll write again tomorrow.

Love,

Jordy

My head hurts from another night of drinking too much and watching bad movies with Mikael. Spending time with him while he's lucid is what keeps me going. The Order could survive without me. Mikael wouldn't. He's too raw and freaked out by the new people. They don't understand him and treat him like a sideshow freak.

The only routines I keep are going to the gym and writing in the thick, leather-bound journal. It started off as an outpouring of grief, but now I write to Jasper every day.

Yesterday, I told the team that she's still alive. No one believes me. Only Mikael does, but he doesn't talk about her very often.

I'd like to talk about her.

I open my laptop and scroll through my emails, like I do every night.

Spam. A Nigerian prince wants help.

Spam. The dating site I've never heard of says I have fifteen matches.

Spam. Make my penis larger for monthly payments of $9.99. *I'm good, thanks.*

Mikael. He's too tired to come over but will visit tomorrow.

Now that I have nothing to do, no plans, I give up on caring about anything. My beard is itchy as hell and when I drag my ass into the bathroom, I can see why. Probably haven't shaved in a few weeks. I go through the routine of showering, scrubbing off the sweat and grime of today's brutal workout and the mess I made rearranging the heavy furniture in the apartment. When the hot water starts to run out, I dry myself off, lather my face with shaving cream, taking my time to make sure I don't cut myself.

My reflection reveals a different man. Someone younger with possibilities and a future he might actually want.

The real me, the one that's exhausted and tired of life, throws on a pair of shorts and climbs into bed.

The illusions are strong tonight. I swear I can hear walking into my room, feel the bed shift when she sits next to me. Feather touches run through my hair. I like this one, so I hold onto it as I begin to drift into sleep. I hear her voice in the wind.

Find me.

Order of Vespers

ACKNOWLEDGMENTS

It took a tribe to write this novel. My husband, Omar, has been my rock. His steadfast support and encouragement is the reason I had enough confidence to show my work to the world. He also tolerated the bouts of writer's block, weeks of ignoring the world, sleepless nights, and threats to delete the entire manuscript. The DD runs have been spectacular.

Special thanks to Shana, my writing mentor, cheerleader, task master, and friend. Without her nudging and advice, Vespers would be in my personal slush pile. Shout out to Kevin Candela, my editor, who cheerfully accepted any scenario I threw his way. Thanks to Rachel Higginson and Rebecca Heyman who read early drafts.

My tribe of extraordinary women: Shana, Jessica G., Liz M., and Michelle K. Thank you for talking me off the ledge on numerous occasions and for your faith.

Without the support of my family and in-laws, none of this would have happened.

And finally, you, the readers. Thank you for giving the world of Vespers a chance.

There's so much in store for Jasper, Jordy, Mikael, and Dakarai. I hope you accompany them on this history-altering journey.

ABOUT THE AUTHOR

Elyse Reyes grew up in the Bronx, NYC, lived in Los Angeles, and now resides in South Florida. She has been an environmental justice advocate, researcher, special education teacher, recruiter for an MPA program, program director for a lupus organization, and a nonprofit consultant.

She believes life is about having experiences that will make great stories. Twist her arm hard enough and she'll try just about anything once.

As a writer, Elyse is obsessed with pithy dialogue and dry humor. She dabbles in different genres including: new adult, paranormal, urban fantasy, science fiction, and non-fiction. Her major influences are diverse: Kevin Smith, Jon Stewart, Chris Hardwick, Jim Butcher, Karen Marie Moning, Christopher Moore, Brent Weeks, and Chuck Wendig are current favorites.

Elyse loves chatting with her readers, so once you finish one of her novels, please leave a review, follow her on Twitter and Facebook, and drop her a line.

2/23/'26

Made in the USA
Middletown, DE
17 September 2016